WHAT
MY
HUSBAND
DID

BOOKS BY KERRY WILKINSON

Standalone Novels
Ten Birthdays
Two Sisters
The Girl Who Came Back
Last Night
The Death and Life of Eleanor Parker
The Wife's Secret
A Face in the Crowd
Close to You
After the Accident
The Child Across the Street

The Jessica Daniel series
The Killer Inside (also published as *Locked In*)
Vigilante
The Woman in Black
Think of the Children
Playing with Fire
The Missing Dead (also published as *Thicker than Water*)
Behind Closed Doors
Crossing the Line
Scarred for Life
For Richer, For Poorer
Nothing But Trouble

Eye for an Eye
Silent Suspect
The Unlucky Ones
A Cry in the Night

The Jessica Daniel Short Stories
January
February
March
April

Silver Blackthorn
Reckoning
Renegade
Resurgence

The Andrew Hunter series
Something Wicked
Something Hidden
Something Buried

Other
Down Among the Dead Men
No Place Like Home
Watched

WHAT MY HUSBAND DID

KERRY WILKINSON

bookouture

Published by Bookouture in 2020

An imprint of Storyfire Ltd.
Carmelite House
50 Victoria Embankment
London EC4Y 0DZ

www.bookouture.com

ISBN: 978-1-83888-860-2
eBook ISBN: 978-1-83888-859-6

SUNDAY

Richard puts the car into reverse and edges backwards until he's out of sight from anyone inside the shop. He's at the rear of the forecourt and there are no vehicles at the petrol pumps.

Alice is in her big red coat and she stops to look across to the far side of the road. The dewy fields lie beyond, with the hazy lights of Leavensfield glowing from the bottom of the valley. On evenings like this, when the sun sets early and frost clings to the verges, the wintry scene from the top of the hill is like a painting.

Alice tightens her jacket's zip – but it won't be much of a match for walking home over the fields in this weather.

Richard pulls up the handbrake and leaves the car idling as he gets out and then beckons the girl across. She glances quickly at the shop, takes one step towards the road – and then seems to change her mind as she crosses to where Richard is standing. He reaches a hand towards her shoulder but she shuffles a couple of paces away, her arms crossed.

'I can give you a lift home,' he says.

'But Mum—'

'Don't worry about your mum.' Richard glances towards the shop, where, because of the angle, there's no chance of Alice's mother spotting him. 'If she says anything, I'll deal with it. She doesn't have to know.'

Alice bobs from one foot to the other. The cold, dark walk home across Daisy Field can't seem too appealing. She's only twelve.

'She's told me not to get into a car with strangers.'

Richard forces a smile, but the icy, needly wind scratches at his face and he ends up offering something closer to a grimace. 'Come on… I'm not a *proper* stranger, am I?'

Alice eyes him and he can see the conflict within her. She should say no – except nobody wants to walk home on a night like this. Besides, what mother lets a twelve-year-old walk home in the dark? Even in a place like Leavensfield?

'It's only down the hill,' Richard adds, nodding towards the village in the distance. 'Not far.'

A car passes on the way down to the village. Alice watches it go and then nods shortly, before slipping into the vehicle.

Richard moves quickly as he returns to the driver's seat. *Just a short ride*, he tells himself. *Just a short ride.*

ONE

Harriet Branch is a massive cow.

There. I said it. Okay, I didn't *say* it, but I did *think* it. It sounds like something that should be written on the wall of a toilet cubicle. Maybe *I'll* write it on the wall of the pub toilets. I would if I had a pen. Okay, I wouldn't – and not only because of the pen thing. It's because I'm almost forty.

I'd *like* to write it on the wall, though.

Harriet claps her hands together and turns to take in the group of women who are sitting in a circle around the back room of the pub. I bet those hands have been treated with something expensive until they're as smooth as the marble countertops with which I imagine her kitchen to be filled. She probably imports the moisturiser from somewhere in Italy, where it's a few hundred quid a tub. That would be *very* Harriet Branch.

'Winter magic, people!' Harriet says. 'That's this year's theme for the masked ball. We need to be thinking winter magic at all times.'

She speaks in exclamation points, with short, snappy, barked instructions. It wouldn't be as bad if it wasn't done with such a smug smile on her face. There are strings of tinsel draped half-heartedly around the corners of the room and she glances up to those, making the point that she wants much more than the tat they have on display here.

Nobody questions what 'winter magic' entails, because of course we don't know. Does it mean I could throw a pack of cards in her stupid face and ask her to guess which one I'm thinking of? If she got it right, there would definitely be magic – *and* it's winter.

Theresa catches my eye a moment before Harriet turns to her. She knows what's coming and gives a mini eye-roll unseen by anyone except me. I suppress the grin but we both know what the other is thinking. Theresa's great at maintaining her cool in these situations. An absolute trouper.

'How are the food preparations coming along for the ball?' Harriet asks.

'Looking good,' Theresa replies. 'It's all in hand.'

'Can Atal make it this year?'

This might seem like a reasonable question but the passive aggression isn't lost on me, nor, I suspect, Theresa. Her husband owns a restaurant on the edge of the village, which is why the food for this year's Winter Festival Masked Ball has been assigned to him. Or, more to the point, to Theresa. It's an all-women planning committee, after all.

'He does have the restaurant to run,' Theresa replies, 'but we'll see.'

Harriet writes something on her pad and finishes with a firm full stop that might have punctured the paper. *We'll see* is not an adequate reply for a woman who deals in firm yeses or nos.

'I'll mark him as a yes,' Harriet says. 'Then if anything changes, it can be switched to a no.'

Theresa nods and smiles through it, managing not to say anything. Nobody talks back to Harriet. She's a professional wife and, in Leavensfield, that's a woman's primary occupation. Up the patriarchy and all that.

Being a professional wife isn't enough for anyone, though. How could it be? Harriet is never going to have a real job – but that means she invents other roles. That's why she set up something called the Lovely Leavensfield Committee, which is as horrendous as it sounds.

Part of that committee's responsibilities involve organising a fundraising winter ball every year. The reason for this is roughly twenty per cent to raise money for charity, twenty per cent to give Harriet something to do, and sixty per cent to give her an opportunity to order around the group of volunteers who are also on the committee.

That includes me.

Although she's chair*woman* of this committee, Harriet's exact role in the planning for the winter ball is unclear. All the jobs have been assigned to other people.

After Theresa's confirmation that there *will* be food at the ball, Harriet continues through her list. It's largely to herself that she mutters 'Sarah's working on the tickets…' – although it's clear to everyone that Sarah isn't at the meeting.

If it was anyone else, there would be offhand remarks about 'needing to fully commit' – but Sarah and Harriet, along with their respective husbands, are the village's power couples.

Harriet taps her pen on the pad and then turns to me. I feel the eyes of the other women in the circle upon me as it becomes my moment in the spotlight.

'How are the bouquets, Maddy?' she asks.

There's a pause as I realise she's done me here. I glance sideways, wondering if she's talking to someone else, but no, Harriet is talking to me.

'*Bouquets?*' I say. 'I thought I was doing dessert catering…? Didn't we agree that last time?'

I look around the circle, although everyone is tactically avoiding any sort of eye contact. Textbook. Only Theresa catches my stare, although even she gulps before replying. It's like the gestapo around here.

Theresa speaks softly: 'I'm pretty sure that is what was agreed last time.'

Harriet turns, nods at Theresa, and then twists back to me.

'It *is* my job,' I say. 'It's what I do for a living…'

Harriet gives me the sweetest of sweet smiles, though she's so full of Botox that the creases have to fight to form. It's a middle finger without the finger. *Is it really?* she doesn't say.

'Everyone needs to be checking the group emails,' Harriet says, punctuating the words with a gentle thump on the table. 'We've got money to raise and it's vitally important that we're all on the same page.'

I try to sit tall, but it's hard not to shrink under comments that are clearly meant for me.

'The desserts are now taken care of,' Harriet adds, as if talking to a child. She turns to take in the circle. 'I was at a charity dinner last week and met someone who was on *Bake-Off*. I don't want to name any names because it's not been advertised yet – but *she's* going to do the desserts.' By the time she focuses back on me, a sinking sensation is growing in my stomach. 'This change was outlined in the last email.'

'I must have missed it,' I reply.

That or deleted it without reading every word. Harriet's emails can make a university dissertation look short.

'You're now on flowers,' Harriet says firmly. 'If you check the email, it's all there.'

'I don't know anything about flowers or arranging.'

'So it's a great time to learn! That's what we always say, isn't it, ladies? You have a whole week. I'm sure you'll be fabulous.'

Harriet's grin remains fixed and I consider letting her know that I'll spend the week learning about flowers so that I can pack them into a neat bundle and find somewhere creative to shove them.

'How does that sound?' Harriet adds.

'I'll see what I can do.'

'Wonderful.' She holds her hands up. 'Aren't we all so blessed to be surrounded by such strong and talented women…?'

There is a mumbling of approval, but I catch Theresa's eye and, even though her face doesn't twitch, I know she's vomiting on the inside.

Harriet continues around the circle, checking on everyone's progress. With the winter ball only a week away, things are getting tight for time. I'm the only person who has had a new job dumped upon them and have surely been set up to fail. This is entirely in keeping with the projects organised by Harriet. Whatever it is, at whichever time of the year, there is always someone who comes out of her schemes looking as if they've messed up their role. It's never Harriet's fault, of course. She has an incredible ability of identifying the hardest part of a venture and then palming it off on someone else. If that's not her greatest talent, then it's the way she can manipulate the village into doing whatever she wants. It's impossible to know why this happens. I'm certainly not immune to her. I am here, after all.

Almost ninety minutes have passed by the time Harriet has finished going around the circle. She repeats that we need to be keeping an eye out for the group emails and then she shows her merciful side by letting us leave.

There's a scratching of chairs as everyone stands and then an orderly line forms as we pick up those chairs and stack them into the corner. It's like being back at school.

People start to drift outside in ones and twos, while others head through the connecting doors into the main part of the pub to have a glass of wine and a natter about the real world. Harriet is still packing her papers away into a designer leather bag.

I'm outside and almost at my car when Theresa taps me on the shoulder. It feels as if winter has landed tonight. The sky is clear, with a speckling of stars winking through the black. Frost is starting to crust along the base of the wall that rings the car park and there's a bristling breeze that leaves me wishing I'd brought a hat and scarf.

Theresa nods back to the pub. 'Fancy a quick drink?'

'I don't want to leave my car here overnight.'

'Only a little one…'

I shake my head. 'Maybe another time? I think I need a break from Leavensfield tonight.'

That gets a slim, knowing smile. The politics of this stupid little place can be exhausting.

We say our goodbyes and then I get into the car and crank up the heat while waiting for the mist on the windows to clear. When it does, I set off onto the narrow road that leads up and away from the centre of Leavensfield. It is lined with low drystone walls which have been here for as long as the village. There's barely a year that goes by without someone misjudging a corner and smashing into the barrier. It usually happens in the summer, largely because of the sheer number of people who pass through the village on their way to the seaside or the motorway. Leavensfield is the type of village that creeps up on a person. One moment they might be driving on comfortable A-roads; the next it's down to narrow lanes with no dividing line and these claustrophobic walls.

Leavensfield itself is a collection of central buildings, with scattered houses along the roads that lead in and out. It's a blink-and-you'll-miss-it Christmas card among an emerald wash of farms and fields.

I continue driving up the winding hill until the rows of houses end and the walls become hedges. Overgrown branches from the wilting trees sway across the road, as it narrows to little more than a car's width.

It's another mile or so until I indicate and then pull onto the drive. There's no sign of Richard's car – but he occasionally parks in the garage if he has no plans to take it out for a few days.

It's a quick, chilled, dash across the path and then I bristle through the front door, into the steaming warmth of the house.

'Richard…?'

My husband's name echoes around without reply. I look to the grandfather clock that stands in the hallway. It's not my sort of thing, probably not his, either – though it once belonged to Richard's father. There's a picture dial atop the numbers, that shows different images relating to the time of day. It's currently showing a crescent moon as it's a few minutes to ten. If I hadn't been out, it would be more or less the time we'd be going to bed. The yawns normally begin at around half-eight and it's a slippery slope from there.

'Richard…?'

I call louder this time, though there's still no response. It makes little sense for him to be out at this time. It's not as if he had anything on. I thought I'd get home to find him under a blanket on the sofa watching a music documentary, or something on BBC Four. Either that, or already asleep.

I try calling but his phone rings and rings without answer. That's not unusual: mobiles have never been his thing. If the phone is in his hand, then it's fifty-fifty as to whether he'll answer. The move from physical buttons to touchscreen was not a good one for him. If his phone is anywhere other than his hand, then it's touch-and-go as to whether he'll hear it. Technology to Richard is like a McDonald's on a high street: impossible to ignore but something that would rather be avoided.

I'm about to try calling him again when the doorbell sounds. Richard will have misplaced his keys in one of his various jacket pockets and will be busy turning everything inside out. His pockets are a black hole of receipts from stores that went out of business years ago, plus a charity shop sale of gloves and hats from winters gone.

When I open the door, it isn't Richard. Atal is standing there, his breath seeping into the cold of the night. He's in a thick coat, with his crimson turban wound tightly on his head.

'Oh,' I say, not expecting Theresa's husband to be here.

Atal says nothing at first. He's panting and turns rapidly from side to side. A black Labrador is sitting at his feet, its tail swishing back and forth across the welcome mat like a windscreen wiper.

'What's wrong?' I ask.

His breath seeps up and into the night. 'Can you call the police? I forgot my phone.'

'Why?'

'There's a body in the stream.'

TWO

After dialling 999, I trail behind Atal as we follow the verge away from the house. His dog, Lucky, is straining at the leash, yanking him forward ever faster, although Atal makes no attempt to tug him back. He's marching at a pace, on a mission to get back to the stream. I'm having to jog to keep up.

The ground is crusty and uneven from the divots and footsteps that froze weeks ago and haven't thawed since. Shadows cling to these corners of Leavensfield for entire seasons and it's not uncommon for mud in the shaded corners to remain hard from November until February or March.

Lucky darts through a gap in the hedges that line the road and Atal trails behind, holding the branches aside so that I can follow. The twigs snap back violently behind us as we emerge onto a wide, empty field. Wind blows icily across the barren space and I pull my coat tighter, wishing I was wearing more layers.

There are no pavements this far out of civilisation. Daisy Field is the one which people cut across if they live away from the village but want to walk to the centre without being on the edge of the narrow road. People have been taking a short cut over this field for as long as I've lived here – and likely for decades before that. In the summer, it's so well used that a path forms from the regular parade of people using the unmarked route.

The stream that slices Daisy Field runs from far up the hill that sits over Leavensfield. It winds snake-like down to the village at the bottom of the valley, cutting around the landscape. It perhaps reflects the time of year better than anything else can. In the wet autumns, it will burst its banks and splay water across the surrounding fields; while, at the peak of summer, it will run dry as children gleefully race across the barren riverbeds simply because they can. A few years ago, it froze in the week between Christmas and new year, and villagers took their only opportunity in a generation to skid and slide their way from bank to bank.

There are no street lights here, only the glow of the moon on a clear night, and Lucky continues to lead Atal across the field as I follow at the side. Atal's eyes are wide and white against the bleakness of the dark. The gaze of a focused, haunted man.

I thought Atal might have been exaggerating. There's often something in the local paper about the latest bit of fly-tipping that's gone on. It might have been a discarded piece of furniture in the stream, or some dark shape that looked a bit like a body.

He's right, though.

Even from a distance, I can see the unmoving body on the bank of the stream. The shape is out of the water, though a red coat burns brightly against the green and brown backdrop of Daisy Field.

Atal and I get closer still, to the point that Atal has to reel in the leash to keep Lucky from getting too near to the body. It's a girl on her side, with her long blonde-brown hair splayed behind her.

Kylie…

My pace quickens for a step or two before I realise that it can't be her. This girl is smaller and younger, perhaps twelve or thirteen.

'Should we…?' I take a step towards her but Atal puts a hand on my shoulder. He doesn't pull me back but it's enough to make me stop.

It's only now I realise that there's a pool around his feet and that he's dripping. His trousers are soaked and there's a trail of water that leads back across the field from where we came. His teeth are beginning to chatter. I'm not sure how I missed it.

'Did you pull her out?' I ask.

He nods, without shifting his gaze from the body. 'I don't think she was breathing. She was already cold.' He pauses and then adds: 'There was blood…'

I move closer, one step at a time. Not *thinking* someone's breathing isn't the same thing as definitely not breathing. In all my life, I've never wanted somebody to be wrong as much as I do now.

Another step and the girl in the red coat is almost at my feet. I recognise her, of course. It's a small village and I've seen Alice Pritchard walking to school in the same bright coat. She is unmoving, with no sign of her body bobbing with breath. I start to crouch – which is when whirring blue lights fill the area.

I'm off balance and rock backwards, startled by the sudden flaring lights. It's an effort to pull myself up and, when I turn to the side, a pair of police cars are bobbing their way across the uneven ground, heading directly towards us. A little further along the lane, an ambulance looms over the tops of the hedges, its lights burning into the black, before it takes a turn through a wide-open gate onto Daisy Field.

I move away from the body, although it's hard to stop watching. Instinct tells me to check that Atal was right about whether she was breathing. The girl must have been lying freezing on this bank for at least the fifteen minutes it would have taken Atal to get to mine and then for the pair of us to come here.

Everything happens quickly when the vehicles arrive. A police officer beckons me across to where Atal is standing and I do as asked. Meanwhile, three other officers and the paramedics descend upon the body in the red coat and form a protective circle around her.

The officer with Atal and myself is young and fresh-faced. She has her back to the scene as she signals us to move further away. Lucky is still pulling at his lead, although Atal is giving him little length to stretch any further.

'Did you find the body?' the officer asks, looking to me.

I stumble for a second, thrown by the use of the word 'body', as if she's definitely dead. My voice cracks and doesn't sound like my own. 'No, I just called it in.'

She turns to Atal, who nods glumly. He's usually full of jokes and joy, though the change is hardly a surprise. It's like this is a twin of whom I wasn't aware.

'I was walking the dog,' Atal says. 'I saw something red when I was crossing the field, so went to see what it was. When I got there, I—'

He's cut off by a babble of voices close to the stream. One of the police officers has darted back to the cars and there's a shout of 'She's breathing.'

Atal gasps and turns to me, mouth still open. He doesn't need to say anything because I can see the horror within him. He thought she was dead and can't believe he left her for so long. I wish I'd checked myself. Perhaps I'd have seen the shallow breaths? Perhaps I could have done something before the police arrived?

It makes little difference now because, as the other officer dashes back towards the stream, the policewoman in front of us shifts Atal and me further back until our view is blocked by the ambulance. She has a notepad out, although I have no idea how she's managing to hold that and a pen without her fingers trembling in this cold. She takes our names and contact details as Atal repeats that he was walking his dog when he saw something red.

'I didn't have my phone,' he says, 'so I went to Maddy's house.'

The officer turns to me and I nod over the back of the field towards the lane on the other side. Through the gaps in the hedge, I can see that I've left the lights on inside the house. I left in such a rush that I'm not even sure I locked the door.

'I live over there,' I say. 'I was waiting up for my husband when Atal rang the bell.'

'You called 999?'

'Exactly.'

The officer nods along at this and notes something new onto her pad. As she does so, a third police car turns from the lane onto Daisy Field. Its spinning blue light blazes bright across the ground as it bumps its way towards us. The officer puts her pad back into a pocket and blows into her hands.

'You should return to your house,' she says. 'It's cold out here and there's not a lot you can do now.'

'What happens next?' Atal asks.

'I don't know,' the officer replies, 'but someone will probably contact you tomorrow.'

She steps away as the newest car pulls to a stop alongside the others. Two more officers clamber out of the vehicle and I don't think I've ever seen this many police officers together away from a big city. They must have been called in from a neighbouring area.

Lucky is still trying to pull his way towards the stream but Atal tugs him away and we walk silently together back across the field in the direction from which we came. We pass through the main gates onto the road and then follow the verge back towards my house. The roads are deserted and, aside from the glow of the moon, the only light comes from the orange haze seeping from the windows of the house.

I'm expecting to see Richard's car on the drive. He'll be curious about where I am, either oblivious to what's gone on a little up the lane, or wondering why there are blue spinning lights creeping through the trees.

His car's not there, though.

The front door is locked, so I must have remembered to close it. I let myself in and then hold the door for Atal to follow me in.

'I should get home,' he says. 'Theresa will be worrying.'

'I'll text her,' I reply. 'Let her know you'll be on your way soon. We can wait here just in case the police come knocking…'

He nods with acceptance, even though we both know that's not the reason. I don't want to be alone at the moment – and I doubt it's any different for him.

Atal lets Lucky off the lead and the dog starts sniffing around the corners of the hall until I beckon them into the kitchen. When we get there, Lucky bounds along the edges of the room, snuffling the corners of the low cabinets in search of crumbs. Atal unzips his coat, though doesn't take it off as he slumps into one of the seats around the kitchen table. He sighs and scratches at the edges of his turban as I set the kettle going, before sending a text to Theresa.

'Do you reckon she'll be okay?' he asks.

'Theresa?'

He shakes his head and I feel silly for not realising.

'At least she was breathing,' I say.

Atal inhales deeply, as if to imitate the point. 'I thought…' He tails off to nothing and we sit quietly at the table, watching as Lucky completes his lap of the kitchen. He has seemingly found nothing on which to feast, so comes to rest on Atal's feet. As he's doing that, my phone buzzes with a reply.

Theresa: *Why's he at yours?*

Me: *He'll explain. Long story. He forgot his phone.*

I leave it at that. It's somewhat cryptic but Theresa will forgive me when she finds out what's going on. There's too much to explain in a message.

'Where's Richard?' Atal asks.

'He went to meet one of his old colleagues this morning.'

'One of his old lecturer friends?'

'Right. I thought, um…' It's my turn for a sentence to disappear off to nothing. I almost said I thought he'd be home by now. He should have been home hours ago but saying that out loud would make it too real. I check my phone again but there are no missed calls and no texts.

The kettle bubbles to a stop and I get up to pour myself a tea. It's way past the time when I might usually have one – but this is anything but a normal evening.

'Do you want a tea?' I ask.

'I don't think so,' Atal replies. He shuffles on the seat and then reaches down a hand for Lucky to lick. 'I should probably be going. Are you going to be okay by yourself?'

'Of course. Richard will be back any minute.'

Atal nods and pushes himself up. Lucky lifts his head expectantly and then trots over so that I can tickle his chin by way of a goodbye. Atal heads back through to the front of the house and then puts Lucky on his lead before I open the door. The cold blusters in as he treads out into the night and then I stand with my arms crossed, watching as Atal crunches across the drive and then disappears around the hedge.

There's still no sign of Richard's car, let alone Richard himself.

Back in the kitchen, I try calling him again. When there's no reply, I send a text asking where he is. It's unlikely he'll see it, so there won't be a reply, but I don't know what else to do.

I sip my tea and then pace around the house. There are pictures that need straightening; skirting boards that need dusting. All sorts of little jobs that I'd not normally notice.

Somehow, it's half past eleven. Ninety minutes have passed since Atal rang the doorbell. I'm in the living room straightening the book spines when the patter begins. I'm confused at first but only for a moment. When it rains, the chitter-chatter always echoes through the rooms at the front of the house as if we live next to a train line. Despite the years I've been living here, it never fails to make me jump. Rain is such a common part of life – but it's only since I moved to the village a few years back that I realised how sudden it is. One moment there's silence, the next there's that rush of needles.

As I look through the window, a blue haze continues to seep through the bushes in the distance. I watch for a moment before turning back to the drive, where there's no sign of Richard's car.

There have been times in the past when he's been late. Punctuality was never his strongest point – but there's a difference between being fifteen minutes past a time and simply not coming home. He's not great with his phone but, if something was holding him up, I'm certain he'd have found a way to tell me.

I try calling him again, though the rings seem to last longer this time. There's no answer and I go for one last attempt, which is again unanswered.

There's only one thing to do – so I head up the stairs to bed, knowing there is no chance of me sleeping tonight.

TEN YEARS OLD

The car heaters are blowing so loudly that I can't properly hear the radio. That's not the only problem. I have to sit tall in the front seat to be able to see through the window, which leaves me straining against the tightness of the seat belt.

It's dark and there's also a mist on the inside of the window that makes it hard to see anything outside, no matter how high I sit.

Dad glances quickly towards me before turning back to the road.

'Only about fifteen miles until we get home,' he says.

'How long will that take?'

'Maybe half an hour?'

He reaches and turns down the heat a little, which allows the voice from the radio to come through louder. I think there's a football game on somewhere and the men are talking about it. I'm not certain – but that's what Dad is usually listening to when we're in the car.

I keep sitting as tall as I can, watching the trees blur by. The windscreen wipers flash back and forth at top speed as the rain continues to fall. It's been so wet today.

The lights of the car flare deep into the distance before being swallowed by the dark. There's nothing out here in this weather… until there is. At first I think I'm the only one to see it. There's a man on the side of the road and, as soon as the lights fall across him, he turns and sticks out his thumb. We're going so quickly that we're alongside and past him before I've even taken him in properly. I turn and watch through the side window as we pass but then the car slows and I hear the gentle ticking of the indicator.

Dad pulls the car to a stop on the edge of the road and then twists to look through the back window. 'I'm just going to check he's all right.'

Dad opens his door and there's an instant storm of rain and wind. The water seems to be coming down sideways and pours into the car until Dad is outside and slams it back into place. I fight against the seat belt and try to turn and watch as he disappears out of sight – though it's impossible for me to see around the back of the seat. All the while, the car continues to tick, while the wipers squeak back and forth against the glass.

I'm alone.

I have to fight away the shivers as I hold my hands in front of the vents, wanting to be engulfed by the warm air. Tree branches sway back and forth in front and there's a scratching on top of the car that makes me yelp with alarm. There are no street lights out here: only the dark and the trees and the rain.

What if Dad doesn't come back…?

As I'm trying to force away that thought, there's a clunk from behind and I jump as a shape in a dark coat almost falls through the back doors to the car. A moment later and the front door reopens and Dad slides back into the driver's seat. A second more and the doors are closed again, sealing out the cold from the inside.

'Thanks for this,' says a voice from the back seat. It is a man, but not as old as my dad. It's more like one of the bigger boys who hang around on the benches at the park and smoke. Not quite young but not quite old.

'This is my daughter, Madeleine,' my dad says. 'Maddy, this is Alex.'

The seat belt is still stopping me from turning properly but, when the voice from behind says 'Hi, Maddy,' I reply with a 'Hi' of my own.

'Alex lives close to us,' Dad says, 'so we're going to give him a lift back. No one should have to walk home in this.'

Dad stops the indicator and then pulls away from the side of the road. He turns the volume up a fraction and then we all sit quietly for a moment until the man on the radio gets excited.

'Do you support a football team, Alex?' Dad asks.

The man behind me clears his throat and then says, 'Forest fan.'

Dad laughs at this. 'I saw them play Arsenal a couple of years back. Cloughy was in his pomp.'

'Aye,' the man says. 'Those were the days. I'm not sure we'll be winning European Cups anytime soon.'

Dad laughs again. 'You never know.'

They go quiet again as we continue listening to the radio. Outside, and the trees have turned into houses, while the darkness has been replaced by a string of orange street lights. I know the route home but instead of going straight across the roundabout like he would usually, Dad turns right and passes a row of shops that I've never seen before. He must sense my confusion because he reaches across and taps my knee for a moment.

'It's all right,' he says – and that's all it takes for me to know that it will be.

A few minutes more and he slows to turn into a petrol station. The lights blur bright and white, making me squint as my eyes hurt after the switch from darkness to this. Dad stops the car next to the air machine and then turns to the back seat.

'Is this all right?' he asks.

'Perfect,' Alex replies. 'Thank you so much. I'd been out there ages. Sorry for getting all the wet in your car.'

'No problem at all. I hope Forest turn it around for you.'

There's the sound of the car door, a 'thank you again', and then the door closes. I get my first proper look at Alex as he walks around the front of the car, gives a little wave in our direction, and then disappears behind the back of the pumps. He's not very tall and his coat is almost as big as he is. He's wearing a woolly hat, though there are sprouts of long hair poking out around his ears.

'Do you know him?' I ask.

Dad turns to me and squeezes my knee harder this time. He looks down and smiles, which makes me feel warmer than any vents could do.

'Never met him in my life,' he says.

'Why'd you stop for him, then?'

My dad's grin grows wider, before he shrugs his shoulders and turns back to the front. 'Because, Mads, sometimes people need help. You can be one of those people who drive by and pretend they're not there – or you can do your bit.'

He reaches for the gearstick but stops when I speak.

'What if he'd been… *bad*?'

'People are generally decent, Mads. It's always best to give them the benefit of the doubt.'

THREE

MONDAY

The sun is late to rise the next morning, not that it makes much difference to me. I was unlikely to sleep anyway but the consistent thumping of the rain was like a drumbeat into my soul. I've long told Richard that we should have taken a bedroom at the back of the house – even if it meant having a smaller one. This seemed ridiculous from his point of view: the master bedroom was ours, regardless of its positioning. That was an easy choice for him, seeing as he can sleep through anything. Also easy as he was here before I was.

There's still no sign of Richard this morning. It's been almost twenty-four hours since I last saw him and he hasn't called or texted. I keep trying to tell myself that there's an easy explanation for it all, although it's hard to imagine what that might be. He's not the sort of person who might disappear for days at a time.

My phone tells me I have made fourteen unanswered calls to Richard's phone. I've thought about calling the police to report him missing – but it's a small police force around here and they must have more pressing issues with what's happened.

There's also a voice that keeps telling me that he'll come through the door any moment with a story about a dead phone battery and a car breakdown in the middle of nowhere. I'm old enough to remember the days before mobiles, when someone being late – *significantly* late – would always leave that growing twinge of worry. In this new, digital, always-on world, that worry is replaced by texts and calls.

It doesn't help that I can't remember the name of the person that Richard told me he was visiting. The first problem is that, like a father with too many kids, he's reached the age where he'll scroll through a good three or four names before arriving on the correct one. The second is that I don't pay a great deal of attention when he starts talking about where he might be going. If he's not lecturing, it's a common thing for him to set off on a morning to visit an old friend or a colleague. One old friend that I've never met blurs into the next. Broadly speaking, we live different lives away from the house.

If it was any other day, I'd be talking to Theresa about what could have happened to Richard, but this is a day like no other for Leavensfield. I've already had three different messages, including one from Theresa, asking if I've heard more about what happened to 'Little' Alice Pritchard. That will be her moniker from now on, as if 'Little' is Alice's official first name. Only Theresa knows that I was with Atal in Daisy Field. That call of 'she's breathing' continues to haunt me, tempered only by the concern I feel for my missing husband.

'Little' Alice has been named on the village's Facebook page, although nobody seems to know her condition. It's a closed group for which people have to apply for membership in order to read about the comings and goings of this area. Most of the posts are passive-aggressive moans from people wondering who's parked a car outside their house, or asking if anyone else heard a dog barking the night before. It's a triumph of inanity, which doesn't say much for me considering I devour every morsel with glee. Theresa and I will text each other links to new posts with added commentary about how society is in decline because the lid of someone's bin blew off in the wind.

When it comes to this place, if it's not on Facebook, then it didn't happen. In the event of a nuclear apocalypse, then no one will believe it unless a friend has taken a thumbs-up selfie in front of a mushroom cloud.

As for this morning, someone has linked to a note on the local police's webpage where it mentions that a girl of twelve was found with head injuries close to a stream a little outside Leavensfield. The police haven't confirmed Alice's name – but that makes little difference in such a small community.

I don't reply to any of the texts about Alice and instead try to call Richard for the fifteenth time. It rings and rings, then blips through to his voicemail. He hasn't recorded a message, so the automated voice reads out his phone number and then says I can leave a message. There's little point considering the ones I've already left, so I hang up.

I'd set aside today to get on with my work. There's a box filled with new bakeware sitting at the back of the kitchen that I'm supposed to be testing and then writing about. It sounds horribly unexciting but the set was sent to me for free. After a day of cooking, I will put together a piece to send to the broadsheets or Saturday magazines and, if they don't bite, it will go on my website. That will mean more hits in my as yet unfulfilled attempt to get a book deal out of baking and blogging. I've been trying for years. It's as big a first-world problem as they come but hardly anybody seems to care unless a person has had a soufflé collapse on television, or has dumped an unfrozen pudding in the bin.

I unpack the box and then start to read the covering letter. Or, I *try* to read the letter. The words blur meaninglessly into one another, as if they're written in crayon in another language. It's impossible to focus on something so trivial when my husband is missing and a little girl was found face-down in a stream a little up the road.

So much for a work day.

I don't know what to do with myself, so end up putting on my warmest clothes and heading outside. It's colder today than it was yesterday, almost as if the heavens have decided to mark my mood with an arctic blast. There's a light grey wash across the sky and a clamminess to the air that makes it feel as if the rain of last night could be back for a second go.

It's hard not to be drawn to the gap on the drive where Richard would usually park. The whole scene feels wrong as puddles have formed in the divots where the wheels of his car would usually sit.

I head along the drive onto the deserted road. A slim creek of water is flowing down the hill on the other side but the verge nearest my house is still hard underfoot. I walk up, following the trail Atal and I took last night, until I notice the white of a police car blocking the gate that leads into Daisy Field. A single officer is sitting in the driver's seat and appears to be reading a newspaper. He certainly doesn't notice me.

Beyond the car, I can see a fluttering web of blue and white tape set up close to the stream. There's a white tent as well, possibly two, although it's hard to tell from this distance. Aside from the officer in the car, there's not a single person in sight.

I turn and follow the road back down the slope, passing my house and continuing towards the centre of Leavensfield. There's a gap from my house to the next and then a shorter distance to the one after that. There's still no path here and the lane is barely wide enough for two cars to pass. That is especially the case when someone in one of those 4x4 urban tanks heads through. At busier times of the year, there is barely a day without some sort of stand-off between one vehicle going up the hill and another coming down.

At the bottom of the hill, there is a row of houses flanked by the drystone wall at the front – and then it's the Fox and Hounds pub. There's a banner up advertising the Winter Festival Masked Ball and I find myself stopping to stare. It was only last night that I was in the back room of the pub resenting Harriet and her stupid planning committee and now, hours later, it feels so inconsequential.

It's only as I pass the pub that I realise I'm not the only person who has drifted to the centre of the village for no particular reason.

Alice's mother, Gemma, lives a few doors from the pub. She's probably in her early thirties, although I don't know for sure. She has one of those burdened faces that could mean she's anything from twenty to fifty. Either way, it's notable because being a single mother in this village is like having leprosy. A woman can be as unhappy as she wants, especially if she's on medication to help, but she damn well better be married if she wants to integrate. There are occasions when being in this place is like going back in time.

Nobody says anything to Gemma's face, of course. She's silently ostracised. Gemma moved here around a year ago and works on the checkout at the independent petrol station and shop, a mile or so past my house. It's called Fuel's Gold and is a short way outside the village's borders up on the hill. Nobody wants something like that in a village that was shortlisted for the overall Britain in Bloom award two years ago.

The other reason that Gemma's never quite fitted in is because nobody seems sure how she afforded her house here. There was no direct inheritance from within a family, which is what usually happens. Old money breeds old money in a place like this. Rumours are that she got some compensation from a car crash and used it as a house deposit. That's what I've heard, though I wouldn't know for sure – and I don't particularly care.

There's a police car parked outside Gemma's house and a group of nine or ten villagers milling around on the pavement outside, chatting among themselves. Everybody is wrapped up in the full gamut of winter wear, from fluffy snow boots through to puffy goose-feather-filled jackets. There's an urn resting on Gemma's wall, and a neat row of teacups. It's perhaps the most British thing I've ever seen – and entirely in keeping with Leavensfield. People want to appear supportive but nobody fancies a morning without tea.

I suppose I'm not that different. I've arrived here as if drawn by a homing beacon. I consider turning and heading home but the entire reason I'm here is that I couldn't bear being alone at the house any longer. In the fraction of a second it takes me to feel torn, the decision is taken for me. Harriet appears from the back of the crowd and chirps an upbeat 'Maddy.' She's always the first to speak.

Harriet is in her late-forties but could comfortably pass for someone a decade younger. I won't pretend that there's no envy there because she always manages to look perfect. She's in all black this morning: hat, scarf, coat – the lot. She sidles across to me and, though we're more or less the same height, it always feels as if Harriet is looking down upon me. It could be just me – and I've often wondered if it is – but Harriet is the sort that hears a word like 'blogging' and hears 'blagging'. The men around here are lawyers and investment bankers, while the women are devoted housewives.

'You heard then?' Harriet says.

'I think everyone has.'

She makes a deliberate attempt to look past me, up the road towards my house in the far distance. 'Where's Richard?'

I blink at her. It's an odd thing to ask.

'He's away,' I reply.

'Oh…' It's only one word, a couple of letters, and yet there's something unmistakably conspiratorial there. Like a girl at school singing 'I know something you don't know'. She has an uncanny knack of making a word or three sound like an entire paragraph.

'Why?' I ask.

Harriet purses her lips. 'I thought you might already know.'

'Know what?'

'It's just that I saw Richard last night…' She pauses for a beat, relishing the moment, making sure everyone can hear, and then adds an almost gleeful: 'He was with Alice…'

FOUR

I stare at Harriet, waiting for some sort of follow-up, or a punch-line. This is some weird joke that I don't get.

'What do you mean?' I ask.

Harriet shrugs, as if this is something that I should have known.

'They were in the car park up by Fuel's Gold,' she says. This is accompanied by a vague wave towards the hill outside Leavensfield.

'Do you mean inside?' I ask. 'Alice was up there with her mum…?'

A shake of the head. 'I was on the way down to the meeting last night. It was maybe half-seven? Something like that. I wondered why Alice was getting into his car. I assumed he was giving her a lift home…'

I continue to stare, waiting for the 'gotcha' that will surely come. 'She was getting into his car?!'

Harriet shakes her head and I can't work out what she's up to. 'I'm just telling you what I saw…'

'You must have made a mistake…'

Another shake of the head. 'It was Alice getting into his car. I know what I saw.'

I wish she didn't sound convincing – but she does. There is no joke at the end of this, only questions. How could Richard have been barely a mile from home and yet never arrived? Why would Alice have got into his car? Does he even know Alice?

'He must have been giving her a lift home…' It's a stream of consciousness because I can't think of any other reason why a twelve-year-old girl would have been getting into my husband's car.

Bob's, the village shop, opens late, closes early and is often shut for an hour at lunch. It's also closed on Sundays. As well as petrol, the small shop attached to Fuel's Gold stocks a few groceries that people might want.

The petrol station is next to the 'Welcome To Leavensfield' sign and technically outside the village. The village centre, the petrol station and my house form a triangle, in that, if someone wants to get from the village to Fuel's Gold or vice versa, the most direct route is across Daisy Field.

That's the field where Atal discovered Alice's body in the stream.

'When's Richard back?'

I flicker back to the present, though it takes me a second to realise Harriet has asked a question.

'Oh, he, um… I'm not sure.'

I can hardly say he's missing.

Harriet turns in a half-circle, taking in Gemma's house and then the assembled crowd of support.

'I should probably tell someone,' she says.

'About what?'

'About seeing Richard with Alice. He might have been the last person to see her…'

I'm fairly certain that my mouth hangs open as I realise she's right. It's not just that she can't wait to go and flap her mouth, it's that she definitely *should* tell someone what she saw.

'Shall we go together?' she asks.

'Go where?'

Harriet nods towards Gemma's house. 'There are police officers in there.'

I take a step backwards. 'I've got to get home,' I say.

She watches blankly, as if this is what she expected. 'No problem,' she replies. 'I'm sure it can all be explained.'

I almost ask her not to but she's already turned and levered open the gate at the end of Gemma's house. I wonder if she only recently arrived, or if she was waiting for me to appear. She could have told this to the police at any time – and it didn't have to be in person. It's like she wanted me to know.

As she knocks on the door, I turn and walk back the way I came. One of the women waiting outside the house calls after me but I keep walking, pretending I've not heard. By the time I get to the start of the hill and the arcing bend, I'm almost at a jog. I want to get home, to where Richard's car is surely sitting on the driveway and he'll have a perfectly reasonable explanation for where he's been all night. He certainly wasn't at the petrol station outside Leavensfield and of course Alice didn't get into his car.

It's not possible.

The chilled air burns the back of my throat as I gasp for breath. I'm not used to exercise, let alone at this time of year. When I get back to the house, it feels as if my lungs might burst. The cold scratches at me with lengthy talons and I can feel each tendril of air clawing its way into me.

Richard's car is not sitting outside the house.

I hunch over, trying to catch my breath as I stare at the space where it should be. There's no explanation for anything that's happened in the last half-day or so. Perhaps it's this, or maybe the cold has woken me, but there's something about the name of the person Richard was visiting that starts to come back to me. K-something. Maybe Kevin, or Kristian, or…

Keith.

He told me yesterday that he was off to visit an old colleague named Keith.

I hurry inside and lock the door, then head upstairs to where Richard keeps the bulk of his work things. It's the smallest room in the house and, although we both call it an office, it's more of a dumping ground for books and folders that Richard has the urge to keep. He's not a hoarder, not quite, but he does seem to keep everything and anything that relates to his work.

I have to shove the door in order to enter the room and, when I get inside, I realise it's because there's a box full of cardboard folders in the way. There is something on every surface and most of the floor is covered with either books or printer pages.

As well as the rainforest of papers, there's also a small table, on which sits an old desktop computer. Every time Richard turns it on, the fan at the back of the main unit whirrs so loudly that it echoes through the floor and I can hear it when I'm in the kitchen. It's like a helicopter taking off, although Richard refuses to replace it because he doesn't want to have to learn how to use a new one. I've offered to teach him some things on the laptop I use to run my website and write articles, but he insists that he's got by for long enough with how things are, so there's no need to learn anything new. I've never pointed out that he would be incredibly unhappy if any of his students used the same argument…

Next to the computer is a rolodex of address cards. Every card has been organised in alphabetical order by last name. There are phone numbers and addresses listed in neat block-capital letters, although I can't claim to know many of the people named. I flip from page to page, skipping over someone named 'Miller, Keith' because I'm almost certain that the name my husband mentioned yesterday morning was longer than that.

I have to go through almost the entire circle of people, starting again at the letter 'A' until I stumble across the name 'Etherington, Keith'. Considering the name was lost among my memories barely an hour ago, it now feels so clear and close that this was the person Richard said he was visiting.

There's a phone number listed, although it's an 01 landline, instead of an 07 mobile. Not surprising, really.

I call the number from my mobile and listen as it rings six or seven times before the call drops with no hint of an answer machine. I scan the rest of the card. There's an address listed, although it's around a ninety-minute drive away.

I'm considering whether I should get in my car and head out that way when my phone starts to ring with the same 01 number I've just called. I press to answer.

'Hello…?'

It's a man's voice. 'Who's this?' he snaps.

'Is that Keith?'

There's a momentary pause and then a snipped: 'Who's this?'

'My name's Madeleine King. My husband is Richard and—'

'You're Dickie's wife?'

'Right…'

The nickname sounds unfamiliar, largely because nobody I know ever calls Richard 'Dickie'. I've heard it before – but only ever from some of his older work friends. It feels like it belongs to a person I don't know and certainly not the man I married.

'How is he?' Keith adds. 'I've not heard from him in donkey's years.'

The room feels like a freezer. I try to reply but nothing comes out.

Keith must sense the confusion because he quickly comes back with: 'Oh, he's not um… is he?'

It takes me a moment to understand what he's talking about – and then I realise that he thinks I'm calling to say that Richard has died.

'No, nothing like that,' I say. 'Richard's fine. I'm just clearing up his contact numbers and have been calling around to check everything's still up to date.'

There's another pause and I wonder if Keith thinks this is as unconvincing as it unquestionably is.

'This is still my number,' Keith says.

'Excellent. I'll make a note of that.'

Another gap. It's certainly an odd conversation.

Keith clearly decides that I'm wasting his time as he offers a short: 'Make sure you say hello to Dickie for me. Tell him it would be great to get together some time.'

'I will.'

We say goodbye to one another and then I hang up. I'm not sure what makes me do it, other than that it feels important – but I use my phone to take a photograph of the card before flipping around the rolodex until I reach Keith Miller's entry. I consider calling him, wondering if I've mixed up the name, but I know I haven't. Richard definitely said he was off to visit the man to whom I've just spoken. The man who hasn't heard from him in donkey's years…

I feel lost, trying to make sense of everything that's happened. If it was only Richard missing, then that would be bad enough… but then there's what happened to Alice. And what Harriet says she saw.

The doorbell echoes through the house and it's such a contrast to the silence that I find myself shrieking with surprise.

It's Richard.

I'm halfway down the stairs when I remember that I've been here before – when Atal was at the door last night. I thought then that Richard might have misplaced his keys. I was wrong then and, deep down, I know I'm wrong now.

I already know who's at the door moments before I open it. That is why it's no surprise to see a man in a suit with a long knee-length coat over the top standing on the doorstep.

'Mrs King?' he asks.

'That's me.'

'I'm Detective Inspector Dee Knee. Can I come in?'

FIVE

I hold the door open, allowing the inspector into the house. He passes me a card that shows his name is Detective Inspector Brian Dini, even though I would never have guessed the spelling of his last name from the way he said it.

As I close the door, he wipes his feet studiously on the mat and then asks if he should take off his shoes. I pass him back his identification and tell him he should. I'm not particularly bothered and Richard never does – but there's something about the way he speaks with authority and confidence that leaves me feeling cornered. At least this is one way for me to maintain some degree of control.

It's hard not to notice the shine of Dini's shoes as he removes them and, though I'm no detective myself, it seems clear he can't have been trampling around fields all morning.

Once he's done removing his shoes, Dini edges further along the hall and looks up and around the walls.

'Nice house you have,' he says.

'Thank you.'

His focus switches back to me. 'Is Mr King around?'

'Richard's out at the moment.'

Dini nods, although it's with an assurance that I suspect means he already knows. He's probably a little older than me, although that's more of a guess from his swept-back grey hair. There's a brightness to his brown eyes that could easily mean he's younger. He's one of those men that are likely better-looking in their forties or fifties than they ever were in their twenties and thirties. Some men grow into their looks… like Richard, I suppose.

'Do you know where he is?'

'No… he, um… he went out yesterday and isn't back yet.'

Dini makes a point of removing a notepad and pen from his inside pocket. He opens it and then scritches something before looking up once more.

'Does he often stay out for a day or two at a time…?' He's wearing a fixed, unassuming smile. The type somebody might offer when trying to sell a used car.

'Do you want a cup of tea?' I ask. 'I was about to make one for myself.'

Dini stares for a second and then takes a step back, giving me a clear passage through the hall. 'Lead the way,' he says. 'I'd love a brew. It's been a busy morning.'

I almost say 'I'll bet' but hold the words as I pass him and edge through to the kitchen. He probably realises this is an excuse for me to try to think of something to say that doesn't make it sound like my husband and I are strangers.

After filling the kettle, I flip it on and then fiddle around with a pair of mugs from the cupboard. I even drag down the teapot, which only usually comes out when we've had people over for dinner. There's no way he could know this, but Dini chuckles, 'I feel blessed' as I fiddle with the tin of loose leaves and the strainer. I ignore him and continue working, trying desperately to think of something that doesn't sound like it's incriminating my husband.

I can sense Dini watching my every move but I ignore the stare that's boring into my back. When I eventually turn and settle with two mugs and the teapot, Dini is sitting at the kitchen table with his knees crossed and the notepad in front of him.

'This is very kind of you,' he says.

'No bother. I was going to make one for myself anyway. Do you want a biscuit?'

He pats his belly. 'Not for me.'

We sit for a moment, staring at the teapot.

'It should only be another minute,' I add, which is a guess.

Dini is unmoved momentarily, before he picks up his pad. 'Where were we…?' I remain silent until he follows it up with: 'Your husband…'

'What about him?'

'Does he often stay out for a day or two at a time…?'

'No.'

That gets a nod. 'When are you expecting him back?'

'I'm not sure. He didn't say.'

'And where was your husband yesterday?'

I take the moment to pick up the teapot and fill both our mugs. I cross to the fridge and grab the semi-skimmed, then dribble a little into my mug before holding it over Dini's.

'Go crazy,' he says.

I dump in as much as can fit into the mug and then return to the fridge. 'Sugar?' I ask.

'Not for me.'

Back at the table and there's nothing more I can do to stall – not unless I want to bake a tray of cookies in an attempt to avoid the questions. I'm not sure Dini's patience would stretch that far – and it's not as if any of the delaying has done me any good. Everything to come is still going to sound awful.

'I don't know where he was yesterday,' I say – which is the truth.

Dini notes something on his pad. 'Didn't he tell you where he was going?'

'He said he was visiting a friend.'

'Did he mention which friend…?'

Dini has a way of phrasing things that makes it sound as if he not only knows the answer already – but that anything I might have to say should be met with maximum scepticism.

This is the moment in which I have to decide whether to tell the whole truth and nothing but the truth. Because he *did* tell me. It's loyalty to my husband, or it isn't.

'I don't think so,' I say.

'You don't think he told you who he was visiting?'

'I wasn't really listening.'

Dini notes something on his pad and then spends a few seconds tapping his pen on the paper. He screws up his lips and then puts down the pad before having a sip of his tea.

'That's perfect,' he says as he places the mug back. 'Just how I like it.'

I don't reply. I've crossed a line, even though I haven't, strictly speaking, told a lie.

Dini examines me over glasses he's not wearing and it feels as if he can read my mind. It's like he can see into my soul. 'Just to clarify,' he says. 'Your husband said he was going to visit a friend, didn't tell you which one, and then you've not seen him in a day…?'

There's a pause and then I answer his question. 'Richard might have said where he was going – but he's a lecturer and knows a lot of people. I wasn't really listening.' I try to match Dini's expressionless face with a breezy smile. *We're both people here, y'know?*

'When did your husband leave yesterday?'

'Between ten and eleven o'clock.'

Dini shuffles up his sleeve to look at his watch. 'A little over twenty-four hours…?' There's a hint of something accusatory in his voice.

'I've been worried. I thought about calling you but didn't know how long you're supposed to leave it.'

'So you think he's missing…?'

Everything's a question with Dini. It all feels like a trap, as if there's no correct answer and that anything I might say could be twisted to mean something else.

'I don't know.'

'Did your husband drive to visit this friend?'

'Yes.'

'What car does he drive?'

I know the answer – I look at it every day – and yet, in the moment, on the spot, I'm lost. I can't even remember my own make and model of car, let alone Richard's.

'It's, um…'

Dini is on me right away: 'You don't know what car your husband drives?'

'I do, it's just…' The words don't come and I'm so flustered that I can't even remember the colour. 'Can I check my phone?' I ask.

'Of course.'

I unlock my phone and flip through the photos until I arrive on one that shows an image of Richard's car. It was taken when we had a drive out to the cliffs last summer. There's a car park that sits almost on the edge and Richard parked there. We stood at the side as a passing couple took our photo. It was Richard's idea, and completely unlike the kind of thing he might usually suggest. He's the opposite of the Snapchat generation.

The photo is a wash of colour. There's the blue of the sky and the ocean, which is offset by the lush green of the grass and Richard's black car.

It's black. How could I have forgotten?

I slide my phone across the table so that Dini can see the photo. 'That's his car,' I say.

'Looks like a Toyota,' he says.

'I wouldn't know.'

'Could you send me that photograph? I gave you my card, right?' He makes it sound like there's no choice, though it's not as if I'd say no.

I use the information from his card to text him the photo. It's only when that's done that I realise he now has my number.

Something beeps from within Dini's pockets, though he doesn't acknowledge it.

'What was your husband wearing when he left yesterday?'

This is a harder question than the car, although the answer comes more easily. 'I can't say for sure – but he tends to wear the same thing most days.'

'And what would that be?'

'Black trousers, with a jacket.'

Dini adds this to his pad, without looking up. 'Was he wearing some sort of shirt?'

'Of course.'

'What colour?'

I almost say white – although I know it wasn't. 'Pink.'

Dini looks up. 'What colour was the jacket?'

'Maybe grey? I don't know for sure.'

I figure he's going to press the point, although he doesn't. That offers no assurance because I genuinely can't remember and it feels as if he knows when I'm offering the whole truth and when I'm not.

'Does anybody else live at the house?' he asks.

'Just us.'

'No kids…?'

I pick up my mug and hide my mouth behind it for a moment as I inhale the sweet, slightly floral fumes.

'I have a daughter,' I say.

Dini nods once more, though he doesn't write anything. The endless sense that he already knows all this leaves me feeling enraged. I've done nothing wrong and yet he's examining every part of my life.

'Where does she live?'

'She's eighteen and she's at Liverpool University. I don't know her address off the top of my head.'

He waves a hand as if to indicate that he doesn't need to know – and then, unexpectedly, he puts down the pad and presses back into the seat with his fingers looped through the mug. 'My boy's in his second year at City University,' he says. 'It's his first time away from home – and he loves it. Probably too much.'

I don't want to smile at this but it's impossible to resist. Suddenly the anger I felt moments before has evaporated as if it was never there. 'It's Kylie's first time, too,' I say.

'Is that your daughter's name?'

'Right.'

'Are you a *Neighbours* fan?'

'More her music.'

Dini nods along and, for a moment, he's no longer a police officer in my kitchen. It feels as if we're friends here for a catch-up.

'I thought my lad would be home last summer but he's enjoying London too much,' Dini says. 'He ended up staying there for work. I only saw him for the long weekend at the end of August.'

I find myself nodding in acceptance of this. 'Kylie's coming home for Christmas,' I say.

'You sound like you're looking forward to it…?'

His gaze pierces towards me and I wonder if there's some sort of second meaning to this. Whether I've given away something that I shouldn't have.

'I am,' I say – and it's probably the first time that I've admitted to myself how much I miss my daughter. We've spoken and we've texted – but I've not seen her in three months. It's the longest we've been apart since she was born.

Dini seems to sense the dead end, or perhaps it's something else. 'Tell me about your husband's job,' he says.

It's only now that I realise Dini hasn't actually told me why he's here. The reason is obvious, given what Harriet said about seeing Richard at Fuel's Gold with Alice – although he hasn't brought it up. Until he got here, he wouldn't have known for sure that Richard was missing. He's managed to keep himself unerringly cool.

'Why do you want to know?' I ask.

He breathes in and then leans forward to put the mug back on the table. I'm not sure he drank from it. 'Because, late last night, a twelve-year-old girl was found face-down in a stream – and we have a report that your husband was the last person to be seen with her.'

I breathe and take this in. *Stay calm. It's not how it seems.*

'I was there when she was found,' I say.

'I know.'

He eyes me but I have to turn away. There's nothing suspicious about Atal knocking on my door, nor with me going to the field. My house is the closest to where Alice was found – and Atal knows me. It shouldn't feel as if I'm guilty of something, even though it does.

'Richard's an English language lecturer,' I say. 'He works at the University of the West of England.' I pause and, when Dini doesn't reply, I find myself talking for the sake of talking. 'I wanted Kylie to go there.'

'So that she'd be closer to home?'

'Yes.'

'She didn't want that?'

'I think she wanted the whole student experience. Hard to get that if you're living at home.'

Dini hasn't written anything on his pad in a while. 'What about your job?' he asks.

'Is that important?'

'Not really. I'm curious.'

I consider telling him that I have nothing left to say, though worry that it would only make me seem guilty of something. I haven't done anything.

'I work from home,' I say. 'I have a food blog and write reviews and recipes for some of the papers.'

There's the merest hint of a raised eyebrow. 'I'll have to look you up. Sounds like the type of thing my wife's into.'

He says this with a smile, although I don't take any bait. I suspect he knows this already. I doubt there's much about our life of which he isn't already aware.

'What did you do yesterday?' he asks.

'I had a bit of work to do. I was in most of the day, then I was at a meeting at the pub in the evening about the winter ball.'

There's the briefest of nods. 'When did you last hear from your husband?'

'When he left.'

'He didn't call?'

'Phones aren't really his thing.'

'Did you try to call him?'

I nod. 'Lots. He didn't pick up. I texted him too. I was worried.' I pause and then correct myself. 'I *am* worried.'

Dini gives himself a second but little more. 'Did you argue before he left?'

'Not at all.'

'How's your relationship?' It's a rat-a-tat-tat of questions.

'Fine… normal.'

Dini doesn't react to this. He inhales a shallow breath and takes me in, eyes narrow and piercing. 'Do you know Alice Pritchard?'

I need a moment. Hearing her first and last name feels so much more impactful than the 'Little Alice' stuff going around.

'Not really,' I say, truthfully. 'I know her to look at. I know her mum – that sort of thing. I've done a few cookery classes at the primary school – just basics, nothing serious. Alice is in that class, so that's probably the most interaction we've ever had.'

It's only once I've said it that I realise Alice is probably too old to go to primary school now. It's at least a year since she would have been in one of those cookery sessions, probably longer.

Dini picks up his pad. 'Does your husband know Alice?'

It's impossible to stop myself from shivering. It's not the cold: it's the feeling that a person has which my dad used to say was someone walking on your grave.

'I don't think so,' I say.

Dini writes something on the pad and then sits with the pen poised over the paper. 'Do you have any idea why she might have been seen getting into his car?'

'No.'

It feels like the betrayal I've been trying to avoid. I should be fighting back by saying that Harriet has it in for me and that she's a liar.

It didn't feel as if she was lying, though. As much as I don't want to believe it, I think she did see Alice getting into Richard's car.

Dini nods along with this, though his eyes never leave me until he re-pockets his pad. Once he's done that, he slides back his chair and stands.

'I think that's everything,' he says. 'If your husband returns, he must contact us right away.'

I look from him to the mug and almost say that he's barely touched his tea. As if that matters. As if anything that trivial is important.

'Should I be worried?' I ask.

Dini gives a grim smile. 'Let's hope not.'

He takes a step towards the hall and I push myself up, before moving past him and guiding the way towards the front door.

When I turn, Dini has stopped next to the grandfather clock. There are two rows of vinyl records on shelves that are built into the wall. He runs a hand across the spines and crouches to take in the titles. 'Impressive,' he says. 'My son started collecting vinyl, even though he's a teenager. Funny how these things go in cycles.' Dini stands and turns to me with a smile that's undeniably friendly. 'Makes you wonder if tapes will come back,' he says. 'Or eight-tracks, or VHS cassettes.' He laughs gently, although it's impossible to join in.

'They're all Richard's,' I say. 'He's been collecting his whole life. There's more upstairs. He's got all sorts going back to doo-wop from the fifties.'

Dini crouches lower and scans the collection from left to right. 'Alphabetical order,' he says.

I don't reply because there's no question there. Dini doesn't need to know, but there are three record players around the house, with one in the living room and two more upstairs.

On the day I moved in, Richard had 'Why Do Fools Fall In Love?' echoing around the house. I knew the song but only found out later that I'd never heard the original. I asked Richard if he'd put it on purposely and whether it was supposed to be a message for us. He laughed and told me it was his favourite song. He was playing the version by The Teenagers, which came out in the 1950s, before either of us were born. I always thought 'The Teenagers' was a bit say-what-you-see in terms of names for bands.

I'm not sure why that fact stuck with me – Richard is full of music trivia from decades back and most of it washes over me. As I stand near the door, I feel transported back to that day, with the youthful *oooh-wahs* booming through the house as it played on a loop. We must have listened to that song at least a dozen times in a row. Sometimes, I will still awaken to hear the strains of it seeping up the stairs from where Richard has got up before me.

'You all right…?'

I blink back into the hall and realise that Dini is now standing and facing me. He's moved across the hall without me noticing.

'Just worried…'

I can't read Dini's expression. I know how it looks. A girl seemingly got into my husband's car, despite having no connection to him. She's found bloodied and face-down in a stream, while Richard is now missing. It couldn't be much worse.

But then I know what can happen when a person is assumed to be guilty…

'If…' I say. Dini cranes his neck backwards a fraction, confused. 'You said "*if*" my husband returns, you want him to contact you…'

Dini doesn't acknowledge this as he crouches to put on his shoes. When he next stands, I shuffle to the side and open the door for him.

'Call me if you think of anything,' he says – and then, without a backwards glance, he heads out to the marked police car.

SIX

The grim sensation continues to grow within me. It's not just that there's something wrong, it's that there's something *catastrophically* wrong.

I've felt this before… but it's been a long time.

I think it's the knowledge that, regardless of what happens now, the world is tilting and life cannot be the same again.

Richard has never been gone for this long before, not unless I already knew the reasons. He's been to conferences and there was a work retreat he had about a year ago. He's had paying engagements to speak at workshops in various corners of the country but, even with that, there was never a time when we wouldn't end up speaking on the phone at some point. He's not the type of person to simply take off.

I have no idea who to contact. Richard's never been one for 'friends', as such. He lived in Leavensfield before me and never seemed to have any close relationships with the people here. I don't know for sure but I think he might have been something of a loner in village terms. To a degree, he still is.

He'd socialise with his colleagues on odd occasions out of work – but it wasn't often and I don't know many of them myself. It's around an hour's drive to where he works at the university and having to make that journey twice a day meant he rarely hung around before driving home. The semester ended on Friday, so there was no expectation that he'd be back at work today. I fully expected him to be home last night and then to spend much of today either sorting through his records, or working on something in his office.

When I check my phone, there's a message from Theresa that arrived while I was in the kitchen with Dini.

Theresa: *Have you seen on Facebook? There's a village meeting at the hall for midday.*

The idea of a meeting for the whole village seems like something quaint, from another age. The sort of thing that might have happened before the internet, perhaps even before phones became widespread. By the time something might be said in a public place, someone else has tweeted it out for the rest of the world to see.

It's almost half-past eleven and the morning has disappeared into an ocean of unanswered questions. I clear the kitchen, partly for something to do, and then put my coat and hat back on before walking down the hill into Leavensfield for the second time today.

There's no mini crowd outside Gemma's house this time – although a single police car remains in place. I hurry past until I get to the obelisk that signals the centre of the village. It's a tall stone monument, with a circle intersecting a high cross. It sits in the place where three roads join and, if anyone is driving through, there's no way out without passing.

A little past that is Leavensfield Village Hall. It is essentially a blocky, grey, stone building with a pair of spires at the front. It looks a lot like a traditional school, with lots of smaller windows around the edge and one large room on the inside.

Off to the side is the village Christmas tree. It's taller than the hall and decorated with lines of coloured bulbs. Nothing too extravagant, although that's likely because Harriet delegated it to someone else.

I don't have to cross the car park to hear the hum of voices from within the hall. It reaches a peak as I get inside to be met by a mass of fifty or sixty people.

It's a Monday but seemingly nobody is at work. Even the children appear to be off school, judging by the number of young people doing knee skids close to the door. By the time they get to eleven or twelve, they're all bussed to the out-of-town comprehensive that serves the surrounding villages. That's if Mummy and Daddy haven't packed them off to a private school by that point.

The bitter smell of instant coffee hangs on the air as I press through the crowd, looking for Theresa. There's no sign of her – but it's easy enough to spy Harriet. She's still in her all-black mourning outfit from earlier, and is up on the stage at the front, a metre or so higher than anyone else. She's standing next to her husband, Gavin, who is the type of clean-cut generic white bloke that I could easily see losing his deposit in an ill-judged attempt to run for Parliament as a UKIP member.

I don't know a lot about Gavin, other than that he works in 'finance'. Every time Harriet speaks about him, it seems as if he's just earned some bonus, or a pay rise. Whenever there are news stories about mass financial fraud, or investors losing all their savings, I wait for the name Gavin Branch to pop up.

Alongside village power couple #1 is one half of village power couple #2. James Overend is some sort of corporate lawyer, although I'm not completely certain what that means. He probably sues chronically ill children for having the temerity to drink the water poisoned by the companies he represents. There's no sign of his wife, Sarah, who was also missing from the meeting last night. Also on the stage are both couples' children. They each have one boy and one girl. Xavier and Beatrice for Harriet; David and Sophie for Sarah. Both boys are seven and the girls are six. It's almost like they planned their copulation dates, or that they did it side by side to try to get their delivery dates to match.

It's little surprise that these two power couples have seized control of the village. Locals, especially the women, do look up to Harriet and – to a lesser degree – Sarah. They also want financial advice from Gavin, or ask legal questions of James.

With that in mind, it's normal for Harriet to be leading this meeting. There is a good proportion of people who will want to hear from her.

After saying something to her husband, she steps across to the microphone and taps it. There's a whine but it's enough to get everyone's attention and for the chattering to subside. The only indication of dissent comes from the boys at the back, who are still sliding across the varnished floor on their knees.

'Hi, everyone,' Harriet says. 'Thanks for coming. I called this meeting because I wanted to reassure everyone, our children especially, that Leavensfield is safe. I've been talking to the police this morning and they're looking into whatever happened to Little Alice last night. They've asked me to say that if anyone has anything to share on that, then they will treat the information in the strictest confidence.'

This gets nods of approval around the room, even though Harriet has literally said nothing that couldn't be figured out with the merest amount of thought.

She reaches and takes her husband's hand and then turns back to the microphone. 'We've not told the police this yet – but Gavin and I are *personally* donating five thousand pounds to help find the person that hurt Little Alice.'

This sets off a chain of mutterings from the assembled mass, although it is entirely in keeping with what I assume to be Harriet's philosophy: that money solves everything.

'How is she?'

I don't catch who shouts up, though it's a man's voice.

Harriet acknowledges whoever it is with a solemn nod. 'I'm not sure how Little Alice is yet,' she says. 'Gemma's off at the hospital and the only information for now is that Alice is very poorly. As a community, for now I think we need to be coming together to support Gemma.'

The speech continues but I'm distracted by a shuffling of people next to me as Theresa appears alongside Atal. Theresa and I nod to one another and then she angles her head towards the stage. We both know what the other is thinking – that it's entirely typical that Harriet has taken over something that doesn't concern her.

Atal doesn't appear to notice as he mutters a low 'hi'. I reply with a quick 'You okay?' and he nods, although doesn't elaborate.

We're not friends as such, it's more that Atal is Theresa's husband. If Theresa and I were to fall out, I doubt Atal and I would have any reason to remain in contact. He is a focal point for the village, however – and not only because he owns one of the two restaurants in the area. He's a Sikh and, with his dark skin and turban, he's perfect to fit Harriet's metropolitan elite quota. The way Harriet courts him to visit her various dinner and garden parties is a long-running joke between Theresa and me. There's even a photo of Atal on the website of Gavin's law firm, which was taken when there was a fundraiser a couple of summers ago. It's almost beyond parody, or it would be if I hadn't overheard James telling Sarah not to invite the 'raghead' to their anniversary party last July.

'How are you doing?' Theresa whispers.

'I'm not sure.'

She leans in to talk into my ear, so that only I can hear. 'Atal barely slept last night. Even Lucky seems down in the dumps. I can't believe you were the ones who found her.'

I don't reply because I don't know what to say.

Theresa continues talking anyway: 'Alice always seemed so happy when I saw her around. She was on the playground a few days ago with some of the other girls.'

I still have no idea of how to reply. I've seen Alice around the village as well – but Leavensfield is so small that I'd likely be able to say the same about any of the young people who live here. I nod up towards the stage instead, where Harriet is still talking. 'Where's Sarah?' I ask.

Theresa follows my line of sight. 'Chest infection, apparently.'

'Who said that?'

She shrugs. 'Harriet, I think. I can't remember.' Theresa turns back to me and then nudges my shoulder. 'Where's Richard?'

I half expected it to be all around the village by now that he's missing. I suppose it's only me and the police who know.

'He's away,' I reply.

Theresa nods, although I can tell from the way she shuffles on the spot that there's something else to come.

'People are saying Alice got into his car last night…' She lets it hang and it feels more like an honest question between friends than anything mean.

'It's only Harriet saying that,' I reply.

'She wouldn't lie about it, though, would she? Not something so important.'

'She lies about all sorts.'

'Probably not this…'

It's impossible to argue. Of course not this.

'Someone said there's CCTV…' Theresa's staring ahead, not looking for a reaction. She's wondering if I know.

'From the garage?' I ask.

'Apparently.'

'Who said that?'

She shrugs. 'Everyone.'

I turn to look at her and Theresa offers a slim smile that almost says a silent 'sorry'. Aside from Richard, she's the only person who knows what happened with my dad. She understands what all this means.

I'm about to reply when I realise the room has gone silent. Harriet is no longer speaking and people have again began muttering among themselves.

'…There is one other thing I should mention,' Harriet says. Her voice resounds around the room and she instantly has everyone's attention once more. 'There are reports that Alice was spotted getting into a car outside Fuel's Gold on Dodds Lanes last night. We all know that Gemma works at that garage and I believe that Alice sometimes cuts across Daisy Field to visit her mum.'

Another shout goes up from the crowd. Another man: 'What are you saying?'

Harriet holds up both hands defensively. 'I'm not *saying* anything. There might have been a perfectly innocent reason for Alice to have got into the car.'

A few heads turn towards me – and then it's suddenly more than a few. It feels as if everyone is looking. Rumours are currency in a place like this.

'The police are aware of all this,' Harriet adds – although it's already too late because everybody seemingly knows that my husband was the driver.

'What type of car?'

Harriet waves away the latest question. 'I think it's best to leave that with the police. I just wanted this meeting so that we could come together as a community. There might be media here in the coming hours – and probably more police. Before any of that happens, I wanted everyone to know that we all have one another's backs. If you've not already got my phone number, then make sure you get it from me on the way out.'

She pauses for a breathy moment – but only to look across towards her children.

'Let's work together to get through this,' she says. 'And let's all be there for Gemma. She's going to need us.'

There's a ripple of approval and then someone starts to clap. A moment later and it feels as if everyone's clapping, including Atal. Theresa shrugs towards me and then she joins in. I probably should, if only to keep up appearances, but the hypocrisy is astounding. The women of Leavensfield would usually be bitching about a single mother with a lowly job, like Gemma. There's no way she would be getting an invite to the annual Harriet Branch Christmas party, but now, with a sniff of publicity on the horizon, it's all change.

It doesn't help that I can still feel hidden sets of eyes boring into me across the room. People know about Richard and Alice – and it's only a matter of time until everyone finds out that he's not been seen since.

SEVEN

I'm in the car park and heading towards the hill and home when a woman appears from between a pair of cars and reaches towards me.

'You're Maddy, right?' she says. 'I don't think we've met properly. I'm Zoe and this is Frankie.'

She motions down towards a boy at her side who must be seven or eight. She has flawless caramel skin with dark freckles peppering both cheeks and a long ponytail of separated braids. Her boy has slightly lighter skin than hers but dark, curly hair with bright brown eyes.

Zoe nods towards the hall. 'Am I late?'

'Kind of,' I reply. 'Harriet was saying there's probably going to be more police arriving, plus possibly media. You can probably catch her if you head in.'

I take a step forward, ready to leave, but Zoe catches my arm. 'How's the girl?'

'Alice? I'm not sure. I've heard she's in hospital but I don't know much.'

Zoe nods along to this. I don't know her as such, although it's hard to miss any newcomers when it comes to Leavensfield. She's a mystery in that she moved into a detached cottage up on the opposite side of the village from me within the past year or so. She is perhaps the only person who has managed to escape the thrall of the various committees and internal politics around the village. Her cottage is near Atal's restaurant and used to be owned by a farmer whose name I've forgotten. After the farmer died, his estate was divided up among his kids and they ended up selling the cottage separately to the rest of the property. Zoe is another single mother although, because she doesn't technically live *in* the village, she gets a lot less attention than Gemma.

In a village where competition means everything, Zoe is an enigma. It might not be out loud, but people will argue over who donates the most to charity, or who volunteers for the most causes. There's never a summer that goes by without some sort of bitchy argument about who has the best – or worst – garden. I would guess that parents end up doing a good proportion of their children's homework because nobody wants to have the kid who's bottom of the class. It is impossible to avoid – and yet Zoe seems to drift around the fringes of everything while never getting involved. She does her own thing in floaty dresses and I've often seen her walking barefooted around the streets.

Not today. It's too cold for all that and she's in a pair of Doc Martens.

Being an outsider is usually a bad thing around here – but Zoe is *such* an outsider that it's created something like a competition to figure out who can get closest to her. I was once at the school gates after a cooking session when I heard Harriet telling Zoe that she loved her style. Zoe's reply was a laugh. It wasn't *quite* in Harriet's face but it was close enough. The fact that she didn't drop to her knees and worship at the feet of Her Highness only made me want to know Zoe better. In many respects, that makes me no better than Harriet. I do see the irony.

I also know Zoe's son, Frankie, through the cookery classes at his primary school. Those usually involve making a mess and eating cake – but there are certainly worse things in life than that.

Zoe makes no effort to pass me and head to the hall. 'Does anyone know what happened to Alice last night?' she asks.

'I don't think so. Atal was out with his dog when he found her by the stream. I live up there and called the police.'

I have no idea whether Zoe knows Atal but she doesn't make an indication one way or the other. Instead she turns to her son, who is busy scuffing his feet on the spot and humming to himself.

'Do you know Alice?' she asks.

'A bit,' he replies.

'When did you last see her?'

'Dunno.'

He continues fidgeting and doesn't look up from the floor. He's still humming something I can't quite make out. The noise feels oddly unsettling as Zoe glances up to me and gives a *kids, eh* half-grin.

'Where's your husband?' she asks.

It catches me somewhat off guard, partly because I don't know why she's asking but also because I had no idea she knows Richard. I suppose everyone knows everyone in a place like this – but it's still unexpected. This is the most Zoe and I have ever spoken.

'He's away.' I'm ready to leave it at that, before I feel a surge of confidence. 'Any reason for asking?'

I instantly regret the somewhat aggressive tone as Zoe narrows her eyes as if to ask why I'm being so defensive. That's all it takes for me to realise that she knows nothing of the rumours about Alice getting into his car.

'I know he's a lecturer,' she says. 'I was wondering if I could ask him a few questions about admissions sometime when he's free.'

I find myself backtracking embarrassingly and manage to fire off three quick apologies before composing myself. He might be something of an outsider and a loner but Richard has lived in Leavensfield for a long time. He's a fixture of the village and some of the young people have knocked on our door over the last few years to ask him to look at UCAS applications and the like. It happened around a month ago when the doorbell went on a Sunday afternoon. I opened the door to find a smiling, blonde teenager clutching a laptop, who asked if Richard could look over her application form. He did, of course. Why wouldn't he?

'I don't see why that would be a problem,' I say.

As soon as the words are out of my mouth, I know it's a lie. Richard's missing and the last time anyone saw him, there was a twelve-year-old girl getting into his car. That's the definition of a problem. If Zoe wants him to go over a university form for her, chances are she's going to be waiting a while.

'That would be great,' Zoe says. She takes a step towards the hall and then stops. There's a fraction of a second in which I almost unload my worry onto her. I would tell her that I love my husband but that there's a voice deep inside me saying something terrible has happened to him. I'd talk about my fear of what that means. Of being alone. Then I'd say how all my happy memories of us together feel muddied because he told me he was visiting someone he wasn't. Because he was a mile up the road and a young girl got into his car, before she was found face-down in a stream.

I want to say all of this to someone but I don't feel as if I can unleash it all on a person I don't know. It's too much.

The moment is lost anyway because Zoe turns back to Frankie. 'Shall we go home?' she asks.

Frankie doesn't need asking twice and makes a zooming plane noise as he bounces off towards the far side of the car park.

'Aren't you going in?' I ask.

Zoe shakes her head. 'I guess I've heard all I needed to. I only wanted to know how Alice was doing.'

I walk alongside her until we're at the edge of the car park, when she points towards a red hatchback.

'That's me,' she says.

'I'm on foot.'

'Do you want a lift?'

'Thanks – but the cold clears my head and I fancy a walk.'

She offers a *suit yourself* shrug and then calls Frankie across to the car. He's still humming to himself and it's only when he hurls himself into the passenger side that I realise why it's all so disconcerting.

The tune he's been humming this entire time is something that's been tickling my thoughts since the moment Dini crouched to look at Richard's pile of vinyl.

It's 'Why Do Fools Fall In Love'…

EIGHT

My phone starts ringing the moment I get in the front door. That instant flash of expecting it to be Richard is something that I suspect won't go until I find out where he is. It's not his name on the screen: it's Kylie's.

'Mum...?'

It's such a relief to hear my daughter's voice.

'Hi.'

'I heard what happened with that little girl. Someone WhatsApped me. I can't believe it's happening in *Leavensfield*.'

I can understand her disbelief. This isn't the sort of thing that happens in our village.

'Atal found her in the stream,' I say. 'He knocked on the door last night and I called the police.'

'It happened next to *you*...?'

I find myself sitting on the bottom step, recounting everything that happened with Atal, the stream, Alice, and the police. As sick as it all makes me feel, I know there's a tiny part of me that enjoys having my daughter hang on my every word. It feels like a long time since that happened.

Kylie listens without interruption, other than the odd 'that sounds terrible' and 'I can't believe it'. It's only as I get to the part where Atal left the house last night that she brings me back to the here and now.

'How's Richard taking it?' she asks.

Richard has never been 'Dad' to Kylie. We married when she was fifteen and she spent about eighteen months resenting him, me, Leavensfield, England, and probably the Earth itself. It was only as she grew out of the hating everything stage of teenagery that she started to accept the situation. That was the time when she decided she wanted to go to university – and realised that Richard might actually be useful for that. She didn't quite get the grades to get into Liverpool but Richard's letter of recommendation and phone call seemingly swung it. That was after I told him not to make the call. The whole *not-what-you-know*-thing doesn't sit well with me.

'He's away visiting a friend,' I reply. It's almost instinctive to lie at this point, even to her.

Kylie sweeps past this, unperturbed. 'I still can't believe what's happened. I hope you're okay.'

'I'm fine.'

'Do they think she was attacked, or…?'

'Nobody knows yet. The police are investigating.'

'It doesn't sound good, though.'

'No…'

There's a pause that I have to fight myself not to fill. Kylie doesn't know how bad it is – and I don't want to spoil her time at university by filling her in quite yet.

'Do you think I should come home?'

The offer is so unexpected that I'm left floundering for words.

'Mum…?'

'No, um… I don't think there's any need. You'll be back in a little over a week anyway – and then it'll be Christmas. I'm looking forward to that.'

The line goes momentarily muffled and there's a sound of someone else's voice in the background. I know what's about to happen but there's little I can do about it. This is the first time Kylie and I have spoken to one another in five weeks. We've texted most days but it's not the same. I want to tell her this, to say that I want to hear her voice for a while longer, but the moment has already gone.

The line suddenly clears and then Kylie speaks again. She sounds distracted: 'I've got to go,' she says.

'Thanks for calling. It was good to hear your voice.'

'Yours, too. I'll be back soon anyway.'

There's another sound that's not quite clear and then Kylie says a final goodbye before hanging up. I stare at the screen for a moment, watching as her name fades from view, and part wishing I'd asked her to come home. I'm glad I didn't because it would be for my own selfish reasons, of wanting someone there – but the alternative is an empty house and a missing husband.

I try calling Richard again. It's the first attempt since this morning but the hours passed have made no difference as there's still no reply. Not that I expected there to be.

There is nothing quite like the unknown. Absolutes can be processed, no matter how traumatic they might be. I know that as well as anyone. This is something else.

I glance over to Richard's grandfather clock and then move across to take in the record collection. Dini was correct in that everything's in alphabetical order, although it's not as easy as that because there's no specific standard for how a spine should look. Some have the artist's name, others have the title of the album, single, or EP. Some have both, some have neither. Some have text that faces one way but there are others where it angles the other. Then there are the ones in which the sleeve is so old, all of that has worn away. There is an order – but only because Richard keeps everything so neatly filed. It is probably the only thing with which he's particularly meticulous. His office is an explosion of books, files, papers and everything else. His half of the wardrobe is filled with clothes he's not worn in years, as well as the same combination of trousers and jackets that he wears every day.

His record collection starts with A downstairs and runs through to G. Everything else is upstairs, where there's a bit more space. I head up the stairs and scan Richard's row of records until I've narrowed in on 'Te' ahead of 'Teenagers'. I'm looking for Richard's prized copy of *Why Do Fools Fall In Love*… his favourite record – and yet it isn't here. I check both of the upstairs turntables and then go down to the living room and do the same.

There's no sign of it.

Richard could have filed it in the wrong place – but that seems unlike him. It's only when I google the song that I realise I've been wrong about the artist for all these years. There's a picture of the album cover that reads 'The Teenagers featuring Frankie Lymon'.

I'm not sure how I managed to miss that for such a long time.

I don't have to think hard to be able to hear Zoe's son humming along to a song that came out almost sixty years before he was born. Not only that, he's *called* Frankie. Zoe could be a fan of that sort of music but in the moment, with my husband missing, there's something about the song that doesn't feel right.

I move into the hall to check the row of vinyl downstairs, wondering if the record is filed under F – but as soon as I get within sight, a howling blare of sirens rips past the house. I'm next to the front door and pull it open in time to see a trio of police cars racing up the hill, away from the village.

It's too much urgency for anything routine, which means something must have happened.

TWELVE YEARS OLD

The car vents are blowing so loudly that I can't properly hear the sound of the radio. It's cool air now and I don't have to sit so tall in the front seat any longer in order to see through the window.

It's such a bright day, with the sky so strikingly blue that it's almost white. Dad glances momentarily towards me before turning back to the road.

'Not long now,' he says.

He reaches and turns down the cooling air a little, which allows the voice from the radio to come through louder. It's cricket and, almost as soon as he does this, he thumps the steering wheel gently.

'What?' I ask.

'Another England collapse.'

'Oh…'

I'm not completely sure what this means – but Dad doesn't seem too happy about it.

The sun is pouring through the glass and, even with the cool air, I can feel my skin prickling. If this weather continues, I'm going to ask if we can go to the beach tomorrow or the day after that. Dad might let me take a friend.

It's as we come over the top of the hill that I spot a shape on the side of the road. It's a man in jeans and a long top – which has to be much too warm for the conditions. He's under the shade of a tree with his thumb out and there's a bag at his feet.

There's the moment from when this happened before, where it felt as if Dad was teaching me something. When we felt close.

'Can we stop, Dad?' I ask.

There's no immediate slowing to the car and it feels like we're going to be past the man too quickly. Just as I'm thinking that, Dad glances sideways and then brakes. He indicates off and then pulls in a little past the man.

'I'll find out where he's going,' Dad says. He starts to open his door but, at the same time, the door behind me clunks open and there's some sort of scuffing sound.

Dad puts an arm around the back of his seat and twists to look behind me. 'You all right, mate?' he says.

There's a grunt, although I don't think the man actually says anything. There's a thump and then a bag appears on the seat behind Dad.

It feels different to the last time we did this. When it was raining and cold, and Dad chose to stop for that man, I felt something swelling within me. There was a pride and happiness that we'd made someone's day better. This isn't the same. There's a smell of something horrible that I can't quite make out. It's like when the bins have been left out in the morning but the binmen don't come until the afternoon. Dad seems uncomfortable, too. He glances at me twice although quickly looks away both times.

'Where are you going?' Dad asks.

The man doesn't reply, although he does let out a long, retching cough. When he's done, Dad asks him again and there's a mumbled 'Bristol'.

'I'm not really going that way,' Dad says. 'I can drop you at the services. You might find a lift there.'

'Whatever.'

Dad sets off again but he turns down the radio and he keeps peeping up to the mirror. I want to say something but I'm not sure what would be best. I shouldn't have asked Dad to stop.

We've only been travelling for a couple of minutes when there's a big bump in the back of my chair. I jolt forward and back as Dad turns sideways to look at me.

'You okay?' he asks.

'Yes.'

We continue for a while, with only the sound of the radio as a distraction. It's hard to focus on that, though, because it feels like the smell from behind my chair is getting stronger. I can feel it on my tongue.

'What's your name?' Dad asks.

The only reply is another mumbled grunt. Seconds later, there's a new smell that I do recognise. Dad must sense it too, because he immediately slows and pulls over to the side of the road. He unclips his seat belt and turns to face the man behind us.

'You can't smoke in here,' he says.

I don't understand the reply but can feel my heart thundering as I watch my dad from side-on. There's a vein over his eye that has started to throb.

In a flash, he opens his door and marches around the front of the car. He moves quickly past me and then there's the sound of the door behind being opened. I hear him say 'Out', and then there's a scuffling sound.

I can't see properly but I strain against the seat belt and twist to see through the window as Dad drags the man out of the car by the collar of his top. When the man has been dumped on the verge, Dad reaches into the back seat, grabs the man's bag, and then throws it down on the ground. The man doesn't move from where he's slumped.

Dad slams the door behind me and then charges back around to his side before starting the car and setting off. His chest is rising and falling so quickly and there's sweat dribbling along the side of his face.

'Are you okay, Mads?' he asks.

'Yes...'

As he goes to change gear, I notice there's blood on his hand.

'What happened?' I ask.

'Nothing.'

'You're bleeding.'

He holds his hand up and then licks it away. 'It's nothing,' he says.

'Sorry for asking you to pick him up…'

I watch as my father gulps. He glances momentarily away from the road, catching my eye before turning back. 'Never be sorry for wanting to help,' he says. 'It's what makes us human, Mads. It's just that, sometimes, the odd bad one spoils it for everyone.'

NINE

The blue of the police car lights illuminates the row of hedges that are far up on the hill above where I live. There are no roads that far away from the main route. It's around a mile from my house in a straight line. There is a densely filled copse of trees at the very top of the hill – and then a series of tracks and trails that link back to the main road.

I grab my coat, hat and gloves and then walk on the verge up towards the lights. If I was to keep going, I'd end up at the petrol station where Harriet says she saw Alice getting into Richard's car. Instead of going that far, I clamber over a stile and follow a slim, muddy trail that tracks a line of trees up towards the woods. The one thing that everybody living in Leavensfield has in common is that we all own a decent pair of walking boots.

The tree branches hang low at this time of year, like spindly, muscle-free arms swaying back and forth. It's colder under the wooded canopy. There is a crystallised mash of leaves from the autumn that have partially mulched into the undergrowth, with a wide slick of mud that stretches over the trail. When it rains hard, an impromptu river will form along here as the water flows down towards the stream in the gully below.

As I reach the top of the hiking trail, it merges with a rocky track that's used by farmers to get their tractors onto the furthest fields. There are wide metal gates on both sides of the track and more further back towards the road. This is more or less the furthest any vehicle can get. There's a dead end – and then nothing but miles and miles of fields.

There is one police car blocking the gate on this side and another a little further back, preventing anyone from coming along the track. The blue lights are no longer spinning. If I'd walked up the way the tractors come, I'd have been turned around. Sometimes, a little local knowledge goes a long way.

I slip unnoticed around the front of the police car and then cross the deserted track to the gate on the other side. There are two uniformed officers standing a little inside the second field, though both have their backs to me.

It's immediately apparent why.

Parked at an angle and hidden in the corner of the field is Richard's black Toyota.

I stare at it, barely able to believe it's actually here. The bottom half of the car is caked with mud and the front wheel has sunk to the point that it's almost entirely buried in the sludge. Because of the positions of the hedges and the way the car is almost wedged into the corner, the car isn't visible even from a few paces away on the track. It certainly can't be seen from the road.

I wonder who found it. It must have been someone like a rambler or a farmer. Without that, the car could have been hidden in plain sight for days or weeks. Maybe even months.

There are tyre tracks that lead from the gate through to where the car now sits. The number plate is obscured by the spray of mud.

I've moved closer to the scene without realising I've done so, almost as if I've sleepwalked across the mud.

Over the back of the hedge, out of sight but barely steps away, is a steep drop to the stream. The water runs further down the hill towards where Atal found Alice.

One of the officers turns and jumps at the sight of my presence. With the other police car blocking the track, there's no way they'd be expecting someone to be up here. He's tall and starts walking towards me with his arms wide.

'You have to turn around,' he says.

The second officer has noticed now. She reaches towards the radio on her lapel and says something into it that I don't catch.

'It's my husband's car…'

The first officer doesn't realise what I've said at first. He keeps walking towards me, shooing me backwards like a naughty puppy. He's already started to say 'back' when he clocks what I've said.

'You know whose car this is?' he asks.

'My husband's. Have you found him…?'

He glances over his shoulder to where his colleague is still talking into her radio. 'You should return home,' he says. 'Someone will be in contact.'

I ignore him, stepping to the side as he tries to motion me away. He stands in front, trying to block my view – but that only makes me continue moving to the side in an attempt to see around him. We're like dancing crabs as we mirror one another's movements.

'Have you found him?'

The anguish in my voice surprises even me. The officer must pick up on it because he drops his arms, while his stony expression slips into something more conciliatory.

'We can drop you home if you want,' he says. 'Someone will come out to talk to you as soon as there's any news.'

I take a step forward and he takes one back.

'Has he been in a ditch this whole time…?'

The officer doesn't answer and I take another step ahead. I angle around the officer's body, squinting toward the ditch that's on the other side of the car. There are some rocks and some shattered wood, though it's hard to work out from where it could have come. I take another step to the side. It could be that slight difference in the way the light is reflecting but I can now see something red close to the front wheel that's sunk in the mud.

I stretch around the officer, who has his hands out once more to keep me away. 'Is that blood?'

He turns to glance towards where I'm pointing. 'If you just—'

I push against him, edging him backwards. He stumbles slightly but keeps his balance. 'Don't tell me to leave. That's my husband's car and he's been missing since yesterday. How would you feel?'

'I underst—'

'You don't!'

I look into his eyes and he has to turn away, towards the red. It feels as if I'm out of my body, watching myself. This manic, angry woman isn't who I am.

There's a silent stand-off now. The other officer is still talking into her shoulder radio – and then, from the other side of the car, Detective Inspector Dini appears. His shoes aren't shiny any longer as he's caked in mud almost up to his knees. He wears a grim expression as he lifts his legs high to almost wade around the back of the vehicle before he crosses towards me. He nods at the officer in front of me and the man in uniform lowers his arms and then moves away to the side.

'How'd you get up here?' Dini asks.

'Does it matter?' He waits until I can't resist the urge any longer. 'It's Richard's car,' I say.

He nods shortly in that infuriating way that I suspect means he already knows. I can imagine this little tic to be the sort of thing that would drive his wife crazy over the years. It brims with a purposeful arrogance. That *I-know-more-than-you* head tilt which says way more than words ever could. One day, you're madly in love; ten years down the line, you're hurling their clothes out the window because he's given that nod one too many times.

I point towards the red mark on the ground. It looks different now, more solid than before. 'Is that blood?' I ask.

Dini glances over his shoulder towards the front of the car. 'No.'

That's one thing, I suppose. A small comfort. 'What is it?'

He sighs and licks his top lip. The reluctance pours from him, but he replies anyway: 'It's a hairband.'

'A *what*?'

He takes a breath and looks me dead in the eye. 'It's a red plastic Alice band. Like the sort little girls wear…'

TEN

Now he's said it, I can see the plastic curve as clearly as if it was in my hand. I can't understand why I ever thought it was anything other than a hairband.

Dini reaches forward and catches my arm. At first, I wonder what he's doing – but then I realise that my knees are crumpling and that he's holding me up.

'Have you found Richard?' I ask as I straighten myself.

'Not yet.'

'But—'

'I know…'

I allow him to guide me away from the car, back through the gate and onto the rocky track.

Dini nods across to the female officer who was on her radio. 'Any sign of the SOCOs?'

'They got lost,' she calls back. 'Ten minutes away, tops.'

He peeps upwards towards the greying sky and it's only now that I realise there's a clinging misty rain. I'm soaked and have somehow not noticed.

'How did you get up here?' Dini asks, although it takes me a second to realise he's talking to me.

I point towards the gate on the other side of the track. 'There's a trail down there,' I say. 'It comes out near my house.'

'Don't you have pavements around here…?' He laughs gently, though I don't join in. 'Let's head back to your house,' he adds. 'You lead the way.'

I could say no, perhaps I should, but Dini is offering something that nobody else is at the moment. Company.

We press through the wide cattle gate and then follow the trail back towards the roads. In his suit, Dini is not dressed for this in any way – and, with his regulation black shoes, he's constantly slipping on the mud, else trying to keep to the parts on which there is still grass. By the time we get to the road, most of his lower half looks like he's done a Tough Mudder.

I lead the way along the verge but do catch the moment when Dini waves towards a small white van that's winding its way up the hill. I assume this will be more people off to check on the site where my husband's car now sits, close to the red Alice band.

When we get to the house, I unlock the door and take off my boots on the welcome mat, before tucking them in on the rack by the door. Dini waits patiently outside, hands behind his back.

'You can come in,' I say – and he does just that. He also removes his shoes – although they're a good sixty per cent mud at this point, and then he rolls up his trouser legs to expose black socks and a hint of hairy, pale leg. When we catch one another's eye, I know I'd be laughing in other circumstances. In many ways it is still funny – except that it doesn't feel like there are any laughs within me.

'Where can we go?' he asks.

I head through to the living room and take a seat on the sofa. Dini doesn't wait for an invitation as he presses back into the armchair where Richard would usually sit. The record player sits on the small table at his side and there is still a small crimson stain on the carpet from where Richard spilled red wine last summer.

'Nice tree,' Dini says, nodding towards the Christmas tree in the corner, near the window.

'It's fake,' I reply. 'We've had that for years.'

It stretches high to the ceiling and there is a winding band of fairy lights looped around. It's a sorry sight at the moment, with the lights switched off. Like a shop window display that's about to be torn down in January.

'I need to ask you something,' Dini says.

'You asked lots earlier.'

'Something else.'

I leave it there, waiting for him to fill in the gap before wishing that I hadn't.

'Can we search your house?' he asks.

Even though I suspected this must be coming, the request is still a surprise. As far as I know, nobody has ever gone through my things. I've never been burgled and I haven't lived with housemates in the way some people might. I'm used to privacy.

'Do I have a choice?'

'If you say no, we'll ask for a warrant based upon witness reports of your husband and Alice Pritchard being seen together. There's a very good chance that application will be accepted.'

'It would take you longer to do that, though…' I look across to Dini, hoping he's uncomfortable or sweating. Wanting him to show some degree of being worried. Instead, he matches my stare and it's me who has to look away.

'It will be granted,' he says firmly. 'It might take a few hours, it might be tomorrow, but we'll get a warrant.'

'So why are you asking me?'

'Because it shows good faith if you let us.' There's a politician's pause. The deliberate, ponderous type that all public speakers now do, to the point that it's lost almost all its impact. 'Sometimes, juries like that sort of thing…' He leaves it hanging, like the promise of a last meal in front of someone on death row. The outcome will be awful either way, but at least there's one thing that isn't terrible.

'I've got nothing to hide,' I say.

'Does that mean you'll let in a search team?'

'Do whatever you need.'

Dini pushes up from the chair and says he'll be right back. He heads into the hall and then possibly the kitchen. I can't tell, though I can hear a muffled voice, presumably talking into a phone.

A minute or so later and he's back.

'I think you've done the right thing,' he says.

I ignore that. Anyone who gets their own way thinks the other person has done the right thing. I go to stand but Dini coughs in a way that sounds fake. When I look to him, he's smiling grimly.

'It might be best if we wait together,' he says.

'Why?'

The smile remains. That annoying, cocksure confidence. He doesn't reply because we both know the answer.

I make a point of crossing the room and switching on the Christmas tree lights. Pink and green bulbs wink into existence and continue flashing on and off as I retake my seat.

'Is that okay?' I ask. 'Is there anything else I shouldn't be doing in my own house?'

Dini says nothing – and then neither do I. We sit in silence for probably ten minutes until there's a knock on the door. I go to stand – but Dini moves quicker. He strides across the living room, into the hall, and opens the door. I'm a few steps behind and arrive as a uniformed officer waits on the precipice. She passes Dini a wedge of forms and he turns and gives them to me.

'Can you sign this?' he asks. 'It gives us permission to search.'

I scan the page, though don't read it properly. I don't think I'd be able to focus on the words anyway. It seems legitimate enough, so I head for the kitchen, grab a pen, sign the form, and then hand it back to Dini – who has, of course, followed me.

'Are there any outbuildings on your property?' he asks.

'There's a shed at the end of the garden.'

'What's in there?'

'Not much. A couple of chairs. Sometimes Richard goes there for a bit of peace in the summer. I don't think he's been down there in a couple of months. It's mainly gardening tools. There's a key by the back door.'

'Thank you.'

Dini returns to the front of the house and mentions the shed to the person who'd brought the papers. With that, he leads me back to the living room and then a parade of officers pour into the house. I watch through the living-room door as anything up to a dozen people pass by one after the other, like clowns getting out of a comedy car. There's the sound of footsteps going upstairs and then of people moving around above. From the kitchen, it sounds as if cupboards are being opened.

'How did you get so many officers together so quickly?' I ask.

Dini shrugs the question away and mutters something about 'resources'. It's nonsense, of course. He's been ahead of me since the moment he turned up on my doorstep this morning.

He presses back into the armchair. With his rolled-up trousers, he looks like a granddad on a beach. With little other choice of what to do with myself, I curl into the corner of the sofa.

It's not long before there are shadows of people funnelling back through the house, past the front windows to where I presume their cars are parked. The front door opens and closes with such regularity that it might as well be left open. The house is draughty at the best of times and I find myself holding my arms across my front.

'Do you need something warmer?' Dini asks.

'I'm fine.'

He glances towards the laptop at my side.

'You can't take that,' I say. 'It's mine. I do all my work on it.' I open the lid and turn around so that he can see my stupid picture of a dog in a high chair on the welcome screen. 'Richard doesn't even know the password. I can't get things done without it.'

'The blogging?'

'Yes, the blogging.'

He looks to the computer one more time as I close the lid. 'There are a few more things I need to ask you,' he says.

'Will you let me keep my laptop?'

'I can't say yet.'

'Richard has his own computer. It's a desktop in his office upstairs.'

Dini doesn't react to this. It's not as if the search team are going to miss it. He purses his lips. 'I don't suppose you can remember the name of the friend your husband was visiting, can you? I know sometimes things can slip the mind. It certainly happens to me…'

It's a second chance that I probably don't deserve. Phrases like 'perverting the course of justice' and 'aiding an offender' bounce around my mind. I still can't believe Richard is involved in whatever's happened. He's my husband. He's not that sort of man. If Alice did get into his car, then there's an innocent explanation.

I *know* him.

I also know that Dini won't give me a third chance…

'It might have been someone who's name begins with a K,' I say. 'Like Kevin, or… Keith.'

It's an odd situation in that Dini must know I'm putting on something of a show. He goes with it, though.

'What would Kevin or Keith's last name be?'

'A longer name. I don't know Richard's friends. If you let me look at his rolodex, I could probably work it out.'

'Where's the rolodex?'

'In Richard's office.'

Dini examines me for a moment, perhaps wondering if I'm lying. Perhaps knowing that I am, even if it's not about anything serious.

'Wait here,' he says.

Dini crosses to the door and calls across one of the officers who is in the process of returning from the cars. He says something that I don't catch and then waits in the doorway until the officer appears a minute or two later with Richard's rolodex. He hands it across and I flip through the entries until I get to Keith Etherington's card.

'I'm pretty sure this is him,' I say.

Dini unhooks the card from the rest of the mechanism and then takes a photo of it with his phone. He then takes a see-through bag from one of the officers in the hallway and drops the card into it, before letting them take it.

'Who's Keith Etherington?' he asks.

'I don't know. Richard works too far away for there to be much crossover between his colleagues and anyone here.'

This gets little reaction, although Dini must see that it's the truth. He returns to the armchair and takes out his notebook.

'Your husband's forty-eight,' he says. It's somehow a question, even though it isn't.

'We married three years ago,' I reply.

'And you're, what, ten years younger than he is…?'

'Is there a problem with that?'

'No problem. I just want to make sure all the facts are correct. Are you Richard's first wife, or…?'

'Why are you asking if you already know?'

I want a reaction – even if it's a demand to answer the question. Instead, Dini remains passive and calm, his pen poised. It's *so* annoying.

'India died about six years ago,' I say. 'She was Richard's first wife. I never knew her. I didn't know Richard back then.'

'How did you meet?'

There's a bang from upstairs and we both stop.

'Are they trashing my house?' I ask.

'Not purposely.'

'What happens to the things you're taking?'

'You'll get a receipt for everything. Once we've run any necessary checks, everything will be returned unless it needs to be held as evidence.'

More shuffled footsteps come from the stairs and then the front door sounds again.

I don't know why Dini wants to hear about how Richard and I met. It can't have any bearing on now – and yet, as I consider telling him that it's none of his business, I realise that I *want* to talk about it. I miss my husband and, for now, memories are all I have.

'I was a mature student,' I say. 'I'd gone back to university to study English. I ended up dropping out because I didn't like the course – but I guess something clicked between Richard and me.'

'He was your lecturer?'

'Yes.'

It sounds worse than it was. People hear 'teacher–student relationship' and it has connotations. It was hardly love at first sight but Richard and I were both adults. *Are* both adults. I knew what I was doing and so did he. I'm not embarrassed by any of that, even though, every time I talk about things, it feels as if I should be.

'What happened with India?'

Hearing the name of Richard's first wife sends me spinning back into the room. I'd been temporarily back in the university building.

'I don't know for sure,' I reply.

'But you must have some idea.'

'So must you…'

It gets no reaction and we sit quietly for a moment as the bangs continue from above.

'She fell off a cliff,' I say. 'I don't know exactly where. She and Richard were hiking somewhere in Scotland. You can google her name. It's all online.'

'Have *you* googled her name?'

'Not recently. Why would I?'

Dini notes something on his pad but doesn't expand. I'm not sure I like the insinuations – because there's definitely a question there that he didn't dare ask.

He looks up abruptly and traps me in a stare: 'I read about what happened to your father.'

'I—'

I'm so taken aback by the change in direction that I can't breathe. The air is trapped somewhere on the way out and I launch into a series of small coughs until it's passed. It's already clear that Dini's done his homework, so no particular surprise that he knows this. It's still shocking that's he's mentioned it.

'I don't see how it's relevant,' I reply.

'It could be.'

'My dad is dead – so I don't see why it would.'

He opens his mouth but then closes it again, perhaps thinking better of whatever he was about to say. It doesn't matter anyway because his phone starts to ring and he removes it from an inside pocket. He checks the screen, then holds it up and says, 'I've got to take this.' With that, he hurries into the hall and pulls the door firmly closed.

I'm alone in my living room, even though it doesn't feel like mine any more. Perhaps it never did: it's almost entirely Richard's things in here, after all. I moved into his house after we married. He said it was 'ours', but I'm not sure it's ever quite felt like that.

I'm still stuck by the mention of my father. I don't like it when people bring him up. Richard learned this early enough and never does. Not even Kylie knows the full truth. I wonder how much Dini knows for sure…

It's another five or six minutes until the door opens and Dini reappears. There's a cardboard folder in his hand, which he passes across without comment. When I open it, there's a large photograph inside.

'It's from the CCTV camera at the garage just up the road,' he says. 'If you check the timestamp, it's from 19:54 on Sunday night.'

It takes me a moment to process the twenty-four-hour clock. Six minutes to eight on Sunday – and it's as plain as anything could be.

Little Alice Pritchard is in a red coat, with a red Alice band across her head, and she's getting into Richard's black Toyota. His hand is on her shoulder as he stands next to her on the passenger side.

I didn't believe Harriet was lying, not really, but here it is for certain.

'Madeleine…' Dini speaks my name with such softness that it makes me want to cry.

I look up, partly because I'm not used to hearing my full name. 'What?'

'Can you think of any reason for your husband to be helping Alice Pritchard into his car?'

I turn from Dini to the photo. My fingers are trembling. 'Perhaps he was giving her a lift back to the village so she didn't have to walk…?'

When I next look up, Dini's lips are pressed together. 'Perhaps…' he says – although it sounds as if doesn't believe his own reply.

ELEVEN

The search takes most of the afternoon. Officers started drifting off in ones and twos, almost without me noticing. Eventually, only two were left – and they went through the living room as Detective Inspector Dini and I sat in the kitchen. At least Richard's part-time hoarding is no longer an issue, seeing as the police have now relieved him of his papers, computer, files and journal. His office is more or less bare.

They let me keep my laptop. I'm not sure if that was always going to be the case, or if it's because I answered all of Dini's questions. I think he might have felt sorry for me, although perhaps that's what he wanted me to believe. It's hard to be sure of anything at the moment.

Dini left me the photo from Fuel's Gold – and I'm glad he did. Without looking at it every five minutes, I'm not sure I'd be able to comprehend what was happening. It would be bad enough if it was just Richard missing – but the double hit of him being gone and Alice being found in the stream has left me floored.

I've not eaten today, but, as I look through the cupboards, I see only Richard. There's the Shredded Wheat that he has for breakfast every day, the peaches he eats straight from the can, the Diet Coke that he drinks all the time, the extra-mature Cheddar because he doesn't like any other cheeses.

Richard is everywhere around me, but he's nowhere.

I'm not sure why but I take the key from the hook by the back door – and then head down the garden and into Richard's shed.

The house is a patchy mess of things the police took and things they didn't – but, here, as far as I can tell, it is untouched. There wasn't much in the first place. It's mainly tools for the garden that I've never used and with which Richard has only patchily bothered. Last summer, he got a gardening company in to keep everything in order.

The rocking chair remains in the corner of the shed, along with the pile of blankets that have been out here since before I moved in. There's a wide hamper built into the back wall that's filled with things like boxes and manuals for various electrical items in the house. I don't know why Richard keeps everything.

I sit in the rocking chair and let it bob back and forth.

The rain has stopped now and the cold has descended once more. I have to clamp my jaw together to stop my teeth chattering. Despite that, I close my eyes and lean back. I can see why Richard spends time here. The silence is perfect and beautiful. There's nothing: not even wind or chirping birds. It feels like another place. It gives me the space to consider everything that's happened.

I lied, maybe, to Dini – although I suspect he knows.

Of course I've searched the internet for the name India King. After filtering out the obvious results about Asian monarchs and takeaway shops, there's quite a lot about Richard's ex-wife. Which second wife wouldn't read every single word available on the first? Definitely not me.

Richard only told me he'd been married before after we'd been to bed for the first time. Not that there was a bed involved.

It was the next morning when I went home and spent the best part of a day reading up on the woman who came before me. I still remember almost all of it, certainly the important parts.

It was six years ago that India King was hiking with Richard in the Cairngorms, Scotland. She was forty-one, older than I am now, when she slipped and fell. There was a line in one of the reports that I can recall perfectly – 'Mrs King's devastated husband watched but could do nothing'. I thought about the word 'devastated' for a long time afterwards. Anybody would have been *devastated* if they'd seen such a thing.

Apparently, the air ambulance attended but they couldn't land. Richard was left at the top of wherever they were, waiting for someone to come and retrieve India's body. He must have known she was dead because of the height of the fall – but he was stuck and alone, not able to be certain.

Who wouldn't be *devastated*?

Eighteen months had passed from then to the time I started viewing Richard in a different way than simply a lecturer. After reading the article, it was hard not to wonder if his love for his first wife would impact on whatever he might end up feeling for me.

There was one other thing I wondered about, too. I'm only human and who wouldn't have those thoughts? It was covered by another line at the end of the report, almost as a throwaway, even though I'd bet anyone who read it had that as a first thought.

'Police say there are no suspicious circumstances involved.'

I wondered if it was alluding to there *actually* being suspicious circumstances, like some sort of police double bluff. Or if it was to do away with the snidey whispers that would accompany any story of this type.

It probably sounds strange but in the end, I kind of… forgot. I fell in love and Richard was in love with me. What went before didn't matter. It's not as if he's ever shown any sort of violent or abusive tendencies towards me or anyone. I'd have to really think as to whether I've heard my husband raise his voice to a person. It isn't his way.

Back in the shed and it's too much effort to stop my teeth from chattering any longer. The cold feels as if it has seeped all the way into my bones. It's tiring just to keep my eyes open – and yet, at the same time, I'm too exhausted to move. I want to stay here, in this small space, and wait for everything to go away.

The only reason I don't do that is because my phone buzzes with a text. My body aches to move and my fingers are stiff and arthritic.

Theresa: *Where are you?*

I think about ignoring the message – and the only reason I don't is because I'm not sure I'm going to have many allies in the coming weeks.

Me: *At home*

Theresa: *Answer the door then!*

My joints creak as I push myself up and attempt to hurry back to the house. I lock the back door and then move through to the front and open up for Theresa. She presses inside quickly, blowing cold air into her hands.

'I thought you might want some company,' she says.

She's wearing the kindly smile of someone who's heard all about my missing husband and the way Alice was last seen getting into his car. If it wasn't already the case, then everyone in the village will know by now.

'I was out back,' I say.

'What were you doing there?'

'Not much.'

She unwhirls her scarf and takes off her coat, hangs both on the hook by the clock and then starts to head for the kitchen. It's when she's passing the living room that she notices the mess that's been left. 'What happened in there?' she asks.

'The police searched the house.'

Theresa stops, turns, and takes me in – and then, from nowhere, there are tears pouring down my face. I don't cry too often, something that goes back to when I had to be the strong one around Dad. This is the first time in years.

It's an ugly cry. A chest-heaving, throat-burning, energy-sapping explosion of the person I pretend I'm not.

Theresa sits with me on the stairs and does nothing other than lay a hand on my knee and let me rest my head on her shoulder.

It's hard to know if I'm crying for Richard, Alice, myself, or a little bit of everyone… except that I do know. I'm crying for myself. That makes me feel selfish, which only has me crying even more.

Time passes. We don't talk because we don't need to. That's what a real friend is, I think.

There's a pile of balled tissues at the bottom of the stairs and, when it's finally over, Theresa helps me put them into the bin. We head through to the kitchen and she fills the kettle and then sits with me at the table. There's not such a mess in here. Unless the police chose to confiscate a packet of half-eaten chocolate digestives, I don't think there's much in here to interest them.

'Are you okay?'

Theresa speaks so earnestly that I shift from tears to laughter in an instant. It's too much for her and, before we know it, we're both cackling as if we're at the end of a drunken hen night.

By the time I've finally got it out of my system, the kettle has clicked off and Theresa makes us both a tea. Back at the table we sit quietly for a moment. Tears still feel close.

'They say Alice is still in intensive care,' Theresa says.

'Does that mean she's going to be all right?'

'I don't know. Hopefully.'

I half expect her to ask about Richard but she knows me too well. I can barely think about him at the moment, let alone talk. I don't know if I'm worried or angry. If I want him to come home, or I don't.

We make small talk about a bake sale next month, for which I've committed to make some cookies and cake bars. Another thing in the calendar after the Winter Ball. There's always something else.

I know Theresa's trying to get me to look forward not back – and I go with it. I'm not sure what else to do. I've still got work to do, though I have no idea how I can write about such triteness given what's happened. How can life continue as normal when there is no normal?

Theresa takes our empty mugs to the sink and rinses them out.

'You've got school in the morning,' she says.

'Huh?'

When I turn, she nods towards the calendar on the wall. I can't read the words from the distance but, as soon as I've realised what she's said, I know she's right. I'm supposed to be running another cookery class at the primary school in the morning.

'I'll have to cancel,' I say.

'Why?'

'Why do you think?'

'Might give you something to concentrate on. It's a bit late to cancel now anyway…'

I don't reply, although I can't see how I can coach a group of children through making a pineapple upside-down cake, or whatever else I might do. It's something for the morning.

Theresa returns to the table. 'What would you like to do?' she asks. 'Do you want to go out somewhere? We can drive to a pub in the country where nobody will know us. Get something to eat, if you want.'

The thought of food makes my stomach lurch.

'I should stay here,' I reply. 'Just in case…'

'Do you want to watch something on TV? Or you can teach me how to make that walnut loaf you were telling me about…?'

I feel stuck in my seat, not wanting to do anything and yet not wanting to sit still either. Everything is a contradiction.

'Can I ask you something?' I say.

'Of course.'

'About India…'

There's a pause. This is territory into which I've never ventured with Theresa. She has lived in Leavensfield for longer than me and she knew Richard's first wife long before I came along. It feels dangerous.

Theresa shifts awkwardly on her seat. 'What do you want to know?'

'I'm not sure. I just don't know much about her…'

A sigh: 'Why now?'

I can't reply, partly because I'm not sure of the answer.

Theresa doesn't push it and, after a few seconds, answers as if this is completely normal. 'I liked her,' she says. 'We weren't really friends, but you know what it's like around here. We'd end up in the same places and doing the same things. She was always sociable.' Another pause. 'I think you'd have liked her.'

I'm not sure how to take that. It's not an insult but I don't feel particularly overjoyed that Richard might have swapped one India for another.

'You're not *that* similar,' she adds quickly, reading my thoughts. 'India was friends with Harriet and that lot. She wasn't all-in, like some of them around here – but they'd organise things together. I think India might have been there when Xavier was born – if not at the time, then shortly afterwards.'

'Do you think that's why Harriet hates me?'

I've often wondered if this is the reason why I've never quite felt a part of the village. Harriet and Sarah were too close to India to ever accept someone taking her place. India was one of them: a housewife who was into yoga and herbal tea. I know all that because, among other things, I cleared out her yoga mat and years-old tins of tea after moving in. Richard had never got rid of her things in the years since she'd died.

'I don't think Harriet hates you,' Theresa says.

'She does.'

'That's how she is. Everyone's an asset to her – but it depends on how useful they are in any given moment. When you get your cookbook deal, she'll want to be your best friend. When they invite you onto *This Morning* to do a cooking segment, she'll want to come with you. You'll see.'

There's something about Theresa's relentless optimism that leaves me both grateful to have her and yet dismayed that I don't feel like that about myself. Any sort of book deal feels a long way off. Any more than that feels less likely than a lottery win – and I don't even play the lottery.

'Harriet and India were close towards the end,' Theresa adds.

'Why?'

'I'm not completely sure…'

She glances away and I don't have to call her on the evasion for her to elaborate.

'India and Richard were arguing a lot that year. I think India had been leaning on Harriet for support.' She holds her hands up. 'I don't know for certain.'

Theresa has no reason to lie about this. If she was simply gossiping, she'd have told me at some point in the past. She's only saying it now because I asked. This is the first time I've heard of any sort of conflict between India and Richard. I wasn't around then – and I suppose there would be no reason for anyone to tell me. Certainly no reason for Richard to do so.

'Why were they arguing?'

Theresa squirms again. 'It was all gossip. I don't *know*.'

'What did you hear?'

'That Richard wanted kids – but that India didn't. I saw them having an argument in the village.'

'When?'

'About a week before…'

I almost ask 'before what' – but the way Theresa can no longer look at me makes it clear to what she's referring. I don't know what to say. Richard is not the type of man who goes for public anything. Displays of affection are a definite no – and I can't picture him raising his voice to argue in front of anyone, let alone *in public*. I nearly ask if Theresa is sure it was them – but of course she is.

'Where were they?' I ask.

'Back of the pub, near Bob's.'

That's the bit-of-everything shop which is a mainstay of any village. About as public as it gets in Leavensfield.

'What did you overhear?'

'Not just me. I was outside the pub on the tables they put out when it's sunny. A bunch of us heard it. He said something like, "I don't understand why you have to be like this" and then she shouted back, "It's my body – and we never talked about having kids." They went quiet after that, but I guess it was too late. The village spent the week gossiping about it. You know what people are like. Then they went to Scotland…'

Theresa leaves it at that. She doesn't need to explain what the village were talking about in the days and weeks after India fell.

My immediate reaction is to wonder how I never heard any of this. The answer seems simple in as much that it was almost two years later that I showed up. I never asked because I had no reason to – and nobody ever told me because why would they.

'It's nothing,' Theresa says. 'I shouldn't have said anything. Richard's a good guy. I've known him for years.'

'I know him, too. But I never thought he'd disappear – and I never thought a girl would end up in a stream after getting into his car.'

She reaches across and rests a hand on mine. 'It will all be okay.'

I take a breath and can't reply because, deep down, I know that it won't.

TWELVE YEARS OLD

Byker Grove is on the TV when the doorbell sounds. I wouldn't usually move but Dad calls 'Can you get that?' from the kitchen – and so I do as I'm asked. There was one time about a month ago when one of Dad's friends came knocking. He answered it and they got talking on the doorstep, in the way that always seems to happen when one of Dad's mates is at the door. The main problem was that Dad had been cooking beans for my tea at the time. I was watching TV then as well – which is when the smoke alarms went crazy. There's still a scorch mark on the bottom of the pan.

I head along the hall and unlock the door before pulling it open. I'm expecting another of Dad's friends – but, instead, it's a police officer in uniform. He's tall and his uniform is smart. He crouches slightly, angling himself down to my level.

'Is your dad in?' he asks.

'Are you a policeman?'

I don't know why I ask it, other than that I've never been this close to an officer before.

'I am,' he says. 'Is your dad around?'

'I…'

The shout of 'Who is it?' booms through from the kitchen and the man straightens.

'Is that your dad?' he asks.

'Yes.'

'Can I come in?'

I hold open the door, feeling unable to say no. The officer passes me but waits for me to close the door before I lead him through to the kitchen.

When we get there, Dad is spinning a frozen pizza on his finger. He spots me first and launches into a 'ta-da!' before he sees the officer. 'Oh, um…'

He puts the pizza onto a baking tray and then quickly turns back to the policeman.

'Sorry about that,' he says. 'What's going on?'

'Are you John Evesham?'

'That's me.'

'Can I have a word?' He nods towards me and I know what's coming a moment before it does.

'Will you go upstairs,' Dad says.

'But—'

'No buts. Upstairs.'

I look towards the policeman, wondering if he might somehow give me a reprieve. I let him in, after all.

No such luck.

I stomp upstairs, making it clear that I am not happy about this development. Each step involves a new *thump* until I'm at the top, where I jump up and down for good measure. I then sit on the top step, clenching my teeth and squeezing my face from the inside, trying to make my ears work better. Unfortunately, Dad has closed the kitchen door, meaning the only thing I can hear is muffled voices. It's like wearing headphones when someone's trying to tell me something.

A few minutes pass and then there's the sound of the kitchen door opening. I watched the Olympics a few years ago but I swear nobody can move as fast as me in instances like this. Before anyone could possibly know it, I'm up and off the top step, across the landing, and through my bedroom door. I hurl myself onto my bed and then lie there waiting with a magazine.

It takes another minute or so until Dad knocks on my door. I call him in and then flip a page of the magazine to let him know that I've definitely been reading it while he's been downstairs.

In an instant, none of that matters. There's something in his face that I can't make out. Not unhappiness… I think it might be worry.

'I'm going to take you next door,' he says. 'Polly's going to look after you for a few hours.'

'Why?'

He shakes his head and holds out his hand. 'Not now, Mads. Let's go.'

I don't move. 'Where are you going?'

'I've got to go to the police station.'

'Why?'

'Let's not talk about that now. Polly's waiting for you. I'll be back later.'

There's a pain in my chest, something I've never felt before. When I reach out, Dad takes my hand and we head for the stairs.

'Are you going to be okay?' I ask.

'Course I am,' Dad replies. 'But it's time to go.'

TWELVE

TUESDAY

I stay up for large parts of the night rearranging the house and tidying up after the police. I think about cross-checking everything on the list given to me by the final officer who left, in case there might be something else that's missing. I don't in the end, mainly because I realise that I don't care. Almost everything in the house belongs to Richard anyway.

When I sleep, it's in short bursts and wherever the urge takes me. I have two naps on the sofa, another in the armchair, three in my bed and one at the kitchen table. I'm like a narcoleptic cat.

In between leaving the house on Sunday morning and being seen with Alice, there are around eight or nine hours in which I have no idea what my husband was up to. We've never been the sort of couple who has to do everything together, or who keeps tabs on one another. He does his thing and I do mine – and then, sometimes, we do things together. It works for us.

Except for now.

I'm now left wondering if, on all those other times he told me he was visiting work colleagues, whether that's what he was actually doing. I've seen those stories about men who have second wives and families. Secret kids halfway across the country. That sort of thing. I always wonder how they get away with it – but now I'm left seeing myself as one of those 'I never knew'-women.

I'll be on the front of those magazines that end up near the till at supermarkets. A person to be mocked.

I only realise I've not drawn any of the curtains when the sun begins to creep through the living-room window. There's a bluey hue over the crest of the hill atop Leavensfield and the sky has turned a dim purple. After the rain of the past few days, it looks as if today will be a crisp winter postcard of a day.

As I head into the kitchen to set the kettle boiling, I spot the calendar and remember that I didn't cancel my morning class at the school. According to the town's Facebook page, it was closed yesterday because of everything with Alice. Nobody has messaged or called to say that any classes are cancelled today.

I stare towards the box of new bakeware at the back of the kitchen. Probably unsurprisingly, the police didn't bother with searching through that. I'm not in the mood to be working and yet Theresa's advice – *Might give you something to concentrate on* – rattles around my mind. She's probably right. It's got to be better than moping around the house enduring wild mood swings. One moment I'm desperate for Richard to return, the next, I think I'd be better off if he never does. There's a constant battle and I have no idea what I actually want.

Then I think of my dad and what happened to him – and there's a renewed determination that I can't let circumstantial evidence win out. Richard was giving Alice a lift home like the kind person I know him to be – and something else happened that had nothing to do with him.

For now, life has to go on.

It seems trivial now, but when I moved into this house, one of the things that excited me was the near empty cupboard at the back of the kitchen. I realise that makes me sound like quite the pampered elite but I don't care. People are allowed to get excited over cars and footballs, so an empty cupboard that I've turned into a baking pantry is fine, too.

The police had a bit of a look yesterday but it was more moving things around than creating any real damage. I fill a couple of bags for life with flour, sugar, oil, cocoa powder, bicarbonate, cooking chocolate, icing sugar – and a giant transparent tub of sugar strands. The school already has a cupboard full of cooking equipment, so the only other thing I need are a few muffin pans.

By the time I've packed everything, I realise that I'm looking forward to something for what feels like the first time in weeks. It's only days, of course, but yesterday felt like it would never end.

I head upstairs and take a shower before tidying myself up enough to make it look as if I've had a half-decent night's sleep. When all that's done, I carry my bags out to the car and pack them into the back.

The sun is completely up now and the sky is a searing blue. The hill over Leavensfield is as green as I've seen it, except for a dusky white peppering of frost across the bottom.

I'm going to be early but I'd rather be at the school with people around me than I would alone in this house.

It's a short drive down the hill into the village centre and there's no police car outside Gemma's house this time. There's also no obvious sign that anything is amiss with the village.

The school's staff car park is next to the main building and it's only half full when I take the spot furthest away from the school, leaving those closest for the teachers. That means waddling awkwardly across the frost-dusted tarmac with my overflowing bags for life.

Because I've been doing this semi regularly for the past year and a bit, the school issued me a swipe card to get in through the staff door. I think the main reason was that it saved the secretary having to come down two flights of stairs to let me in. There's also the logic that nothing bad ever happens in Leavensfield, so why would it be a problem for me to let myself into the school?

There are probably only a hundred or so children at this school and it serves Leavensfield and a handful of other local villages and hamlets. It's the type of place that might be hard for someone to imagine if they're used to inner-city schools with thirty kids in a class. As with many things around here, there's a cosy safety that inhabits everything about the school.

I balance the bags with my knees and fish around my pockets for the swipe card, before letting myself in. The walls are plastered with drawings and posters created by the various year groups as I follow my way around the corridors to the reception area of the school, where the students enter. It's there that I have to stop to put everything down.

One of the teachers, whose name I can't remember, is standing near the doors while tapping something into her phone. She turns at the sound of me nearly dropping the bags, and then catches my eye.

'What class are you with today?' she asks.

'Year threes.'

That gets a nod before she twists back to the front – and does a double take that's so pronounced that it's impossible to miss.

I follow her eyeline out towards the playground. There are children towards the back running around with a ball – but, away from them, off to the side, it's as if a pause button has been pressed. The kids have moved away, forming a path through which Harriet is descending the steps to the playground. She's in full goddess mode today, in some sort of matching all-white outfit, with a furry collar. Like a snow queen descending from her throne. She's even wearing a pair of huge sunglasses, the type of which are usually only seen among celebrities who allegedly don't want to be spotted.

Xavier and Beatrice are walking in front of her and they're all keeping pace so perfectly that I wouldn't be surprised if they've practised this beforehand.

That's not why the teacher did a double take, however.

Walking at Harriet's side is Gemma.

The toll of what happened with Alice hangs in every step that her mother takes. Harriet walks tall but Gemma is slumped, with her shoulders drooped and low. Her skin is pale, while her dark hair hangs loose and unwashed. She's in leggings, with a tatty coat – a complete contrast to what Harriet has on.

None of that is surprising – but the fact Gemma's here genuinely is. Alice is surely at the hospital and yet her mother's at the school her daughter is too old to attend.

Harriet and Gemma stop at the bottom of the school steps – which is when I realise a pair of photographers with long lenses and camera bags are with them.

I follow the teacher out onto the playground as the photographers' camera shutters click away in rapid succession. The two women are suddenly inseparable and, though Gemma had been looking to the floor, she blinks upwards to take in the attention. Other parents have gathered and the children at the other end of the playground have stopped running and started to mass.

There are people I assume to be journalists holding their phones at arm's length out towards Gemma and Harriet. By entering the staff car park, I seemingly missed the beginnings of whatever this is.

Harriet is treating it like an impromptu press conference. She holds up a hand and there's instant silence. This would be impressive anywhere, let alone at the edge of a school playground.

'Gemma won't be answering questions today,' Harriet says. 'She is asking everyone to respect her privacy. This is all she has to say on the matter.'

If it wasn't here, in this moment, it would be laughable. Harriet's been watching too many court dramas.

Other teachers have joined the huddle, although they're looking to one another with something approaching confusion. This probably shouldn't be happening, let alone on school property

– but there are cameras and reporters here. Who would be brave enough to step in?

As Harriet speaks, Gemma continues to look around the gathering. She's suddenly standing taller and she starts to smooth down her hair. I can picture her as that teenager who's picked on by the cool kids but who then gets a chance to join the gang. Her daughter is in hospital and yet I can see how a part of her must be flattered by whatever it is that Harriet is doing here.

Some people think that others can only be traumatised if they're crying into their hands, or hiding away. Anything less than that means they're guilty of some sin, imagined or otherwise.

Harriet takes a step forward and rests a hand on each of her children's shoulders. Gemma shifts ahead, too. It's as if there's an invisible shield around them – and people *keep* moving as Harriet edges towards the school. Gemma keeps pace as they get closer to the main entrance.

I only realise what's about to happen when it's too late. I'm frozen on the spot as Harriet stops a few paces away from me. Gemma is staring, wide-eyed, as if she's prey and I'm the lion.

I shouldn't be here. It was a massive misjudgement to think that I was up to this – or that anyone would want me to be here.

It's not only Gemma who is staring. Xavier and Beatrice are both open-mouthed, as are, seemingly, all the other children and adults. I'm a pheasant in the crosshairs as Harriet clears her throat dramatically.

'Well,' she says, 'this is awkward.'

THIRTEEN

Harriet nods past me towards the school beyond. 'Are you *sure* this is the best place for you to be today, Madeleine?'

It's a question, but it's not. It's also none of her business – but it is. She says my name like my dad used to do when I was in trouble. I was 'Mads' when things were good, 'Maddy' at other times – and then 'Madeleine' if I'd overstepped the line. Nobody ever calls me that nowadays. I don't think I've ever introduced myself to a person using my full name. Now there's Dini and Harriet in the space of a day.

Harriet takes a moment to stop and make a deliberate point of looking to the surrounding children, as if I'm some sort of danger. None of the watching journalists, parents or teachers say anything. We're all in Harriet's thrall.

Children are massing around me now. It's as thrilling as it is frightening to see adults argue. I should go. Except the image of my father drops into my head and I know I can't let it go like this.

'Are you accusing me of something?'

Harriet opens her mouth and then closes it again. She won't be used to dissent, let alone directly to her face while people are watching. She'd have expected me to meekly fold away and disappear.

This is probably why she takes the moment to play the trump card with which I can't argue. She turns sideways to look to a muted Gemma. 'I just think that with everything that's happened to Alice and with the fact that your husband is missing – plus everything else – that a school might not be the best place for you.'

'Why?'

Harriet stares at me. I've surprised myself by standing up to her. What's she going to do? Accuse me of beating a child half to death and leaving the body in a stream? Harbouring an attempted murderer? Not even Harriet will go that low.

It's Gemma who speaks. Her voice is croaked and it sounds like she has a cold. 'Do you know where your husband is?'

It feels as if everyone is looking at me. As far as I know, it's not been reported that Richard is missing, nor that there's any connection between him and Alice. That makes no difference in a place such as this, though. Once one person knows, everybody does. Everyone around me, probably including the children, will know that Alice got into Richard's car. She was dumped in a stream, while he's not been seen since.

'No,' I say, although I'm unable to meet Gemma's stare. 'If I did, I'd say.'

I glance up and Gemma has turned sideways towards Harriet.

'Maybe we should take this inside?' Harriet says. 'We'll talk to the headmistress.'

She sounds polite – but only in the way somebody does when they're calling a new haircut 'brave'. What I didn't realise until now is that the damage has already been done.

It's unclear who says it – but the voice belongs to one of the group of women standing directly behind Harriet. 'I don't want her alone with my kids.'

'I'm not—'

'Someone call the police.'

'You don't—'

'Paedo!'

I'm left in a spin, trying to see who's talking, while also attempting to reply. The final word leaves me stunned. I've no idea who said it, other than that it was a woman. I don't know everyone here – and parents do drive their children in from other places – but this is my home. I'm a part of this community.

Or I used to be.

One of the teachers begins to speak – but Harriet talks over her.

'I'm sure Madeleine isn't involved in any of this. I don't think we should be throwing around words like that.'

The chattering around her subsides – but it's not lost on me that she's the one who whipped it up in the first place. Like someone shouting 'fire' in a cinema and then admonishing people for not forming an orderly queue to leave.

There's a hand on my shoulder and someone at my side. When I turn, it's Louisa – Mrs Peartree – the teacher with whose class I'm supposed to be helping. I can see in her sad but firm expression that I wasn't expected today, despite the scheduled class. That I shouldn't be here.

'I thought someone had called you,' she says softly.

I'm defeated, with nowhere to go from here.

'I just need to get my stuff from inside,' I say.

Louisa nods a solemn acceptance before Harriet steals the final word.

'Madeleine…?'

'What?'

'I was thinking it's probably best if someone else takes care of the flowers for the winter ball…'

I stare towards her. I'd forgotten about the job she'd given me. The one I didn't want. I also can't believe her stupid event is still taking place considering everything that's happened. It's systematic of the hypocrisy in the village. My husband's suspected actions have left me ostracised, even though I've done nothing. Meanwhile, nobody is questioning why Gemma's daughter was free to walk across darkened fields in the middle of winter.

'You know what, Harriet? You can take those flowers and shove them right up your—'

Louisa grips my shoulder a little harder this time and I stop. Tears feel close again and there's no way I'm going to cry in front of a crowd. Louisa guides me inside and I let her. She leads me towards my bags and picks one up, leaving the other for me.

'Where are you parked?' she asks.

'In the staff car park.'

She nods. 'I'll show you out, then.' There's a momentary pause and then: 'Perhaps it's best if I take your pass, too.'

FOURTEEN

The house is cold and desolate. Sometimes the central heating turns itself off for seemingly no reason. Richard says it only happens when I set it. He perhaps has a point – but he's never gone out of his way to show me how it all works.

I've already taken off my coat when I decide to put it back on again. I leave the bags in the hallway, unable to deal with putting anything away quite yet. Who cares about a stupid pantry? I almost wish the police were back to do another search because at least there would be someone here.

I consider calling Theresa but don't. It's the daytime and she has her own things with which to be getting on. Word will go around about what happened at the school anyway. Chances are, she'll call me at some point.

I think about contacting Kylie but don't do that either. She doesn't deserve any of this to be dumped upon her, although I should tell her about Richard before any of this reaches the wider news cycle.

I need to first find out where Richard was on Sunday. He lied to me but there has to be a clue somewhere – even though the police took many of his things. The only items left in his office are some random books and stationery. When I find nothing of note there, I go into our bedroom and hunt through the pockets of the jackets and trousers still hanging in the wardrobe. There are receipts that go back years, £40 in notes spread across three jackets, a comb, a pair of nail scissors and a random key that looks like it should fit our front door, even though it doesn't turn when I try it.

It's as I'm dropping the banknotes into the spare change pot that Richard and I share that I have an idea.

Richard and I have had a joint bank account and shared credit cards since around a month before we married. We also each have our own savings accounts that date back to before we were together. I've never felt the urge to ask about his and he's never asked about mine. He's more old-fashioned than I am when it comes to money. He prefers to use cash and deal with any issues in a branch. I can't understand why more places don't let me tap my card, while I use online banking for as much as I can.

I retrieve my laptop from the kitchen and log myself into my bank's website. I check the credit card first – although there have been no transactions since I filled my car with petrol on Friday. I almost close the tab – but then remember that Richard uses his debit and credit cards interchangeably. They're both the same colour, so it's not entirely his fault – although it can be annoying when he pays for something expensive that takes us either overdrawn or close to it.

A single click of the tracker pad and there it is.

I stare at the transaction from Sunday, knowing it was nothing to do with me. Richard spent £38 at somewhere called The Willow Tree. I've never heard of it, but, when I google it, I find the place immediately. It's a country pub with an attached restaurant that is around twenty miles away.

Although I've not heard of the pub by name, I know where it is. I've probably driven past it once a month or so when heading for the motorway. One of those places to which I've never paid attention. I close the laptop, grab my car keys, and then head out once more.

It's hard not to feel edgy as I drive past Fuel's Gold on the route away from Leavensfield. I slow without meaning to when

I'm near the tarmacked area a little away from the forecourt. This is where Alice and Richard were pictured together. There's a tall, metal clothes recycling bin off to the side, with some sort of large, rusting, cylindrical fuel tank behind that.

If I'd been thinking straight this morning – and there hadn't been the crowd – I might have asked Gemma if she was working on Sunday. I could have found out if she knows why Alice was out here, or why her daughter might have got into Richard's car. The police will have asked those questions but they're hardly likely to share the answers with me.

I'm only aware of the car in my rear-view mirror when it swerves onto the other side of the road and disappears into the distance with a honk of the horn. It spurs me back to the present and I accelerate away and towards the deepening shadows that criss-cross the road. The hedges are higher the further I get away from the village. Evergreens sway low across the lanes, with overgrown branches scraping across the roof of the car. The verge soon disappears as the road narrows to little more than a single track. I have to pull in a couple of times in order to let someone pass who's coming the other way but, other than that, the route is deserted.

The Willow Tree sits at the bottom of a valley, close to a stone bridge that crosses a river. There is even more green out here than there is around Leavensfield. The fields stretch to the horizon and beyond before melding with the blue of the sky. The pub is in the middle of nowhere – although that's part of the appeal. People will travel from miles around to eat here.

The first indication that there's something wrong is the near-deserted parking area. There are only another two cars anywhere in sight and they're close to the bridge, meaning they probably belong to hikers or dog-walkers who've parked up and then headed off along the river bank.

It's only as I spot the closed doors at the front that I realise I'm far too early. The lack of sleep and premature start to the day has me feeling like it's mid-afternoon, even though it's only a little after half-past ten. When I check the sign next to the door, it says that they open at twelve, which leaves me a fair bit of time to kill. Going home, sitting for fifteen minutes and then coming back makes no sense and, given that I don't really know this area, I don't seem to have a lot of options.

As I'm pondering my choices, someone in a grubby hatchback pulls up close to the river. A man opens the back of the car and a huge dog that might have been cross-bred with a pony leaps down. The dog seemingly knows where he or she is because, without prompting, it starts cantering along the riverbank with the owner trailing behind.

Because I don't know the way, I follow them, although the dog and owner are both walking faster than me and it doesn't take long for them to disappear into the distance.

There is something about this area that feels very Richard. He's not a big walker when it comes to things like fields and trees – but he likes the views. Being in the Cairngorms with its steepling mountains and mind-blowing valleys is entirely the sort of break I know he'd enjoy – as long as there was a B&B room in which to sleep at the end of a day. I can also easily picture him ambling along this riverbank while saying hello to the various dogs that pass. He could have come here for some peace and a walk, before getting himself a bit of lunch at the end of it.

All perfectly explainable… except he told me he was meeting a friend, who ended up knowing nothing about it. That can't have been an accident. Whatever Richard did on Sunday was planned – and kept secret from me.

I head over a second bridge to get to the other side of the water and then it's a long, meandering route back to the car park before recrossing. My cheeks feel flushed from the cold and the chill is tickling my nose – but the walk has been worth it to clear my head. There's a focus that I didn't have before and the cloud of exhaustion has passed.

It's almost 12.15, and the doors of the pub are open. Inside, and the immediate warmth is as welcome as a cosy armchair after a long day and I follow through a second set of double doors until I'm in the main area.

There's a large carvery hatch against the back wall, with a second sign and an arrow pointing to a 'vegetable station'. This is the type of place that will be rammed with people throughout a Sunday afternoon as families pour in one after the other to fill their plates with meat and gravy.

I sit at one of the high stools at the bar and grab a food menu, so that I don't look completely out of place. There's seemingly only one barman working, although there are no customers, other than me. He's got that shaved sides and stubbly thing going on that all young men seem to copy at the moment.

'Can I help you?' he asks.

'Do you do coffee?'

'Only from a machine.'

'That's fine. I'll have a cappuccino.'

I pay and then he drifts off to the other end of the bar, before returning a couple of minutes later with a frothy cup, plus a small biscuit.

'I've never been here before,' I say, unsure what to talk about.

He picks up a glass from behind the counter and starts to wipe it down with a tea towel. 'Where do you live?' he asks.

'Leavensfield. I suppose I should venture further afield…'

He smiles in the polite way waitstaff do when someone's boring them. I don't blame him.

'Were you here on Sunday?' I ask.

He puts down the glass and picks up a second, which he begins to dust. 'That was my day off.'

'Is there anyone in who might have done?'

'Only my manager.'

'Can I speak to him, please?'

The barman gives me a quizzical frown and I sense he's almost about to ask 'why?' before he thinks better of it. 'Sure,' he replies, before adding that he'll be right back.

He disappears through the door on the other side of the bar, leaving me alone in the pub. The flashing lights of the quiz machine near the door flicker on and off and there's a distant hum of some inoffensive music that I don't recognise. I pass the time by scanning the menu, until a man in a suit emerges behind me.

He offers his hand for me to shake, introduces himself as Darren, and then says, 'I gather you wanted to talk to me.'

'Were you working on Sunday?' I ask.

'Most of the day.'

I take out my phone and load a photo of Richard, before holding it up for Darren to look at. 'Did you see this man?' I ask.

His expression turns into a scowl. The recognition is obvious and I have to resist the urge to jump in too keenly by asking why my husband is so familiar.

Darren checks over his shoulder before ushering me away to a booth in the far corner of the pub, leaving my coffee abandoned on the bar.

My heart is thundering as I sit. There was no squinty look of confusion. Darren knows Richard for a reason. He slots in next to me and glances to my phone again.

'I don't want any trouble,' he says.

'What do you mean?'

Darren looks from the phone to me and then straightens himself. 'Who are you?' he asks.

'This is Richard,' I say, holding up my phone. 'He's my husband.'

Darren's eye twitches and he stays quiet as a couple enter through the main doors. There's a silver-haired man in a suit with a woman who's a good fifteen or twenty years younger than him. They dither nervously at the front before noticing the 'please seat yourself' sign. They then spend a good thirty seconds tripping over one another in not making a decision about where to settle. I wonder if they're having an affair. The pub is remote enough that it's unlikely any aggrieved partners might find out where their husbands and wives happen to be.

'I've already been through this once,' Darren says.

'Through what?'

'The police were here yesterday.'

This stops me slightly – although I suppose it isn't surprising. I'm always bemused by those mystery dramas where some random bloke will always be two steps ahead of the authorities, who have almost limitless resources at their disposal. Once the police heard about a link from Alice to Richard – not to mention my lack of clarity about where he was on Sunday – they'd have been trying to find out his location. If they didn't do the same thing as me by checking our bank statement, they might have seen him on a traffic camera. There are probably other things I wouldn't know about, too.

'What did the police ask?' I say.

Darren stands abruptly and pushes himself away from the table. 'I shouldn't say.'

I slide sideways out of the booth and follow him across the floor. 'You can at least tell me what he was doing here…?'

'You should leave.'

I glance across to where the couple from before have finally decided on a table in the furthest corner, far away from prying eyes.

'I can ask a lot louder…'

Darren stops and I can see him weighing it up. He could definitely get me removed from the premises, but is it worth it? He glances towards the couple and then back to me.

'Fine!' he says. 'But don't say you weren't warned.'

'Warned about what?'

'He was with another woman.'

TWELVE YEARS OLD

I never realised there was a room inside a police station where the walls are the same yellow as the ones on my bedrooms at home. There's also a pair of sofas in here, which I didn't expect. I thought I might be in some sort of white room with a table in the middle. That's what it looked like on a show Dad was watching one time – with a policeman on one side who was shouting at a woman on the other. I didn't really understand it.

Nadia – who called herself a 'welfare officer' – says this is a special room where they talk to young people. I wonder if that's why the policeman in front of me called himself 'Thomas', instead of whatever police name he has.

'Do you remember the afternoon I'm asking about?'

I can tell that Thomas is using a voice with me that isn't his own. He speaks softly but there's the odd word that he says faster and more deeply. I look to Nadia, who nods at me.

'Yes,' I say.

'What happened on the afternoon?'

'You should ask Dad. He was there too.'

'I'm asking you, Madeleine.'

'Why?'

'Because you might have seen something that your father missed.'

'Like what?'

'I don't know. That's why I'm asking.'

Nadia leans closely and whispers, 'It's okay' into my ear. Dad told me I should trust her, even though I'm not sure that I do. He also told me that I should tell the policeman everything that I saw and not tell lies – except that I'm not sure about that either. I can't explain why but it feels… *wrong*.

'A man got into the car,' I say.

Thomas doesn't reply at first, although he's still smiling in a way that doesn't fit his face. I know he's faking.

'What about before that?' he asks.

'When?'

'What happened *before* the man got into the car?'

'Dad stopped the car to let him in.'

'Did your dad say anything when he did this?'

'No. I asked if we could pick up the man.'

Thomas nods a little. He hasn't stopped smiling since he came into the room. 'Why did you do that, Madeleine?'

I don't like the way he says my name. The first part is louder than the second, like when the girls at school call me Mad Maddy.

'Because it's good to help people. He looked like he needed help.'

Thomas looks towards Nadia, although neither of them speak to each other.

I squish myself further back into the sofa. It's much comfier than the one at home – but it's deeper and I can't bend my legs when I'm at the back. There's a tape deck sitting on a table at my side, like the one I use to record the charts on Sunday – but bigger. Nadia told me they use this to record everything I say in case they need to check it.

'Why do you say that?' Thomas asks.

'Because people only stick out their thumbs when they need help, don't they?'

Thomas nods again, although I wonder if I'm wrong. He's not said anything but the way he looks away makes it feel as if I might have misunderstood something.

'So you saw the man with his thumb out – and then you asked your dad if he could stop the car…?'

'Right.'

'What did your dad say to that?'

I try to think. I'm sure he said something but I can't remember what. It feels important – but I don't know what the better answer would be.

'I don't know.'

'But your dad did stop the car?'

'Yes.'

'And then what happened?'

'He was going to talk to the man – but then the door behind me opened and the man got in.'

'Did you see him?'

I stop to think, even though I know the answer. I wonder if I should say yes – and almost do – except that they might ask me what he looked like. If they do that, then I won't be able to answer without making up something else. They'll know that I'm lying about that – and then they might not believe anything else I say.

'No.'

Thomas nods again. I thought he might write something down but he doesn't have a pad or a pen.

'What happened then?'

'The man started smoking.'

'How do you know this?'

'I could smell it – and the smoke came into the front.'

'What then?'

'Dad told him he couldn't smoke in the car.'

'That's good, Madeleine. You're doing very well.' Nadia rubs my back gently but I don't like it, so I wriggle to the back of the seat, even though it makes my legs uncomfortable. She takes her hand away and whispers a soft 'sorry'.

Thomas is still watching me. 'What happened after your dad said the man couldn't smoke in the car?'

'Nothing.'

There's a gap and Thomas glances momentarily towards a mirror on the wall to the side. I follow his eyeline, though can't see anything other than the reflections of me, him and Nadia.

'Nothing at all?' he asks.

'Nothing at first. Dad stopped the car and then got out and opened the back door. He told the man he had to get out.'

'Did the man get out?'

'Yes.'

'Did you *see* him get out?'

It feels dangerous to answer, although I don't know why. It's like there's something in the room that I can't spot. Something's tickling the back of my neck, even though there's nobody there.

'I was looking the other way…'

Thomas looks towards the mirror again and I follow his stare. When I turn back to him, he's watching me again.

'Did you turn to look?' he asks.

'No.'

'Did you hear anything after your dad opened the door?'

'I don't think so.'

'But the man definitely ended up out of the car?'

'Yes.'

Thomas shifts in his seat and it's Nadia who speaks next. 'You're doing really great, Madeleine.'

'Is it going to help my dad?'

There's a momentary pause. 'I'm sure your dad would want you to tell the truth.'

I think through everything I've said. It's what happened and I can't see any way that it wouldn't help him.

Thomas talks to me next: 'Did you see anything that happened outside the car?'

'No.'

'Nothing at all?'

It's hard to keep the annoyance from my voice: 'I said no.'

I'm hoping Thomas will react to this. Perhaps say that he believes me, or let me leave. He doesn't: he keeps going.

'How long was it until your dad got back into the car?'

'I don't know. A minute. Maybe less.'

'Could it have been longer?'

'I don't think so.'

He lifts his wrist and presses something on the side of his watch. 'Shall we see how long? How about I'll say "now". If you think about when the man got out of the car – and then tell me to stop when you think it's about the time that your dad got back into the driver's seat.'

I tell him okay, even though I'm not sure I can remember. Thomas says 'Now' and then we sit and wait. He keeps watching me but I don't want to look at him, so I pick a spot on the floor instead.

It's a guess when I finally say 'now', mainly because I really can't remember. It definitely wasn't long.

Thomas presses his watch and then has a quick glimpse towards the mirror once more, even though he says nothing about the time.

'Was anything different about your dad after he got back into the car?'

'Like what?'

'I'm not sure. Perhaps something with his hands…? That sort of thing.'

I find myself wriggling on the seat and, though it was fine a few minutes ago, it now feels itchy and uncomfortable. 'I don't remember.'

Thomas says nothing, although I can tell from the way he's watching me that he doesn't believe this.

Nadia shuffles and I think she knows as well. I'm not sure that I'm a good liar.

'If you thought a bit harder, do you think you could remember anything?'

Thomas knows.

I wonder what will happen to me if he decides that I'm lying. Will I end up in prison? Do people get away with things like this if they're only twelve?

'Maybe,' I say.

'Think about when your dad got back into the car. Was there something different about him?'

'I think there was blood.'

'Where?'

'On his hand.'

Thomas leans in and I know this is what he wanted to hear. I wish I'd not said anything but it's too late now. It feels like he can read my mind. 'Did you ask how the blood got on his hand?'

'No.'

'Did he say how it got there?'

'No.'

Thomas nods. 'I need you to think very hard about this next answer, Madeleine. Do you understand?'

I'm trapped now. It's like he has me frozen to the seat, even though all he's doing is looking at me. 'Yes.'

'Did the man in the seat behind you say anything to threaten you?'

'No.'

'Did he say anything to threaten your dad?'

'No.'

'Did he *do* anything that made you feel threatened?'

'The smoking.'

That gets a nod and one more glance towards the mirror. 'I've only got two more questions for you. You've done so well.'

I say nothing. It feels as if I've already spoken too much. Dad told me to tell the truth but perhaps that's not what he wanted at all. I shouldn't have mentioned the blood.

'After your dad pulled away, did you look behind?'

'I couldn't.'

'Why?'

'My seat belt.'

'So you didn't see or hear anything from the man after he left the car?'

I'm not sure what to say. It feels like there is no right answer. 'No,' I say.

'Last question: Did your dad ever talk to you about what happened in the time he was outside the car?'

My throat is dry and, even though I haven't done anything, I feel so drained by all of this.

'No.'

Thomas smiles one final time and then exchanges a look with Nadia. 'That's everything,' he says. 'Thank you very much.'

I turn to Nadia but she's watching the mirror. 'Will Dad be okay now?' I ask.

Nadia stands and gently touches my shoulder. 'Let's get you home,' she replies.

FIFTEEN

I stare at Darren. The fact he says Richard was with another woman is somehow one of the biggest shocks of my life – and yet not surprising at all. I think the lie about where he said he was going means I had already braced myself for it.

'What did the woman look like?' I ask.

Darren tugs at his shirt and winces. 'I don't know – a woman. I think she had dark hair, but she was wearing a hat. They were sitting outside and I only saw them once.

'How did you remember him when the police came?'

'The pink shirt – and the fact they were outside. It wasn't warm out there.'

I suppose this kills any doubt I might have had for Darren's story. He has no reason to lie – and Richard was definitely wearing a pink shirt.

'It was busy,' Darren adds. 'I didn't pay them a lot of attention. It was only when the police came yesterday that I thought about it again. 'They wanted CCTV but there are no cameras in that corner.'

'Is that what you told the police?'

'That's what happened.'

He takes another step away but there's something about the way he won't look at me.

'What…?' I ask.

A shrug. 'I think they were arguing. She was pointing at him and looked kinda angry. I wasn't close enough to hear anything.' Darren takes another small step away and then reaches into his jacket before pulling out his phone. 'I've got to take this,' he says, before holding the phone to his ear. The fact it wasn't ringing is obvious to us both – but he's already told me enough.

When my husband told me he was visiting a man named Keith, he was instead here with a woman.

I have very little to go on, other than that my husband was arguing with a woman who might have had dark hair and was definitely wearing a hat. They were sitting outside in the cold, so it's no surprise she had that on. She was likely in a coat as well. It's interesting that they chose to sit outside, despite the temperature. I wonder if there was a specific reason. I'm also curious as to whether the police know who the woman is. They've had a day longer than me to process this.

I don't want to judge Richard quite yet, not after what happened to Dad.

By the time I realise where I am, I'm almost home. I've been driving along the lanes on autopilot. I've already indicated to turn onto my driveway when I notice someone sitting on the wall at the front of the house. There's a moment in which my heart surges and I think it's Richard. He'll be able to explain everything and people will find out that none of this is what they've been speculating it to be. They can cancel those magazine covers about how I was oblivious for the past three years.

It's not him, though. It's not even a man.

It's Sarah Overend.

Harriet's meeting about the winter ball on Sunday night seems like half a lifetime ago, even though it wasn't even forty-eight hours. Sarah would usually be Harriet's right-hand woman – but she was away and Theresa reckoned she had a chest infection. We're no more friends than I am with Harriet, so I have no idea why she's here.

I park the car and then wait by the driver's door as Sarah makes her way along the drive towards me. She's in a thick woollen coat, with fluffy snow boots that I'd swear are the same ones Harriet has.

She says my name as she reaches out her arms towards me. Before I know it, she's pulled me in for a hug and it's too late to avoid it. I have no idea what's going on: we've barely exchanged more than a handful of sentences in the entire time I've lived in the village.

'I heard what happened at the school,' Sarah says. 'I hope everything's okay with you…?'

I almost tell her that of course it isn't. I was called a 'paedo' in front of the village. My husband is missing. A girl nearly died. How is that okay?

'I guess so…'

Sarah sets off towards my house and I feel compelled to follow. I don't invite her in, but she essentially does that herself by trailing in behind me after I open the door. I could tell her to leave but it's a bit late now. I'm not sure what's happening.

Even though I don't post much on Facebook myself, I am friends with both Harriet and Sarah. I even have alerts set up for whenever they post – because, when they do, it's gold. Sarah once took a selfie of herself giving a homeless person a sandwich. She posted it to Facebook and, within two hours, there were over a hundred likes – plus almost as many comments from people saying what a caring person she is. The lack of self-awareness is barely believable.

We're not friends – and I very much doubt we have anything significant in common.

We're standing in the hallway where the bags of unpacked baking ingredients still sit. There's a twinge of embarrassment that I haven't tidied it all away.

'Let me put the kettle on for you,' Sarah says. 'Which way's the kitchen? Down here?' She points in the correct direction and so I let her lead me through to my kitchen. She wanders around, pointing to various appliances and saying how wonderful it all is. Anyone would think she'd never seen a mixer before. I let it all play out, mainly because I'm interested to find out where this is going.

By the time she's filled the kettle and fiddled around with the teapot, she's used the word 'fantastic' four separate times, including to describe the spice rack.

It's as we're sitting at the table, each with a mug in front of us, that she gets to the real reason she's here. She isn't even subtle about it.

'I was wondering if you'd heard anything?' Sarah says.

'About what?'

'About Richard.'

I assume she's fishing on behalf of Harriet – and that whatever I say will be on the village grapevine within minutes of her leaving. I should tell her to get lost, but burning bridges in a place like Leavensfield is rarely a good idea. Sooner or later, there will be no people left. Because of that, I decide to go with it.

'Nothing,' I say.

'What about from the police? I heard they found his car.'

'I think you're asking the wrong person. Why would the police tell me what they're up to?'

Sarah stirs her tea absent-mindedly but I can see something twitching around the corners of her eyes as the thoughts swirl. She must've missed out on the Botox session when Harriet went.

'Fair point,' she says. 'They probably think...' She stops and stares off into nothingness.

'What?'

'I probably shouldn't...'

I know what she's doing but it's hard to resist joining in. 'Shouldn't what?'

'Will you promise you won't get mad?'

I stare at her and it's like we're hormonal teenagers. This is ridiculous, but it's the game we play. 'I won't.'

Sarah looks at me earnestly, with wide, concerned eyes. No wonder she and Harriet are such great friends. 'They probably think you're a suspect.'

It sounds like she thinks this should be some major revelation to me. As if the thought never occurred that, with my husband seemingly involved, the police might think I could be, too.

'Probably,' I reply, drily.

'I heard that Alice walks across Daisy Field to Fuel's Gold most weekends when her mum's working.'

'Was Gemma working there on Sunday?'

'I think so. That's what somebody said. I thought it was odd for a twelve-year-old to be walking in the cold across the field when it's dark. I wouldn't let my two do that.'

For the first time since she arrived, it sounds like Sarah's saying something that isn't geared towards getting information from me. Kylie was fifteen when we moved to the village and I don't think I'd have let her traipse across fields by herself in the dark. That's not to say I don't understand why it could happen. It's a shortish walk from the village to the petrol station – and Leavensfield is remote enough that the chances of anyone noticing would be low.

Still, Alice is *twelve*.

'Sophie's not sleeping,' Sarah says, talking about her daughter. 'Because of this?'

'She's worried that someone's going to leave her in the stream. I'm not sure that David's taking it too well, either. He says he's fine but he was sleepwalking last night and he's not done that in a couple of years. It's got to be hard for the kids, hasn't it…?'

I nod along. Sarah's right – except that this is the type of thing she might share with another mother who has children the same age as hers. Or something she might talk about to a friend. Why me?

'Have you spoken to Gemma?' I ask.

This gets a partial arching of the eyebrows and a blank gaze. 'Gemma?'

'Harriet was with her this morning at the school. I assumed you were all friends now…?' Sarah's eyes narrow. 'You said you'd heard what happened at the school…?'

We stare at one another and it's as if we've been speaking in different languages.

'I did,' she says. 'I just didn't realise it was Gemma…'

'Harriet never told you she was there with Gemma…?'

Sarah shakes her head slowly and I get the sense that I've missed something. Perhaps she has, too. Even with everything that's happening, there's a small stab of satisfaction that everything might not be paradise between the village's two power couples.

'How's the chest infection?' I ask.

Sarah blinks and touches her chest delicately. 'I'm still a bit husky,' she replies – although she doesn't sound it. 'You know what it's like.' She sips her tea and then licks her lips.

It could be nothing, it probably is, but there was something about the confident way she entered the house with me…

'Have you been here before?' I ask.

She looks up to the ceiling, avoiding me. 'Once.'

'When?'

'James and I came for lunch one time with Richard and, um…'

'You can say her name.'

She gulps. '…With Richard and India.'

'Did you know them well?'

From being in charge of the situation, Sarah suddenly seems caught out. She picks up her cup and holds it to her mouth. She doesn't drink, she simply holds it in place while she looks anywhere except at me. It is a few seconds until she puts it down again.

'Not really. Richard has lived here forever. I was more friends with India. James and I came along because she invited us as a couple.'

'When was that?'

A shrug. 'Years ago. Long before she, um…' She tails off and then adds: 'I still can't believe what happened to her.'

It sounds like a figure of speech but I wonder if there's something factual there. Whether she *literally* doesn't believe the story of how India died.

It's like she's drifted from the room but then, in a flash, she's back and alert. 'Not that it's anything against you.'

Sarah sits up straighter, perhaps remembering why she's here. She reaches into her bag and then passes across four rectangles of card.

'Tickets for the ball,' she says.

I scan the calligraphy on the front. 'Why are there four?'

'There were some spares and I figured you can bring anyone you want.'

'I can't believe it's still on. Even if it is, I'm not sure if it's the best thing for me to go…'

Sarah bites her lip and then leans in. 'I think we should be better friends going forward, Maddy.'

'There's not a long line of people who want to do that at the moment.'

'Which is exactly why we should spend more time together. We should do this regularly.'

I wonder if there's some sort of sarcasm, or a joke I've missed. She seems genuine – although I'm not convinced anything I could say to her wouldn't end up back with Harriet.

'We'll see…'

It's not a commitment – but Sarah doesn't seem to mind. She finishes whatever's left in her cup and then returns it to the table.

'Harry's full steam ahead for the winter ball,' she says. 'She's going to run it as a fundraiser for Gemma and Alice. Well, assuming Alice is okay…'

'Do you know how Alice is?'

A shake of the head. 'I heard she was in a bad way – but that was yesterday.'

We sit and ponder that for a second. There's a twelve-year-old girl fighting for her life in hospital and I realise I've let much of that pass me by because I've been consumed by my own problems.

'It was Harry's idea,' Sarah adds.

'What was?'

'To make the ball a fundraiser.'

I don't reply because I don't know what to say.

Sarah waits a moment and then nods. She glances up past me towards the clock and then slides her chair backwards. 'I should probably go.'

I stand as well and, as we get into the hall and she finishes putting on her coat, Sarah stops to rub my arm gently. I might have been annoyed at this two days ago, but the human contact is undeniably welcome.

'If you need a friend, or whatever, you've got my number,' Sarah says.

'It's in my phone.'

That much is true – except we've never contacted one another. Phone numbers do the round for everyone on the village's various committees.

Sarah puts a hand on the door but doesn't open it. 'Do you think they'll find out who hurt Alice?' I'm unsure what to say but Sarah isn't done yet anyway. 'I'm sure it wasn't Richard…'

'Who's saying it was?'

Sarah starts to say something but stumbles over herself and ends up going silent before she's made any sort of reply.

'I should go,' she says – and then, after one more long and deliberate sigh, she does.

SIXTEEN

I'm not sure how I missed it before. It's only when Sarah talked about lunch with Richard and India that I realised we've never had couples over since I moved in. Some of that might have been because Kylie was living here – but there must be more to it than that.

There is another thing that's been niggling me. Richard told me he was visiting his old colleague, Keith – but I wonder why he specifically chose that name. It might have been random – but why would he have been thinking of an old work friend he'd not seen in years?

I consider calling Keith a second time but, by now, I suspect the police will have paid him a visit. He probably told them I called him with some nonsense story about updating Richard's contacts list, though there's not a lot I can do about that now. He likely won't be receptive to a call.

When I check the photograph on my phone of the rolodex card containing his name and number, I again take in the address. I eye the bagged baking items in the hall, knowing I should put things away. I also have work to do, although I can't imagine writing a piece on something as trivial as a bakeware set at the moment. Instead, I head for the car and enter Keith's address into my phone. The directions say it should take eighty-three minutes in current conditions and, seeing as I have nothing better to do, I set off into the country lanes once more.

The blue skies of the morning have faded to something closer to a light grey, while the air is clammy and dank. It feels like it could rain again soon. There is no sign of any vehicles up on the farmer's track any longer, nor of any police cars at all. The road out to Fuel's Gold is clear and I resist the urge to slow this time. The image of Alice getting into Richard's car is burned into my mind anyway.

One clue as to why Richard might have chosen to tell me he was visiting Keith is because the route I'm sent on by my phone takes me past The Willow Tree pub. If for any reason someone had reported back to me that he'd been seen here, he could have easily said they were meeting in the middle.

I've never thought of him as conniving – but perhaps that says a lot more about me than it does him.

The phone directions take me over the road bridge and through the winding roads, out towards the coast. The further I get from home, the more the wind picks up until it's buffeting the car on a series of wide-open straights.

Keith Etherington lives on the outskirts of a typical British seaside town. There's a pier and a row of shops along the front that sell fish and chips or ice cream. In the summer, it will be packed; at this time of year, it's a ghost town.

There's one road in and out, so I drive along the front to get out the other side – and then continue up towards the cliffs. Keith's home is a cosy cottage that sits by itself in a dead end near the base of the rock face. There's nowhere to park, other than on the side of the single-track road. Whether he likes it or not, this means Keith has been blocked in.

The wind is so strong that it almost blows my door closed as I get out of the car. I have to fight to hold onto it and nearly trap my fingers in between the frame and the door. As I'm doing that, a gust grabs my scarf and partially unwraps it. By the time I've finished battling with the gate to Keith's cottage, I'm exhausted.

A 'sea view' is supposed to be one of the things that people crave while looking for somewhere to live, or retire. Although

Keith technically has that, the current sight is of a raging torrent of foamy water a couple of hundred metres from his house. The sea roars as the wind howls – and a sea view feels like the least appealing thing going.

The doorbell is one of those that offers no indication it's actually gone off. I press the button twice in quick succession but hear nothing. It's as I'm about to try the bell a third time that a light goes on beyond the front door. Moments later, the door swings open to reveal a familiar stranger of a man. We've never met and yet, on first glance, it feels as if we have. He dresses like my husband, with cord trousers and a blue jacket atop a shirt that's too big. Even without entering the house, I can see the crammed bookshelves that stretch along the hall.

'Are you Keith?' I ask.

His eyebrows are bushy and overgrown. They meet in the middle when he frowns towards me. 'And you are?'

'Madeleine,' I say. 'We spoke on the phone yesterday.'

His expression softens – but not by much. 'Dickie's wife…?'

'That's me.'

He puts a hand on the door frame. 'I don't think we should be doing this.'

'Have the police been?'

Keith has started to close the door but stops. 'Did you know? When you called me, I mean. Did you know what they're saying he did?'

I shake my head. 'Not then. Later.'

He eyes me with suspicion – and I don't blame him.

'Can we talk?' I ask.

'About what? I'm nothing to do with whatever this is.' He sounds cold and uncomfortable, which is perhaps not a surprise.

'I think Richard might have involved you whether you like it or not…'

He stares at me, one eyebrow twitching and his hand still on the door. The stand-off lasts a few seconds until he sighs and pushes open the door wide enough for me to enter.

As soon as I get inside, I see that the hall is far more cluttered than it first appeared. Not only are there filled bookcases running the full length of the wall, there are dozens of small piles across the floor. It's like a tornado hit a library.

He leads me into a living room, where there are even more books around the walls and on the floor. There are pulp paperbacks, chunky hardbacks and weighty textbooks. Some look old and handed-down, others are near enough new. There seems to be no order to any of it. There are no photographs on the walls to indicate a family, nor anything to show anyone lives here other than Keith.

If Richard lived alone, I can imagine it wouldn't take too long before his house would end up in a similar state to this. Before I moved in, I know he got in a cleaner to help tidy the place.

We sit in a pair of leather armchairs that are firm and uncomfortable. I explain that Richard told me he was off to visit Keith on Sunday – and I've not seen him since. I don't mention anything about the woman with whom he was seen at the pub.

As I tell him this, Keith pulls at his errant, greying hair, while crossing and uncrossing his knees like a demented Sharon Stone in *Basic Instinct*.

'We've not spoken in probably two years,' Keith says breathily. 'Why did Dickie say he was coming here?'

'I have no idea. I thought we might be able to figure it out between us…?'

If there's one thing that Keith can do with astonishing ability, then it's frown. His face isn't particularly wrinkly until he objects to something, at which time it turns into a dropped cauliflower.

'What would you like to know?' he asks.

'I suppose we could start with how you know each other.'

He crosses and recrosses his legs while wagging a finger. It feels as if I'm about to be told off, although he answers normally.

'We taught in the same department for about five or six years until I retired a couple of years back.'

'Have you been in contact since?'

'Not really. We might have swapped a departmental email or two – but nothing major. We've not spoken.'

'Not at all?'

He snaps back with: 'That's what I said, isn't it?'

There's such annoyance that it leaves me temporarily silent.

It's Keith who speaks next, only marginally softer this time. 'Were you a student of his?'

'Yes.'

'What was your maiden name?'

'Evesham. Maddy Evesham.'

'Did I ever teach you?'

'No. We've never met.'

Keith picks up an e-cigarette from the table at his side. It's one of those with a pouty plastic nib and a long tube. He sucks on the tip, making a popping noise with his lips, before he blows a bluey haze into the air. It only takes a few seconds until I can smell the fruity grimness. I've never smoked – but I'd take tobacco over this any day. He sucks on the cylinder a second time and then puts it back on the table.

'Dickie always had an eye for his students…'

Keith speaks deliberately, his words chosen with purpose. It doesn't sound as if there's malice, only truth. I suppose I'm the greatest proof there could be.

'Did you tell the police that?'

'I told them everything they wanted to know.'

Of course he did. Why wouldn't he? I wonder if he said these words to the police in the same way he did to me. 'An eye for his students' sounds so brutal.

'It was usually the older ones,' Keith adds. 'I'm not entirely surprised he married one of you.'

A shiver whispers its way around the back of my neck.

One of you.

'How many others?' There's a quiver to my voice that I didn't know would be there. I don't know why I want to hear this and realise I'm gripping the arms of the chair so tightly that my knuckles have turned white.

Keith pouts his bottom lip. I don't think it's deliberately mean, but it is dismissive. 'I don't know. I'd heard Dickie had been in trouble a couple of times over the years.' He licks his lip and then adds: 'Not trouble, I suppose. That's the wrong word and I apologise. We're all adults, after all. Let's just say that observations were made.'

He leaves it there and I wonder if there's more to come. Perhaps I suspected this all along? Maybe the true reason I came here is that I needed someone to say it?

'We got together about four years ago,' I say. 'We were married three years ago. Do you know if there were any, um… *observations* after me?'

Keith smiles, though there's nothing kindly there. I suddenly realise that he's finding this amusing – and that's why he invited me in. I thought I was leading the conversation but now he has me where he wants.

'I don't know you,' he says. 'And I *definitely* don't know what Dickie did and did not get up to in his private time.'

'Did you know his first wife?'

Keith picks up his e-cigarette again and wags it towards me as if it's an extension of his finger. 'I didn't know he had a *first* wife, let alone a second.' He has a puff on the device and then holds it in his palm. 'I didn't want anything to do with this. I didn't want the police to come here and ask questions – and I did *not* invite you here either.'

'I didn't mean—'

'It doesn't matter what you meant.' He's loud now, shouting. 'Why do you think I live in a place like this? It's not so I can have police knocking on my door.'

He stands abruptly and I mirror him instinctively.

'You should go,' he says, ushering me towards the front door. 'And please don't contact me again. If Dickie does turn up, make sure he knows that he should do the same.'

SEVENTEEN

I sit at the opening to the lane that leads to Keith's house with the car engine running. The sea is in front of me and it's raging with a fury I can understand.

It's not necessarily the implication that Richard might have cheated on me, it's more that the last few years of my life feel like some sort of inevitability.

I'm not entirely surprised he married one of you.

It makes me feel like I had no choice in the relationship. That I was one in a line. Everybody wants to feel special, or unique – not one of many.

Can it be true?

Keith was annoyed at having his privacy invaded, so perhaps he was trying to hurt me? The worst thing is that, after everything that's happened, I don't know what to believe. Do I still trust my husband?

My phone rings, jolting me away from those thoughts. Even though it's an unknown number which I would usually ignore, I answer it.

It's a man's voice: 'Is that Madeleine?'

'Yes.'

'It's Detective Inspector Dini. Are you at home?'

I picture him standing outside my front door, already knowing that I'm not.

'No.'

There's a pause in which I suspect he's expecting me to fill the gap by telling him where I am. Instead, I remain silent.

'Can you come to the station?' he asks. 'The one at Beaconshead.'

'Why do you want me?'

There's another pause that I don't realise is a break in the connection until the hairs on my arms have already stood up. It can't be anything good. When the line kicks back in, Dini is halfway through a word.

'…tify some clothes we've found.'

'What clothes?'

'We think they might belong to your husband.'

The wind is so strong that the vehicle is rocking from side to side. The air's been sucked out of the car.

'Madeleine…?'

'I'm here.'

'Do you want me to send a car for you?'

'No. I'll be there as soon as I can.'

I hang up and then stare at the screen for a few seconds, wondering if he might call back. I should set off but it doesn't feel as if my body is able to do what I want it to. I'm shattered and my thoughts are quicksand.

When I do finally get going, I end up crawling the car along the seafront like a pervy guy in a red-light district. Nobody on foot seems to notice because they're too busy rushing along the pavement from dry spot to dry spot.

I only pick up speed when I get back to the country lanes. The further I get inland, the more the wind ebbs away. The sky changes from the grim grey of the coastline to a glimmering silver. I pass The Willow Tree for the third time today and, now that it's later in the afternoon, the parking area is around a quarter full of cars.

On and on through the lanes, following the route that Richard must have taken on Saturday. There's so little out here, other than farms and blink-and-you'll-miss-it hamlets. Past the petrol station and then my house, before I follow the road down into a deserted Leavensfield and then out the other side.

Beaconshead is the closest big town to Leavensfield, even though it isn't actually that large. It's where the secondary school sits that serves the entire area – and it's also the location of our local police station. Long gone are the days where villages might have their own bobbies.

As I take the turn onto the road on which the police station sits, I brace myself for some sort of media scrum. There are bound to be reporters and photographers hanging around… except there isn't.

I park on the street and walk the short distance to the station, where the only person outside is a woman in a large coat who's shouting at a traffic warden. A police officer is there too, probably caught up in the commotion outside his workplace. He has both hands out, trying to calm the situation, though the woman then starts shouting at him for good measure. I don't catch much but I do hear the words 'joke', 'you lot' and 'I know my rights'.

I head up the steps and through the front door of the police station. There's a man behind a tall glass divider that's on top of a reception desk. He's reading something on a computer monitor but glances up as I enter. I'm about to tell him who I am but he seemingly already knows. He calls out that he'll be right back, before disappearing through a side door.

The reception area has a U of uncomfortable-looking blue canvas chairs with the foam spilling out. Above those are a selection of posters with slogans like, 'Lock It Or Lose It' and 'Drug Drivers Are Dopes'. The second has a close-up of a man with reddened eyes sitting in a wrecked car. The ol' sledgehammer approach.

There is another that tells people how to keep the beat of 'Stayin' Alive' by Bee Gees when giving chest compressions if someone doesn't appear to be breathing. There's an almost identical poster next to it, offering the same advice but telling people to use the beat of 'Another One Bites The Dust' by Queen.

As I scan the walls, the door next to the seats opens and DI Dini appears. He has one hand in his trouser pocket and the other holding open the door. 'Do you want to come through?' he says.

I head through the door as he lets me pass, then he closes it and leads me off along a corridor.

'Did you park okay?' he asks. 'It's a nightmare around here.'

'It's fine.' I'm not in the mood for small talk.

He takes a couple of quick turns, although the greying, bleak corridors all look the same to me.

'I went to The Willow Tree today,' I say.

Dini takes a couple more steps and then stops to look at me. 'You know it, then?'

'I didn't: not until today. I spoke to the manager and he said he'd already talked to you.'

The inspector presses himself against the wall as someone heads towards us from the opposite direction. I follow his lead and the two officers nod to one another before Dini turns to take me in.

'In here,' he says, nodding towards the closest door.

I follow him inside but stop on the precipice, staring at the pair of sofas. There's a rainbow on the wall and cuddly toys in the corner. It's like a quiet room from a nursery that's been transported to the police station.

'It's where we talk to vulnerable witnesses, or children,' Dini says, noticing my hesitation.

'I know,' I reply.

'You don't have to come in. There's nothing formal here – but it sounded like you had something to say…?'

I have to force myself to take the couple of steps into the room, where the door swings closed behind me. It's not the same room as from all those years ago but it's close enough.

Dini sits on one of the sofas and there's a compulsion for me to do the same.

'Did you know about the pub?' he asks.

'Not when I spoke to you yesterday. Only after I checked our bank statement and saw it on there.' I have to force myself to look away from the rainbow on the wall. 'The manager told me Richard was there with a woman…'

Dini scratches his chin. 'What are you asking me?'

'Was he?'

'I could ask you the same question.'

'I don't know.'

He continues to watch me and it's like he's trying to read my thoughts. To figure out if I'm lying. 'I can't talk about an active investigation.'

'If there's something shocking about to come out, would you tell me before everyone else?'

His eyes narrow but it doesn't feel harsh. 'I can't say. It depends on what that something might be.' He hesitates and then adds: 'What do you think might come out?'

'I wish I knew.'

Dini hitches up his trouser legs, about to stand, but I keep talking.

'Did you find anything among all the stuff you took from the house?'

He settles back onto the seat. 'I can't comment on that.'

I hold onto a frustrated sigh. I'm in the middle of everything but appear to know the least. 'Is there anything you can comment on?'

'Not much.'

'What am I supposed to do? Supposed to think? You must know what everyone's saying about Richard and me when I'm not around.'

'I can't control that, Madeleine.'

'I think…' The words slip away. I can't explain why I'm confiding in the man who is investigating my husband and possibly me. The only thing that comes into my head is that I know I've done nothing wrong. I want Dini to know that. I want everyone to.

'What?' he asks.

'I think there might have been other students before me.'

He pauses for a second, eyes narrowing, but then the expression clears, as if it was never there. 'In what way?'

'What way do you think?'

We both know what I'm talking about and Dini doesn't push it any further. He waits a moment before moving onto something else.

'I was going to ask you this after you'd looked at the clothes – but I might as well do it now,' he says.

'What?'

'Would you do an appeal for your husband to come home?'

It's not what I was expecting. Not even close. If it's a trick, then I'm not sure what it is.

'We're keeping the investigations separate at the moment,' Dini adds. 'To some degree anyway.'

'How do you mean?'

'Your husband is a misper – a missing person. If you were to appeal for him to come home, it doesn't have to have any link to Alice Pritchard.'

It feels odd, it *is* odd – but I'd almost forgotten that Richard is missing in his own context. Everything feels tied to Alice.

'Why would you do that?' I ask.

'Because Richard might have some evidence. There might be a reason that he's disappeared that has nothing to do with Alice.'

I'm expecting some sort of punchline. This is what I've been trying to tell myself ever since Harriet told me Alice got into Richard's car.

'It's only an idea,' Dini adds. 'You don't have to decide now.' He pushes himself up and steps towards the door. 'You coming…?'

I follow Dini back into the corridor and then he sets off into the labyrinth of identical-looking passages until it feels as if we must have done a couple of laps of the building. He eventually leads me into a small room with a table in the middle, on which sits three large transparent bags. There is an item of clothing inside each. The first thing I see is the pink.

'Where did you find these?' I ask.

'I can't say… Do you recognise anything?'

I move closer to the table. 'Can I pick them up?'

'As long as you don't open the bags.'

I go for the pink shirt first. One of the arms is caked with mud and there's a slight rip across the cuff of the sleeve. There is a single black slip-on shoe in a second bag – and then a torn pair of dark trousers in the other. I don't have to look any closer to know the answer.

'They're not Richard's,' I say, trying to conceal the relief.

Dini has been so good at keeping up the mask that I'm stunned when his eyebrows leap up. 'They're not…?'

'No.'

'Are you sure?'

'The shirt is too small and the shoe isn't his size either. Whoever these belong to has to be quite a bit shorter.'

Dini rocks on his heels and, just as it feels as if he might be about to accuse me of lying, he takes a step to the door and opens it.

'Thanks for coming,' he says. 'Have a think about that appeal.'

EIGHTEEN

I have never lived alone. Before Richard, there was Kylie and, when she was young, there was her father. I lived with my parents before that. I'm almost forty – and this is the first time.

I sit in my car on the driveway, trying to convince myself to enter the house. It should be simple – I've done it thousands of times – and yet I don't think I can face the emptiness. I never realised how reliant I am on others for company until now.

Theresa doesn't answer her phone, so I send her a text, asking if she fancies having a drink. I'd love there to be an instant 'yes' – but nothing comes through.

I consider driving somewhere like a cinema, or a shopping centre. There will be people and things to do that might be distracting enough to tire me out before I can face the house. I turn the key to start the car and am resting on the handbrake when I change my mind. I've done so much driving today that I don't think I can face any more of that either.

Instead, I wrap myself up in my coat and scarf, grab the paperback that's always left in the glove compartment, and then walk down the hill into Leavensfield. The light is starting to fade as the sun dips low to the horizon. There's a crisp chill to the air again and a dampness that makes it feel like there might be overnight snow. Living in a valley makes the weather unpredictable, so little would surprise me. This time last year, we were basking in temperatures in the low teens.

The school bus has parked on the verge close to the cross – and a line of local children who go to the secondary school in

Beaconshead are filing off. They mass in small groups, saying their goodbyes, before heading off to their various homes. The engine of the bus roars and it chunters off towards the hill, ready to drop off more young people in the next village along.

I head for the Fox and Hounds because they do food for a few hours every evening. There's no Deliveroo or Uber Eats out here – not even a standard pizza place – so, if people don't want to cook at home, or drive somewhere, this is the natural alternative.

Someone might think the village's only pub might be above the point-scoring that goes on around here – but that couldn't be further from the truth. There was a campaign last year to rename the place, which I think was backed by the Anti-Hunting League, or something like that. I was only aware of it when Harriet sent round an email saying that the campaign had to be fought 'tooth and nail'. There were hundreds of words about 'our way of life' and 'townies who don't know what it's like'. I think she mentioned tradition a good seven or eight times.

In the end, the name of the pub remained and life went on. It wouldn't be Leavensfield if there wasn't a manufactured drama every few weeks. Until now, there were so few real problems that people have to invent their own.

The pub is the sort of place that American tourists can't quite believe actually exists. It's all low beams, thin carpets and large dogs ambling around in case someone's dropped something on the floor. The walls are decorated with browning photographs that show the village as it was in decades gone by. That is to say that it's more or less the same now as it was then.

Heads undoubtedly turn as I walk into the pub. It's mainly villagers – but I quickly spot a small group of men I don't know who are having a beer in the back corner. They could be journalists, or they could be people passing through on the way to somewhere else. I don't want to risk being anywhere near them, so head to the opposite end of the bar.

Zoe is in the corner, sitting with Frankie in front of the fire. She's reading to him from a slim paperback but stops when she sees me and gives a small wave. I return it and she offers a smile before going back to what she was doing. Frankie is watching and seemingly listening to his mother, though I'm never going to be able to see him without remembering him humming my husband's favourite song.

'Can I get you something?'

The barman is the landlord's son. He's in his twenties and seemingly waiting for the day when his old man pops it, so he can take over the business. I can't think of any other reason why he's steadfastly remaining in the area.

'Glass of red,' I say.

'Big or small?'

'Big.'

He measures out the wine and then tips it into a glass before taking my money. I head off to an empty booth that's not far from the toilets. Hardly a prime spot – but it's out of the way and nobody is likely to bother me.

I start to read my book but it's immediately apparent that I'm not going to be able to focus on anything. The words swim and swirl on the page and I take none of it in. It's still better than being alone at home.

There's some sort of football on the TV, with half a dozen blokes huddled underneath the television chatting and watching. I have no interest in the sport but find myself half watching the screen because it's something to do.

Time passes.

I order another glass of wine and then try my book a second time. It still washes past me and I'm not sure I could even understand a picture book at the moment.

The evening drifts as I leave my coat on the seat and head for the toilets.

If tourists find the pub charming, then the toilets are another matter. All the walls are tiled, which leaves the area freezing in the winter and boiling in the summer. I doubt it's been refurbished at any point in the past twenty years. Probably more.

Among the other issues, there is only cold water in here. I'm busy washing my hands when the door goes. I've been alone in here until now but, when I look up, the newcomer is standing in the doorway and she has venomous eyes that are only for me.

'Hi,' I say. Out of nothing, it feels a degree or two colder.

Gemma's eyes narrow as she looks me up and down. 'You've got some nerve,' she says.

NINETEEN

I dry my hands on a paper towel and then drop it in the bin before turning to the door. Gemma is still standing there, not coming in – but not going back out, either.

'I don't want any trouble,' I say.

Gemma doesn't reply and, when I try to move around her to leave, she sidesteps quickly so that she's in front of me. She's cleaned herself up since we were on the playground. Her hair has been washed and she's in skinny jeans with a dark top – and the furry boots that are either Harriet's, or a matching pair.

'Is everything okay?' I ask.

'You tell me.'

She stares through me with such fire that the hairs stand up on my neck.

'I'm sorry,' I say.

'For what?' The reply fires back before I've barely finished speaking.

I realise that I don't know what I'm apologising for.

Gemma seems unfazed and steps away from the door. She keeps moving directly towards me, leaving me nowhere to go except backwards. It's only a few steps until the sink is pressing into my back and I'm stuck. Gemma is slightly shorter than I am and yet it feels as if she's towering over me as she gets to within a step or two. Her eyes are wide and unfocused.

'Your daughter's at uni, isn't she?'

More chills.

'Yes.'

'How would you like it if someone took her? If someone smashed her over the head and left her for dead in a stream?'

'I—'

'I've been with Alice at the hospital all day. There's a machine breathing for her. They say she might never recover.'

'I—'

'Where's your husband?'

Her eyes bore into me and there's hatred there.

'I don't know.'

She takes another step ahead and all I can do is arch my body backwards against the sink. It presses hard into my lower back, leaving me creased with pain. Gemma is almost nose to nose with me and I have no idea what to do. Should I push her away? Hit her? Should I shout? If I do, then it will take no time at all for everyone in the village to know what's happening.

She's so close that I can smell garlic on her breath.

'Your husband tried to kill my daughter.'

'He—'

'Say it.'

I open my mouth but the words don't come. The crack comes from nowhere. I only realise she's slapped me because of the sound it makes when her palm hits my cheek.

A moment later and there's the pain as my jaw burns. I never saw the blow but there are tears in my eyes, which I try to blink away.

'Now, tell me where he is.'

'I—'

The second slap rings louder than the first. The sound of flesh on flesh echoes around the tiles until it's like it's happening over and over. I try to open my mouth but my jaw clicks and sticks.

I see Gemma's hand rising again – but I'm too quick this time as I put both hands on her chest and shove her away. She staggers backwards, just as the toilet door opens and Harriet appears.

Gemma turns between the two of us, caught in the middle.

'What's going on?' Harriet asks.

I look to Gemma, who glares back at me, before turning away. 'Nothing,' she says, before striding past Harriet and out of the toilets.

When I push myself away from the sink, my head spins and greeny-pink stars race from the edges of my vision. I have to hold onto the sink to stop myself from staggering.

'Did something happen?'

I ignore Harriet and turn to look in the mirror. The right side of my face has already turned scarlet and there's a pinprick of blood close to my eyebrow. I dab it away with my finger and then wash my hands.

I can't remember the last time I was hit. It would have been at school sometime, although specifics escape me. I vaguely remember some sort of clawing fight with a girl whose name I can't recall. I have no idea what we were fighting about and the only clear memory is that she had red hair. That would have been more than thirty years ago. There was that other time – with that girl named Jen – but that wasn't a fight, as such. Violence hasn't been a part of my life. I suppose that's isolated me from what should be an obvious fact: that it hurts to be hit.

When I turn, Harriet has left the toilets and I'm alone once more. Everything happened so quickly that I didn't have time to process any of it.

I fully expect everyone to be watching as I emerge from the toilets. Someone will have noticed Gemma following me in, not to mention Harriet after that. Everyone will know what happened… except that nobody's paying me any attention. It's the teatime rush and people are busy tucking into their evening meals.

My cheek is starting to sting as I pick up my book from the table. I don't want to be here any longer, which leaves home as the lesser of two evils.

I head outside and it's a chilly walk up the hill to the house. The dank air clings to the back of my throat, leaving it tickly and hoarse. I move as quickly as I can, wanting to be away from the village.

As soon as I get through the front door, that indefinable sixth sense prickles my ears. It's like there's an electrical undercurrent running through the hall as I close the door behind me.

I stop and listen to the silence and then… *something*. There's a gentle thud from the kitchen. Perhaps a cupboard opening, or the fridge door being closed. I move slowly along the hall as there's a second, more defined, *thump*. It's definitely the oven door snapping closed on the hinge.

Someone's in the house.

It can only be Richard.

TWELVE YEARS OLD

I'm almost out of the front door when Auntie Kath calls me back.
'I can give you a lift to school, if you want,' she says.

'I'd rather walk.'

She looks to me for a moment and I think she knows. She's about to insist that she'll drop me off at the gates… except that she doesn't. She picks up her second slice of Marmite on toast instead.

'I'll see you later then, love,' she says.

'See ya.'

I close her front door behind me and then walk to the corner before checking both ways and then ducking through the hedge into the alley beyond. The branches scratch at my back but I pull myself through and then continue on until I'm next to the bins at the back of the tower block.

In my practice run, this was the fastest route to get to the safest place I knew of.

There is one major downside, however: the rotting, bitter smell leaves me holding my breath and trying to work as quickly as I can while taking as few breaths as necessary.

It doesn't take me long to ditch the school tie, skirt and shoes into my school bag. I replace them with a longer, tighter skirt, plus my aunt's old work heels that she says she doesn't wear any more. With that done, I put my jacket back on and pull up the hood. There are no mirrors in which to check my handiwork – but it's going to be as good as I can manage.

I hide my school bag behind the bin and then head back the way I came. The one thing I hadn't realised was how difficult it is to walk in Auntie Kath's heels. Her feet are a little bigger than mine and I constantly slide backwards and forwards. That's not the only problem. Even though I've tried heels before, these are higher than my previous attempts. I wobble my way to the bus stop, fighting a non-stop battle with gravity.

When I get there one minute ahead of schedule, there are already six or seven people lined up waiting. I slot in at the back, keeping my hood up and my head down as I studiously avoid eye contact with anyone.

I've got this far – but this was the easy bit.

The bus pulls in a few minutes later and there's a brief wait as someone in a wheelchair is helped off. After that, everyone in the line gets on one at a time. When it's my turn at the front, I drop the stolen change into the driver's hand. He presses a button on the console in front of him and then it chunters out a ticket, which he rips and passes over.

I've been panicking about this moment ever since I figured out what I wanted to do today – except that the bus driver barely even looks at me. If he knows my age, then he doesn't care.

Each step of this plan is likely to be trickier than the last, so I spend the bus journey plotting through the scenarios of what I'll say if anyone challenges me about what I'm doing by myself, or why I'm not in school. My general plan is to say something along the lines of, 'Oh, how kind of you. People are always saying I look young.'

I was going to claim to be seventeen if anyone asks. It's only if they want ID that a real problem will arise.

I get off the bus when it pulls in at the train station – and then get into another line for tickets. When I get to the front, the seller simply says, 'Where to?' I tell him and then ask for a return, before handing over the twenty-pound note that I stole from Auntie

Kath's purse. If she asks, I don't think I'm going to be able to get away with claiming the theft has nothing to do with me. She's like a telepath in knowing when I'm lying.

The man behind the counter is already handing me the tickets and change when he withdraws his hand. I've been avoiding any sort of eye contact but it's impossible now as I realise he's staring.

'How old are you?' he asks.

'Seventeen. I've got a job interview.'

His eyes narrow and I know it's all over. He's going to call over one of the police officers that are hovering close to the gates – and then it will all come out.

'Do you have a young person's railcard?' he asks.

It's not what I expected, and I struggle to get out a 'no'.

'Tell you what,' he says, 'I'll put it through as if you do.'

He presses something on the computer in front of him and reopens the money drawer before passing across the tickets and my change.

'Good luck with the interview,' he says.

'Thanks.'

My heart's pounding as I insert the ticket into the automatic gates. There are two police officers standing barely a metre from me and I angle away from them as there's a fizz. My luck is still holding as the gates open and my ticket pops back up for me to grab.

Almost there.

When I get onto the platform itself, I have to sit on the bench because the shoes are hurting me so much that I'm sure I've already got blisters on both of my big toes. I think about taking them off – except that will only make people look towards me, and that's the last thing I want.

The train is on time and I wait for everyone to file on in front of me before clambering on at the back. There are no seats in the first carriage I try, so I keep walking through and into the next.

My toes are throbbing and spiky jolts of fire burn at my calves. I can't keep walking and, luckily, I don't have to because there's an entire double seat free close to the door. This time, when I sit, I do take off my shoes.

I'm wearing dark tights – but they do nothing to cover up the pooling spots of red on my big toes. I can't touch them because the pain is too much – but it's too late now. I left my school shoes in my bag.

I listen intently to each announcement about stops, paranoid that I might get off at the wrong place. As it is, there are so many announcements – and the signs at the station are so big – that it would be more or less impossible for me to have missed it.

I'm half expecting there to be police at this station – but there isn't. In fact, the concourse is empty aside from a handful of people standing around with newspapers. I walk barefooted, except for my tights, through the car park and onto the street. I'm looking for signs that might help me know where I'm going – except there's nothing other than those listing places of which I've never heard.

I have to stop someone in the end. There's an old woman pushing one of those things that are half-trolley, half-bag. She immediately looks down to my feet, with a concerned expression on her face.

'What happened to your shoes, love?'

'Too sore.'

She starts to say something else – but I get in there quickly enough to talk over her.

'Do you know where the prison is?'

'Are you sure—'

'I'm supposed to be meeting someone.'

She stares at me and she must know I'm too young to be doing this by myself. I can also see something in the way she stops to take a breath that she isn't going to say anything.

The woman takes a hand off her trolley and points back the way I've just come. 'It's that way,' she says. 'Past the station, turn left, and keep going. You can't miss it.'

I thank her and then turn and walk as quickly as my feet will allow. It's hard because I keep stepping on small stones and each one sends sparks of agony through me. I end up having to walk on my heels, because it's the least painful way of moving.

It's not long before I get to the point where I know I'm going to have to sit for a while. My tights have worn through at the back and, when I turn to look behind, there's a series of bloody spots on the pavement.

And then, it appears.

The prison is like an old castle, with huge stone walls and an enormous gate at the front that towers high above me.

For some reason, with the prison now in sight, my feet no longer hurt. I wait at the crossing and ignore the sideways glances from the man at my side, before bounding ahead of him. When I get to the prison gates, I realise this isn't the actual way in. Instead, there's a small sign with an arrow that points around to the side.

Not long…

When I get to the reception of the prison, there's a man sitting behind a counter. He's doing a crossword and pays me little attention until I'm in front of him.

'Can I help?' he asks, not sounding as if he actually wants to do so.

'I'd like to see my dad.'

The man looks up from his paper and creases appear in his forehead. 'Who's your dad?'

'John Evesham.'

He eyes me for a couple of seconds as the creases deepen. 'Wait here,' he says, before pushing himself up with a groan.

The man disappears through a door at the back of his office, leaving me alone in the waiting area. There's little to see here, other than two rows of plastic chairs, like the ones we have in school. There are posters, too, listing the things that people are not allowed to take into the prison. I scan the page – although there's nothing on there that I'm carrying.

I've done it. I know I'd planned it all but I can still hardly believe it worked. All those months of plotting and working. It won't be long now…

There's a sound of something metal clinking and then a second door opens behind me. There's a different man this time – and this one's in a dark uniform.

'Madeleine, is it?' he says.

I almost reply to say that it is – except that I didn't tell the first man my name.

'Who are you?' I ask.

'Your aunt called us,' he says. 'You didn't go to school today, did you?'

He crosses the room and sits on the plastic chair in front of me, meaning that we're at the same eye level.

'She's on her way,' he says.

'Now?'

'Now.'

'Can I see my dad?'

The man in the uniform shakes his head. 'It's not up to me… but no.'

The pain is back in my feet but, this time, it's so much more. Everything hurts. It's like there's something inside, waiting to explode. Suddenly, there are tears on my cheeks. 'I want to see him.'

'I know you do, love.'

'He didn't do it. He didn't kill him.'

The man in the uniform leans forward and tries to put a hand on my shoulder. The only reason he doesn't is that I pull away.

'I'm sorry, love,' he says.

'He didn't do it.'

'There's nothing I can do.'

He reaches for me again but I slap his hand away, creating a sold *thwack* that echoes around the room.

'He didn't *do* it,' I say, pleading and wanting him to understand.

The man doesn't try to touch me this time. Instead he smiles in the way so many adults have in the past few months. He pities me.

'I'm sorry,' he says – but I know that he isn't.

TWENTY

I push open the door and head into the kitchen, where there's a figure stepping backwards away from the oven.

It's not Richard.

'What are you doing home?' I ask.

Kylie turns to look at me: 'I wondered where you were.'

'Why didn't you text or call?'

'I wanted it to be a surprise!'

My daughter drops an oven glove on the table and then steps around the table, holding out her arms for a hug. She's slimmer than I remember and wearing a grey hoody with her university's logo on the front. When she steps away again, I look her up and down properly. There's something unbelievably calming and comforting about having her here, home and safe.

'I like the new hair,' I say.

Kylie touches it instinctively. She has let it grow longer so that it's past her shoulders. There's a lighter tinge now, too. 'I wanted a change,' she says. She waits for a second and then adds: 'Why didn't you tell me about Richard…?'

It takes me a second to realise what she's said. Kylie knows and she has every right to be aggrieved. I even lied to her yesterday when I told her Richard was visiting a friend. That was only a day and a half ago. It's barely believable. I've lived weeks since then.

I sit at the table, needing to be off my feet. 'What did you hear?' I ask.

'It's all over Facebook, Mum. My friends have been texting me too. They say that little girl – Alice – was seen getting into Richard's car before she was found in the stream...?'

It's a question, even though it isn't.

'It's true,' I say. The folder with the screengrab given to me by DI Dini is still on the side and I point her towards it. She removes the picture and then stares at it for a good thirty seconds before returning it to the folder and the countertop.

'I don't understand,' she says.

'Neither do I.'

'...And he's missing?'

'I've not seen him since Sunday morning.'

'Oh, Mum...'

Kylie steps around the table to crouch. She rests her head on my shoulder and clasps her arms around my front. I grip her hands with mine and we stay like this for around a minute until Kylie pushes herself back up.

'I meant to ask... did you go through my room for some reason...?'

It takes a moment for me to realise what she means. 'The police were here,' I say.

'Because of Richard?'

'Yes. They searched the house and took some of his things. His office is mostly empty.'

'Do they really think he tried to... *kill* her...?'

It sounds so brutal... so surreal.

'I don't know what they think.'

Kylie eyes me for a moment and then shakes her head momentarily before crossing towards the oven. She ducks to look through the glass at the front.

'What are you cooking?' I ask.

'Pizza.'

When Kylie first decided she could cook at around the age of eleven, it was because she'd figured out how to put a frozen pizza in the oven. I've not thought about this moment for years but now it's so vivid, it's as if I'm back there in our old kitchen with her looking up to me proudly. She needed my help to get it back out again because she had pushed the tray too far back.

'How did you get back?' I ask.

'One of my friends was driving to Cardiff – but he went a bit out of his way and dropped me in Bristol. I got a bus from there.'

I don't question the 'he'.

'When did you get in?'

'About an hour ago. I saw your car outside and assumed you were home. I've got a bagful of dirty washing for you…' She slips into a grin and then a small laugh that's hard not to reciprocate.

'You had a bag of dirty washing on the bus?'

'I did get a few funny looks.'

I laugh and it feels wonderfully refreshing to be talking about normal things. 'Let's have it then,' I say.

Kylie skips from the room and then heads upstairs before returning moments later with the promised bag that she puts down next to the table.

'Have you washed *any* clothes this term?'

'I did a wash about a month ago but I knew I was coming home for Christmas…'

The smile is there again and, though I feign an annoyed frown, I wouldn't have it any other way. I'm not ready to let her go completely… and it also gives me something to do.

As Kylie watches on, I empty the clothes onto the table and then sort everything by colour and material type. I load up everything for the hot wash first and then set the machine running, before transferring her clothes partly to her bag and partly to the basket that sits by the washer.

By the time that's done, Kylie's pizza is ready. She swaps it to a plate and then sits at the kitchen table as I watch on. The normality of all this is breathtakingly touching to the point that I have to blink away the tears.

Kylie is partway through the second slice when she looks up and takes me in: 'What happened to your cheek?'

I'd forgotten until she mentioned but, now she has, my skin burns.

'Gemma,' I say. 'Alice's mum. I was in the pub toilets and she came in after me.'

She frowns. 'What do you mean?'

'She slapped me a couple of times.'

'She… what? Why?'

'I'm not sure. I guess because she thinks it was Richard who attacked Alice and left her in the stream.'

'You should tell the police.'

'Nobody else saw it, plus everyone will think I deserved it anyway.'

'You've not done anything wrong.'

I know she's my daughter – and I know it's true – but there's still something comforting about hearing this.

'She can't just go around hitting people, Mum.'

'I'd be angry if I were her.'

Kylie stares at me for a moment before realising she's not going to change my mind. She's halfway through the pizza slice and takes another bite before looking up again. 'Do you want a cup of tea?'

I laugh at this and she looks at me incredulously.

'What?'

'It's got to be a good four or five years since you last asked.'

'Take it or leave it.'

'That would be lovely.'

Kylie fills the kettle and then sets it boiling, before returning to her pizza. Perhaps it's the comfort of having her home, or maybe it's because she's the one person I know I could tell without any risk of it getting around. Either way, for the first time, I say the one thing I've been keeping to myself.

'I don't think I should have married him…'

Kylie freezes with a slice of pizza halfway to her mouth. 'Because of all this?'

A shrug. 'I think I regretted it at the time – but I felt too far in to turn away.'

'Why?'

'I think because I was feeling old—'

'You're not *that* old.'

'I'm old enough. You were in your teens and I knew you'd be leaving at some point. I thought it was my last chance to find somebody.'

Kylie looks on but I can see that she doesn't quite get it. Times have moved so fast and young women have a lot more awareness over what they can achieve with their lives. I think they're probably a lot more confident about saying no to things they don't want to do – and that includes boys. She also doesn't yet know what it's like to be single, mid-thirties, with a child.

I had Kylie when I was only twenty and my entire adult life has been given over to raising her. I don't regret a moment of that – but that doesn't mean I could stop myself from thinking ahead.

'Do you love him?'

It's such a simple question and yet there's no simple answer. The truth is that I'm not sure whether I've ever been in love with anyone. It was exciting to be with Richard, certainly at the beginning. Some of that was because of his position compared to mine. Later, when he asked me to marry him, I said yes. I figured there were few reasons not to. I felt safe with him and he wasn't controlling or abusive. He was financially secure and, though I wasn't poor, that held an appeal. More importantly, I didn't think there would be a line of men asking me in the future.

I should have paid more attention to the other signs – that we never did the normal things that couples do. There were no cinema visits or meals out. We didn't have other couply friends and rarely sat down to watch television together. He had his interests and I had mine. I thought that was liberating but, in the end, I think it's probably more dividing.

I don't answer Kylie's question – because I'm not sure of the truth. Perhaps I do love him? Or, maybe, I don't know what that is.

'Oh, Mum…'

It's the second time Kylie has said it – but this hurts more than the first. It's the embarrassment that stings. I feel like the teenager and she's the adult.

Neither of us speak for a while as there's little to say.

Kylie finishes making my tea and, as I sip at that, she eats the rest of her pizza, before rinsing the plate in the sink. When she sits back at the table, she fidgets for a moment and then says what's on her mind.

'What are you going to do?'

'None of this means I shouldn't stand by him.' It's not quite the answer to the question.

'How do you figure?'

'He could be a victim, too.'

Kylie is silently biting her lip.

'He could be,' I say, with a little more insistence.

She still doesn't reply and we're at an impasse, where we remain for a good minute or so.

'What about university?' I ask.

Kylie sits up straighter. It's quite the change of direction. 'What about it?'

'I thought you had exams, or…?'

'I've got coursework due on Monday – but I've already done half of it and I can submit online. Half the people on my course have already gone home.'

'How's it going in general?'

'Fine.' She stretches high and then cricks her neck, before yawning. I know she wants to avoid this conversation and am not convinced it's a real yawn. 'I think I'm going to go to bed,' she says. 'It's been a long day.'

'Do you need anything doing?'

'I don't think so. I'll see you in the morning.'

Kylie hesitates as she passes me, as if she's not sure whether to hug me another time. She's still a teenager, after all. It's only a moment – and then it's over as she continues walking. The stairs creak and then there's the sound of her door opening and closing.

I sit by myself for a little while, knowing I should probably go to bed as well. I'm tired but I'm not. I want to sleep but I won't.

When I check my phone, I've missed Theresa's text. I'd forgotten I'd asked her if she wanted a drink. She says she can't make it out tonight but that maybe we can do it another time. I leave it at that, not wanting to bother her any further.

There's a squeak from above and I realise how comforting it is to hear someone else's footsteps. It's easy to forget how reassuring such small things can be.

I potter around downstairs, finally emptying those bags of baking goods, as well as doing other bits of cleaning. When there's nothing left to do, I take myself up to bed and then lie awake, listening to the barely-there voice from the next room. I assume Kylie is either chatting on her phone to one of her friends, or watching a video on her laptop.

My eyes are open, but then they're not. The clock says five hours have passed. Whatever noise was coming from Kylie's room has now gone silent. Except… there's something tickling the edges of my thoughts. I was asleep but then I heard… something.

A second later and a booming *crash* thunders through the house.

TWENTY-ONE

WEDNESDAY

I head down the stairs, still blurry and confused from the abrupt interruption. It's only the grogginess that stops me from moving so quickly that I miss the splinters now lying across the hallway floor. The white of the moon glows through the newly created hole in the glass of the front door, with the shards glistening bright like a carpet of crystals.

There's the sound of a door from above and then Kylie's on the top step.

'What happened?'

She's speaking with the sleepiness that I feel.

'I don't know… I guess someone…'

Kylie edges down the stairs and stops next to me, looking over the banister towards the half-brick. We both know what's happened.

We're also both barefooted.

'I'll get some shoes on,' Kylie says.

'No. I'll do it.'

'Should we call the police? They might want to see this before it's cleared away.'

'What are they going to do? It'll take an age to get someone out at this time.'

'They might get DNA off the brick, or something?'

I consider it for a moment. 'I think they've got more important things on.'

Kylie doesn't question this, though she does sit on the stairs as I tiptoe around the edge of the glass and pluck my wellies from the rack that's close to the door. I crunch across the carpet and then open the front door. The frozen breeze bristles through and there's nobody there. Whoever threw the brick will be along the lane and on their way back to Leavensfield by now. There's no question it will be a villager who did this. I head across the drive to the road anyway, looking both ways across the deserted tarmac. My car sits untouched on the driveway.

I close the door when I get back inside. Kylie is still on the stairs.

'Anyone there?' she asks.

'No.'

'Do you think it was Gemma?'

'I don't know. Maybe.' I pause and then add: 'You should go back to bed. I'll clean this up.'

Kylie watches me for a moment and then pushes herself up. 'I think you should call the police.' She hovers, waiting for a reply that she doesn't get – and then she heads back to her room.

It's around eight a.m. when the sun finally rises and a sliver of light passes through the window onto the kitchen floor. The long winter nights were starting to bite at me a good few weeks before any of this happened. I've never been much of a fan of this time of year. Christmas is the respite, with the food and drink, the glamorised TV shows – and, when she was younger, Kylie's everlasting excitement at presents. Other than that, the four darkening months from November to February always mirror my moods. Moving to Leavensfield has only made that worse. I lived in a town before this and, though it was no bustling never-sleep city, there were always lights. Always people. It's easy to feel abandoned and forgotten out here.

I blink away from the laptop screen watching the light from the window creep across the floor towards the cabinets. It's probably because Kylie's home that my mind feels more focused this morning, despite the wake-up call. Regardless of everything else, I need to get on with some work. That starts with my emails – with which I only deal on my laptop. The embarrassing typos became far too much when I used my phone.

I skip past a couple of unimportant marketing mails and click onto one from the editor of the food magazine for which I write a monthly piece. Steady, regular work is a glorious bonus when freelancing – and this is the publication for which I've been working the longest.

There's a trick to reading emails from editors and commissioners. They all start off with a general 'Hope you're okay'-vibe. After that, there are either two or three lines of fluff that means next to nothing – and then it gets to the point.

Which is why the fourth line is so galling.

It's probably best if we put everything on hold for now. Hope you understand. Perhaps we can assess once things have quietened down?

I read the entire email back three times, without completely understanding what she's talking about. It's only then that I realise the obvious. Local news is never local news in the age of the internet.

She doesn't live anywhere near Leavensfield and yet she'll have read about Richard being linked to what happened with Alice. She doesn't mention that in her email because she assumes I'll know what she's talking about.

I hammer out an angry reply, insisting that I've done nothing wrong. I've been loyal to her and her readers like what I write. This is grossly unfair… and so on. Then I delete the lot without sending. Then I rewrite most of it, because I really am furious. Then I delete it a second time.

She doesn't want her publication to be linked to a woman whose husband might have kidnapped and then left a young girl for dead. It's hard to blame her for that – but it's the three lines of fluff that particularly grate. I would have preferred the honesty.

I'm attempting a more conciliatory reply when there's a hefty thump from the letter box. I assume it's the postman at first… except that we never get mail in the morning. I head into the hallway, where the temporary fix of the cardboard I've taped to the front door seems particularly abhorrent.

Sitting on the doormat, from where I swept and vacuumed the glass just hours ago, sits a padded envelope. When I pick it up and turn it over, my name has been written on the front in thick capital letters. There's no stamp or postmark – this has been hand-delivered.

I open the front door and head onto the drive, though there's nobody in sight. There's no one on the road, either. The parcel is not particularly heavy or bulky, though I can feel something small and rectangular on the inside.

Back in the house, I take the parcel through to the kitchen and cut open the top with a pair of scissors. I reach inside and remove an old-fashioned mobile; the type of basic model I had before phones came with internet access, email, apps, and all the other modern things. The sort that's used for calling, texting and little else.

There's no box and no note. Nothing except the phone. With no other clues, I twist it around and remove the battery cover before putting it back on. When I press the buttons on the front, the screen remains blank and it takes me a few seconds to realise that the power button is on top.

When I turn it on, nothing happens for a moment until the maker's logo appears. It's a crude animation compared to the high-definition, colour images of now – though it swirls and blurs until fading away to reveal a home screen with no access code required. There are four bars of signal in the top right corner and a notification telling me there is one text message outstanding.

It takes me a couple of attempts to figure out which button does what, largely because I'm so used to touchscreens. Anything else feels alien. When I do finally manage to click on the message, it takes a second to load.

Whatever I was expecting, it wasn't this.

Don't tell anyone about this phone. I love you and I'm so sorry.

TWELVE YEARS OLD

I never realised what chaos a school playground can be until I sat up on the steps above it and watched. There are the boys over on one side who are playing football. There seems to be some sort of instinct about who's on what team because, despite the fact they're all wearing the exact same uniform, they all seem to know who's on what side. It's amazing.

The ball keeps shooting off sideways and cannoning in to random people who've got nothing to do with the game. Each time it happens, there's a big cheer from the players, while the victim clutches whichever part of their body has been walloped and then heads off to a hopefully safer area.

Away from the footballers, there are the girls in cliques of five or six who are standing around while seemingly doing very little. I know from experience that they are, of course, criticising everyone in sight.

There are some lads in the corner opposite the footballers playing on their Game Boys, while two others are trying to climb the tree from which students are strictly banned. Some of the younger girls are hopscotching under the contemptuous gaze of older students who were doing the exact same thing when they were that age.

I continue watching for a while, before looking back to the exercise book that I stole from the shelf behind Mr Garrett's desk a few months ago. It was fresh and empty then – but now it's full of letters to Dad that I know will never be posted.

I'm not sure what to write today. Sometimes it feels easier than others – and today is one of those times where I'm stuck. I don't know what he'd like to hear. School is what it is – and, even if it wasn't, he'd only want to know about the subjects in which I'm excelling. He keeps telling me in his letters that education is the most important thing.

I'm still thinking of what to write when a shadow passes across me. I look up and one of the groups of girls have stopped eyeing the footballing boys and instead climbed the steps to stand in front of me.

'What are you writing?'

It's Jen who does the asking. She's the tallest girl in my year and always the first pick at sports. This is the one thing above everything else that seemingly makes her popular, even though almost all the girls I know claim to hate sport. It's quite the anomaly, though I suspect her popularity is more down to the fact that other girls are scared of her.

I stuff the book and my pen into my bag.

'Get lost, Jen.'

'Oooh… whatcha gonna do? *Kill me?*' The girls laugh as Jen sneers down towards me. 'What's it like in prison?'

I stand and, even though I'm on the step above her, Jen is still a little taller than me.

'Leave me alone.'

She reaches forward and taps me on the shoulder. 'Whatcha gonna do? Get your dad on me?'

She half-turns to make sure the other girls are still laughing – which they are.

I know there's a choice to make here: to walk away and let this continue over and over, or…

Her nose actually crunches when I punch her in the face. I expected it to be hard but it's a lot squishier than I thought.

Jen barely moves as her face explodes, not at first anyway. She stands still, with her eyes wide, like a pig that's seen something it can't quite believe. And then, as the red streams across her lips and down her front, Jen screams.

I look down to my knuckles and they're drenched with blood as well. It's darker than I would've guessed. Perhaps more black than red. I flick much of it away onto the ground but I'm going to need to wash my hands.

Jen screams a second time and then turns so quickly that the blood sprays across two of her friends' clean white shirts.

It's only when she screams a third time that the nearest dinner lady notices. She looks up from the playground below and takes in the abnormally tall twelve-year-old drenched with blood before her eyes go wide.

I sit back down, avoiding the blood spatters and wondering whether the dinner lady will let me wash my hands before she marches me off to my head of year.

It's going to be a very long afternoon – and I suppose this is one more thing I'll be leaving out of my letters to Dad.

TWENTY-TWO

In more than one way, I'm not sure what to do with the phone. In a practical sense, I am struggling to figure out what all the buttons do and how to open anything. Secondly, I don't know what to make of the message: *Don't tell anyone about this phone. I love you and I'm so sorry.*

It can only be Richard. He's not great with phones but, if anything, this type of device suits him far more than any newer smartphone. I've never seen the device before but I could easily picture him having it hidden away in a box under the bed, or something similar. He's never been one to have a big clear-out.

Should I text back? Or call? Or contact Detective Inspector Dini and tell him what's happened?

There's an unexpected noise from the stairs, which reminds me that Kylie's home. I stuff the phone and the envelope down the back of the sofa and then, a moment later, Kylie yawns her way into the living room.

'What did you do about the front door?' she asks.

'Cleaned it up.'

'I mean what *else* did you do?'

'I called the non-emergency line – and I'm going to get the glass fixed.'

She stands with her hands on her hips before her features soften.

'I'm going to make breakfast,' she says. 'Do you want something?'

'No, thank you.'

She gives me a slightly disapproving look – which is more striking in the fact that our roles were reversed a year ago when I thought she wasn't eating enough. Unlike me, Kylie says nothing and heads through to the kitchen, leaving me alone in the living room.

I'm about to retrieve the phone from the back of the sofa, when there's a knock on the door. I'm not sure what it is at first, largely because there's a doorbell that visitors would use.

When a second knock comes, I get up and peep through the front window, to see DI Dini standing on the front step looking at his phone. It's as if he has eyes in his ears as he immediately glances sideways and takes me in.

With little other choice, I move into the hall and then open the front door. Dini eyes the cardboard and then turns towards me.

'I didn't know you were investigating thrown bricks,' I say.

He gives a half-smile but nothing more. 'Can I come in?'

I hold the door wider and he edges in, before taking off his shoes. With Kylie in the kitchen, I almost motion him through to the living room, before deciding against it. Not with the phone down the back of the sofa.

When we get into the kitchen, Kylie is standing next to the toaster, doing a little jig to the appalling music that's playing from her phone. I know all parents think music was better in their day – but that is especially true now.

I cough with Globe-level theatrics and Kylie stops and spins. She steps backwards when she spots Dini standing tall in his smart suit.

'This is Detective Inspector Dini,' I say, nodding towards him. 'And this is my daughter, Kylie.'

Dini stretches out a hand. 'Nice to meet you,' he says.

Kylie eyes his hand and then promptly reaches for the cancel button on the toaster to eject her breakfast. His hand hangs unshaken as she pops the bread onto a plate and then goes to the fridge for the margarine. He only lowers it when she starts smearing the spread. I don't know if I'm proud of, or annoyed, at her.

When she's done with that, she eyes him from bottom to top. She's in her fleecy cow pyjamas that I know are her most comfortable pair, even though she refused to pack them for university. 'What are you going to do about whoever threw that brick?'

Her tone is scornful and deliciously suspicious of authority.

Dini glances sideways to me but I'm not going to help him. 'Someone will be by shortly to check on the damage.'

'What does that mean?'

'We'll look for footprints or any other signs of—'

'Isn't it a bit late for that?'

Dini straightens himself – and this is the most rumbled I've seen him since we met. I can't pretend I'm not enjoying it, even though the adult in me is screaming that I should step in.

He doesn't need me to look after him, however. 'When was the last time you saw Richard?'

Kylie's neck cranes at the abrupt change of direction to the conversation. There's a part of me that's glad I'm not the only one who feels this way about Dini.

'Are you kidding?' she says.

'I have to ask.'

'So arrest me and do it down the station.'

'Kylie…' I do step in this time and my daughter glares between me and the inspector, not sure at whom she should be most annoyed.

'Richard and Mum dropped me off at university in September – and I've not seen him since. Happy? Why don't you ask Mum why her cheek's red?'

Dini turns to take me in and I'm too slow in looking away. I've not checked myself in the mirror this morning, though it still stings slightly, so I can imagine how it appears.

'What happened to your cheek?'

I glare at Kylie, though it won't make the question go away.

'It's nothing,' I say.

'Gemma Pritchard slapped her.'

'Kylie!'

I try to shut her up but my daughter has that chaotic streak about her that sometimes wants to make things worse, if only to see what will happen. We glare at one another and it's Dini who breaks the mood.

'Is that true?'

'It's nothing,' I repeat.

The three of us stand in a triangular stalemate until Dini speaks up.

'I only wanted to check in,' he says. 'I saw the report about your door this morning and thought I'd drop round to make sure you were okay.'

Kylie fires him a suspicious look but I take him at his word. 'I'm fine,' I say.

'If you want that glass refitting, my brother-in-law does that sort of thing. I can leave you his number. Tell him I gave you it and he'll do it for cost.'

'Do you push your family businesses for all your jobs?'

He shrugs dismissively, although there's something in his eyes that might be a tinge of hurt. Either that, or I'm far too soft.

'I'll take his number,' I say.

Dini removes his phone from his jacket and then reads me the promised details before returning it to his pocket.

'Have you thought about the appeal?' he asks.

I'm silent for a moment and it's Kylie who answers: 'The what?'

He looks between us and I know that he's taken this opportunity on purpose.

It's Kylie to whom he replies: 'I asked your mother about doing a public appeal for Richard to come home. I'm obviously aware of all the rumours circulating but, for the moment, he's a missing person.'

I think of the phone that's jammed down the back of the sofa and the message I've read over and over. If I was fully cooperating with police, I'd hand it over… except that I already know what I think of the police because of what happened to my dad. If I'm not strictly cooperating, then I at least have to give the impression that I am.

'When?' I ask.

'Later today? We can set it up and help you with what to say. It doesn't have to be a huge thing. We'd live-stream it on our website and it will probably get written up by some news organisations. Our media relations officer will put together something, plus we'd release a photograph of Richard to try to jog the memories of anyone who might have seen him on Sunday.'

I picture those people at The Willow Tree pub, where the manager saw Richard sitting outside. I'd certainly like to know what he was doing there – and if any of the other patrons remember him.

'I'll do it.'

Dini nods, though he doesn't smile. 'It will be after lunch, so I'll be back in contact with you shortly.' He half-turns back to the hall. 'I should probably be on my way.'

I escort him back and he puts on his shoes before eyeing the cardboard once more on his way out. He hesitates for a moment on the step. Though, just as I think he's going to say something, he turns and heads for his car.

Back in the house and Kylie is waiting for me in the hall. 'Why are you doing the appeal?' she asks.

'Because I want him to come home.'

'But—'

'We don't *know* that he's done anything wrong.'

'Alice got into his car.'

'He might've been giving her a lift home!'

Kylie stares back at me, making her views clear without even saying a word. Richard is not her dad, after all. Never has been and never will be. He was my choice, not hers. It's not as if they don't get on, more that there's little overlap in their lives.

When she realises she's not going to get any more from me she takes her plate upstairs and heads for her room. That's perfect for me, because I head into the living room and retrieve the phone.

Don't tell anyone about this phone. I love you and I'm so sorry.

When I think about it, this is a perfect way to contact me. I check the number that sent the text against the one I have stored in my own phone for Richard. It's different – but then I've seen that police can trace the location of a phone against the mast that's used to transmit data. If he wanted to contact me illicitly, this is probably the most sensible way.

I press to call the number and then listen as the phone starts to ring… and ring… until it goes silent without connecting to a voicemail. It's only a couple of seconds later that a new text arrives.

Can't talk. I'm sorry.

If he can't talk, then he can seemingly text.

Me: *Where are you?*

I wait for around a minute until the next reply comes.

I can't say. Will explain why one day. I'm safe.

Me: *What happened with Alice?*

It's a longer wait this time. I want an instant denial: something that restores my faith in my own decisions. Something that would make me right and everybody else wrong. Something that gives me hope that my life will not be defined by this.

And then it comes.

It's not what people think.

Me: *So where are you?*

I can't say – but I need your help.

I stare at the words and they feel dangerous. There's a choice that's coming which involves picking between my husband and the law.

I don't reply straight away and, as if he's sensing my hesitation, another text joins the previous.

I need you.

It's such a powerful word. He doesn't want something from me, he *needs* it.

Me: *Please tell me where you are.*

I wait and wait. Five minutes pass this time – the longest gap since we started messaging.

When it comes, the reply doesn't answer my question.

Please trust me. I'm safe – but I need you to put some of my clothes and a coat in a bag and leave it at the end of the lane, behind the village sign. Please.

I read and reread the message. Richard has to be nearby if this is what he wants. Has he been hiding this whole time? Perhaps living in the woods atop Leavensfield, or somewhere else that's seemingly far-fetched? I wouldn't have thought him capable – and yet I also cannot explain why Alice got into his car.

The phone beeps again – and this time there is no request.

I love you whatever you do.

TWENTY-THREE

Whenever I see those men or women in front of a board emblazoned with the police logo, I wonder why they blink so much. Now I know. It's because the lights are as bright as the sun.

This is despite the fact that, as Dini promised, it is not a major event. I'm at the front of a small room with the customary backdrop. Dini is sitting in front of me, along with three people who are presumably journalists. At my side is Liz, the media relations officer who spent fifteen minutes telling me what not to say. I'm still not completely sure why that was needed, because she'd already pre-written a statement into which I've had limited input.

Other than that, there's a camera pointing directly at me, which Liz says is being used to live-stream the conference.

Liz is one of those people who is ruthlessly efficient to the point of seeming rude. She rattled through everything I might want to know, asked if I had any questions, and then, when I hesitated for a moment, said 'That's great,' before moving onto the next thing. They should put her onto curing cancer, or something like that.

With everyone in place, she leans into the microphone and angles it towards her. 'Madeleine King is about to read her statement. I'd like to reiterate to you that there will be no questions afterwards. Thank you.'

Liz twists the microphone back to me and then presses back into her seat. When I look up, the three journalists and Dini are all watching me – although, of the four, I'd guess it is Dini who has the most intense stare.

I expected the journalists to be here with pads and pens – but all three simply left their phones on the desk in front of me and are now sitting and watching. I guess that's all it takes nowadays.

I read the statement more or less as it's written. Much of it was put together by Liz before I arrived – although there was little to object about. A lot of it is listing facts, such as when I last saw Richard. Even the personal bits don't sound like me. I say I've been missing him and that I'd like him to come home. The house isn't the same without him. It's a direct me-to-him speech – except that we'd never talk to one another in such a formal way. I even say 'I'm worried about your well-being', even though I'm sure nobody uses the word 'well-being' in real life. It's one of those officialdom words that have seeped into the public's consciousness.

The main thing is that the speech doesn't mention Alice Pritchard, even though everything under the surface is about her. I know the biggest reason the police want me to appeal for Richard to come home is that they're desperate to know why she got in his car. If they already knew – or had any idea where he was – there'd be no need for any of this.

By the time I'm done, I can tell the journalists are confused because of the way they each turn to one another. Like people who have gone to a heavy metal gig, only to find some bloke with an acoustic guitar.

Liz stands and says 'That's it' because nobody seems clear – and then she scuttles to the back of the room to stop the camera. As she does that, each of the journalists head to the front to retrieve their phones. Liz meets them and starts to usher them towards the door, before one of them turns to Dini.

'Is that really it?'

'That's it,' Liz insists.

'What about Alice Pritchard?'

Dini continues to sit, not acknowledging any of them. For a moment, I fear they're about to charge towards me in protest – but a small room at the back of a police station is probably not the best place for that. In the end, despite the temporary stand-off, Liz manages to usher them all outside, leaving Dini and me alone.

'You did great,' Dini says, although it's more of a mumble.

'You're a terrible liar.'

He doesn't acknowledge this and the truth is that I suspect he's a fantastic liar. I imagine he's told a few mistruths to me in the past two days. He's so good at it that he deliberately made this lie sound like one in order to make his others seem truthful.

'I'll get a car round the back shortly,' he adds quietly. 'Then I'll be in contact if anything comes from this.'

I nod towards the door. 'Were they expecting something else?'

Dini shakes his head but he doesn't speak and he's not hiding the fact that he's unhappy about something. It's entrenched in the way he's hunched forward, with angular shoulders and his clenched jaw.

'I have to go,' he says. 'Liz will be back in a moment.'

He strides for the door and closes it behind him, leaving me alone. I focus on the camera at the back, wondering if it might still be on, even though Liz went to turn it off. Would there be some sort of benefit to that? I'm not sure who I trust in all of this – but it's definitely not Detective Inspector Dini, not even with his mates' rates for fixing windows.

I'm about to get up to look more closely at the camera when the sound of raised voices comes from the hallway. I edge closer to the door, trying to make out specific words from the muffled male voices. I'm fairly sure one of them belongs to Dini, although I couldn't be certain. Even if it is him, I can't tell if he's the one being shouted at, or the one doing the shouting.

It all lasts perhaps thirty seconds before there's the sound of someone shushing – and then silence. I hover by the door for a few seconds more before footsteps send me scurrying back towards the desk.

Liz steps into the room and, for a woman who appeared on top of things since the moment I met her, the pink hue in her cheeks now makes her appear slightly flustered.

'There's a car waiting at the back for you,' she says. 'I'll walk you round.'

'Was everything okay?'

'Absolutely fine.'

'It didn't seem like it was fine. Everyone seemed confused. Did they know they were here to hear about a missing person?'

'They were invited here to be given details of an ongoing case.' The vagueness remains, I suppose. It's all deliberate.

'But they would have assumed that would've been about Alice Pritchard…'

'I was always told never to assume.'

She reopens the door to the corridor, making it clear it's time to go. I feel like I've missed something, although I'm not sure what.

I follow her through the corridors until we arrive at a door. When she opens it, there's a dark car waiting, with a uniformed officer in the driver's seat.

'What happens now?' I ask.

'We'll let you know if anything significant comes from this.' She pauses a second and it's as if she then remembers what we've just done. 'I do hope your husband returns.'

It sounds insincere – but that could simply be because of the way Liz is with everything. I thank her anyway and then get into the car, where the driver checks that I'm on my way to Leavensfield, before setting off.

The roads around the village have started to feel very familiar in the past couple of days – but it's easier to acknowledge the sheer majesty when not having to drive. The sweeping green brushstrokes feel endless as they soar up from the road and then swoop down towards the horizon. Even the long, winding drystone walls have a degree of beauty as they criss-cross the fields with rugged precision.

The fields will be filled with sheep come the warmer months but I have no idea where they are now.

The sky is dim as night approaches, even though it barely feels like an hour or two previous that I was in the kitchen when the sun rose. The officer continues along through the roads, passing the centre of Leavensfield and then continuing up the hill towards my house. He slows as he nears the drive but I ask him to keep going.

'Are you sure?' he asks.

'I like walking,' I reply, 'and I need a bit of exercise.'

He doesn't query this and shifts gears as he continues up the winding road until the village sign is in sight.

'Here is fine,' I say.

The driver indicates and pulls over to the side, where I clamber out of the car and then straighten myself as he takes an age to move. I start walking slowly down the verge, waiting for the car to disappear around the bend. As soon as it's out of sight, I turn and head in the other direction, hurrying this time until I get to the base of the sign. It's more than the usual black-on-white 'Welcome to…' notice that's at the entry to almost all places around here. At some point, the parish council found the money to pay for a solid, permanent structure that's around two metres high and five or six wide. Someone painted the welcome message in large, colourful letters, with a selection of bright flowers around the edges as decoration. It's undoubtedly impressive – and very on-brand for the village.

I'm not here to admire the handiwork, though. Instead, I move around to the back of the sign – where there's a clear patch of grass, making it apparent that the bin bag full of clothes I left hours before has now gone.

TWENTY-FOUR

I turn on the phone that's been concealed in my bag throughout the time I was in the police station. The logo swirls until the menu screen loads – and then I wait to see if there are any new messages. When nothing arrives immediately, I start down the hill towards the house. By the time I arrive, there have still been no new messages, so I return the phone to my bag.

I'm not sure if I can explain why I did as asked and left those clothes. I suppose the biggest reason is that Richard's 'Not what people think' feels so real to me. Whenever someone would ask about my father being in prison, I'd use those exact words. There's every chance he was doing a kind act in offering a twelve-year-old girl a lift home when it was dark and cold. What responsible person *wouldn't* do such a thing? After that, something clearly happened – but that doesn't mean it was anything sinister, or down to him.

I look up to the woods that sit above where Richard's car was found and wonder if he might be in there somewhere. Wilderness living does not seem like something of which my husband would be capable – but all sorts of people are capable of all sorts of things when pushed to their limits. The bigger question might perhaps be how he's evaded any police attempts to find him. I consider walking up the fields towards the woods myself and calling his name, except if he wanted me to know where he was, he could have told me in one of his texts.

As I approach the front door, I can immediately see that the glass has been fixed. I even think Dini's brother-in-law might have given the whole frame a clean, because it's gleaming in a way that matches nothing else at the front of the house.

I let myself in and then follow the voices along the hall into the kitchen, to where Theresa and Kylie are sitting at the kitchen table. They go silent as I enter and, though it might have a *bet-you-think-this-song-is-about-you* vibe, the guilty looks they're both wearing make me feel sure they were.

'I came by to see how you were,' Theresa says, before nodding towards Kylie. 'I didn't realise this one was back.'

Ever since they met, Theresa and Kylie have had an easy relationship in the way a girl might have with an aunt or a grandparent. Someone who is close to the mother–child dynamic but slightly off to the side. There were times a little over a year ago when I felt jealous of it. Kylie and I might argue about something silly and I'd find out that she'd ended up getting a freebie at Atal's restaurant, while talking everything through with my best friend. Much of it was nerves ahead of exams or coursework. Few, if any, of Kylie's actual college friends live in Leavensfield, so I think Theresa became a default.

'I didn't know she was coming,' I say.

Theresa moves on and I guess they've already talked about this. 'You should've said you were doing an appeal for Richard. I could have come with you.'

'That came up quickly, too. Did you see it?'

'Not live. There's a video on one of the news sites that someone linked to on Facebook. I can show you—'

'I don't think I want to see it.'

Kylie and Theresa exchange a glance, before both settle back on me.

'What?' I ask.

It's Kylie who replies. 'Have you heard about the march?'

'What march?'

Theresa picks it up: 'Perhaps it's more of a vigil. Harriet sent out an email to the planning committee this morning – and it's on the village Facebook page. There's going to be a march through the village later today to support Gemma and Alice.'

'That makes it sound like she's dead.'

'Critical condition is what people are saying. Not much progress since you and Atal found her.'

Theresa and Kylie swap another look and I don't need to ask what about this time – because Kylie says it out loud.

'Theresa thinks we should go…'

'I'm not sure about that—'

Theresa interrupts me: 'For solidarity,' she says. 'You've got nothing to be ashamed of and you don't have to interact with Harriet, Gemma, or anyone else.'

'I still think it's a bad idea.'

'It might look worse if you don't go…'

I don't have an answer for that.

'Harriet left you off the email chain, even though it went to everyone else on the committee…'

Theresa doesn't need to say more. There's little chance that was an accident, which means there is every chance Harriet is trying to set me up to look terrible. It happened last year, with the summer fete. She sent an email to Pam knowing she was in Malaysia with limited internet access. Then, at the following meeting, when Pam hadn't ordered a pair of signs, her reasoning was that she hadn't checked her email while away. She'd arrived back just forty-eight hours previously and hadn't had time to sort anything. Harriet had, of course, already done the job and turned herself into a hero at Pam's expense. That's how she works.

'I think we should go,' Kylie says. 'I've not been out since I got back.'

She makes it sound like some sort of fun party, though I suspect she's been away from the village for too long.

'The three of us can go together if you want,' Theresa adds.

'When does it start?'

'Sundown.'

I glance towards the window and it's more or less already dark. 'We better go now, then.'

While putting on my coat and other winter items, I take a moment to check the phone that came through the letter box. There is still no follow-up to the earlier requests for the clothes – and no confirmation they were taken, even though I know the bag has gone.

After that, Theresa, Kylie and I hurry down the hill into the village. A glimmering orange radiance makes it easy enough to spot where the march is beginning, even from a distance. Despite the endless social occasions, a march doesn't feel like the sort of thing people do here. Protesting injustice is the sort of thing people do through flowery posts online, instead of actually taking part.

Not today, though.

When we close in on the pub car park, I can see that the glow is from all the adults, who seem to be clutching a lit candle. I have no idea where they've come from but, if nothing else, Harriet is resourceful. It's well within her means to have found a hundred or so candles with accompanying holders in an afternoon.

Theresa goes to grab us some candles from a large box that's resting on a wall at the front. In the gloom of the night, and with the commotion over people collecting candles, it's easy enough to slip around the crowd relatively unnoticed. In doing that, I spot Harriet at the front, alongside Gemma, who still seems to be wearing those fluffy boots that I'm now certain are Harriet's. That's mainly because Harriet is wearing a relatively normal pair of black boots that can't be anywhere near as insulated for these conditions. Even by Harriet's standards I'm surprised at just how easily she's managed to put herself front and centre in this.

Harriet's husband, Gavin, is a step or two behind her, next to James – as well as their combined four children. Power couples stick together. Curiously absent is Sarah once more. I haven't seen or heard from her since she showed up at the house saying we should be better friends.

I spot Zoe and Frankie about two-thirds of the way back in the crowd. Frankie is carrying a candle but Zoe isn't. She gives me a small wave, which I return.

Theresa soon finds Kylie and me again near the back of the crowd – and she has Atal with her this time. It's far too solemn an occasion for extravagant welcomes but he gives Kylie a brief hug and a thumbs-up – which is very him. Kylie did a few shifts at his restaurant last year when he was busy over Christmas and he told her she could have a job with him any time she wanted.

We're too far back to hear the starting call but, all of a sudden, everyone sets off in an orderly line that's up to six people wide at any given time. People are holding their candles earnestly, while walking at a steady pace. We set off as if heading out of the village but then cut along the lane that loops around the back of the school. Nobody speaks and, though I'm usually sceptical of anything Harriet plans, it's impossible to ignore the significance of what's happening. Nothing we do here is going to aid Alice's recovery – except that we're together as a village in showing support to her mother. That has to mean something.

There's a sense of community as Kylie walks at my side and we match the pace of the people in front of us. Theresa and Atal are behind and they do the same.

After circling the school, we get back to the main road and then head towards the high cross monument that signals the centre of the village. The trail of fire stretches for a good hundred metres and I can only imagine how impressive it might look from the fields above.

When we reach the cross, people start to mass into a large circle. If anyone were to try driving through the village, they'd have a long wait – but that's the whole point about Leavensfield. People don't come here unless they need to.

Theresa, Atal, Kylie and I slot in close to the wall, where there are hardly any people. Harriet has found a vicar from somewhere, despite the village not having its own church. He's in the full gown and stands next to the cross as people continue to mass. Gemma and Harriet are side by side in front of the vicar, with the crowd grouping out from around them. I watch as Gavin tries to take his wife's hand, only for Harriet to gently slap him away. Her gaze remains unflinchingly on the vicar throughout and her expression never changes.

When everyone has settled, the vicar holds up his hands and asks for silence, which he gets. With that, he asks everyone to bow their heads, before he says a rambling prayer that covers love, understanding and a few other things to which I'm not really listening.

It's only as he says 'Amen' that I realise there don't appear to be any journalists covering this. Or, if they are, they're out of sight. Whatever media life this story had outside our little enclave, it doesn't seem to have lasted long. I doubt the same would be true if it had been Harriet's daughter who'd ended up in that stream, instead of Gemma's. When Harriet stood on the stage at the front of the hall and told everyone to prepare for what could be a media invasion, it was because she was thinking of what would happen had this been her child. The difference is that Alice is a not a blonde-haired, blue-eyed prodigy of a relentlessly upper-middle-class English couple.

As the vicar continues to speak about what we can all now be doing to support Alice's mother, I watch Gemma shuffle uncomfortably next to Harriet. The moment where she backed me into that sink was only a day ago and yet the pain has gone and it already feels as if it didn't happen. If she even wants my forgiveness, I know I'd give it to her.

I'm so busy watching other people that I somehow fail to notice that the vicar has stopped talking. It's only when villagers start filing backwards that clues me in to the fact that it's over.

Kylie leans in to whisper that she'll be right back – and then she disappears into the mass. With Atal and Theresa in conversation with another couple, I'm left standing awkwardly, unsure whether I should make a hasty exit. I've shown my face, which was the main reason for coming.

It's James who catches my eye. With Sarah absent, his kids busy mingling with the others, plus Gavin talking with Harriet, Gemma and the vicar, he's on his own, too.

I'm not sure we've ever shared more than a casual 'hello', but he seems keen to talk as he strides across to join me.

'Not sure I expected to see you here,' he says.

'Where else would I be?'

'Fair point.'

He twists to take in the rest of the crowd as we stand side by side.

'How is Sarah?' I ask.

'She's resting at home. She's been a bit poorly recently and we figured being out in the cold wouldn't be great.'

'She seemed all right yesterday.'

It takes a second or two for this to sink in – and then he turns to look sideways at me. 'You saw Sarah yesterday?'

'She came to my house. She said she'd had a chest infection but was feeling a bit better.'

He pauses, unsure of himself. 'She came to *yours*?'

'Yes.'

His narrow eyes make it clear he had no idea about this. 'Why was she at yours?'

I start to answer – and then have to stop, largely because I don't know.

'For a chat,' I say. 'Although I'm not sure. She was waiting for me.'

He cups his chin with his fingers and then rubs it before looking away towards Harriet.

'Is that a problem?' I ask.

'No… I just didn't know you were friends.'

I almost correct him to say that we're not – except there is no reason to do so.

I try to remember the conversation with Sarah, wondering if she'd perhaps given some reason as to why she was there. She said it was to give me tickets to the ball – but she could have posted those through the door. I try to remember whether she'd mentioned her husband at all. He seems even more surprised about her visit than I was.

There's no time for any further conversation because he drifts away as Atal and Theresa appear at my side – along with Kylie.

'Atal's going to cook for us,' Kylie says – though the grin on her face tells me a lot more than the words.

'My treat,' Atal adds. 'A welcome home meal for my future manager!' He nudges Kylie with his shoulder but she doesn't take the bait.

I'm not sure I want to spend any longer in public – but the empty house doesn't feel appealing, either.

With that, the four of us walk back towards the Fox and Hounds car park, where Atal has parked on the next street over. Parking in front of someone's house would usually instigate a strongly worded note being left on the windscreen – but everyone's on their best behaviour tonight.

He drives us up the hill on the opposite side of the village to where Richard and I live. It's the road that ultimately leads to Beaconshead and Atal's restaurant is based a short distance past Leavensfield's boundary. A few decades ago, it used to be a second pub in the days when a village of this size seemingly needed two places to drink. Atal bought out what was a largely abandoned site before I moved here and has since converted it into the somewhat originally named 'Atal's'. It's got a rating in the high-fours on both TripAdvisor and Google, which is what matters nowadays.

It's clear something is wrong the moment he pulls into the car park. Two police cars are parked at the building's entrance and there's an officer standing in the doorway talking to a member of staff. 'Atal's' shines brightly above them.

Theresa manages a 'What—?' before Atal jolts the car to a stop. 'Wait here,' he says.

None of us moves as he unclips his seat belt and gets out of the car, before crossing the tarmac. We watch in silence as he approaches the officer who was talking to the member of staff. I'm sitting behind the driver's seat, watching Theresa in the passenger seat. She's hunched forward and I'd swear she hasn't breathed since the moment her husband got out of the car. It's one of those moments in which it feels like nothing good can happen.

The conversation with the officer and Atal goes on for perhaps a minute until they turn and head back down the steps at the front of the restaurant and round the police car.

Theresa finally breathes out as it looks like he's on his way back to us... except that he isn't. The officer opens the rear door of the marked vehicle – and Atal ducks and gets inside.

Theresa doesn't hesitate this time. She's out of the car before I can unclip my seat belt. I only catch her as she's bearing down on one of the other officers. As best I can tell, both sets of officers are set to leave.

'What's going on?' she asks.

The officer eyes Theresa, then me, and then the approaching Kylie.

'Who are you?' he asks.

She points towards the car, in which Atal now sits. It's impossible to see him through the glare of the windows. 'I'm Theresa Bhamra. I'm his *wife*.'

'Oh…' The officer glances sideways, looking for help that isn't there. 'I'm afraid I can't give you any details now.'

'Details about what?'

'Your husband has been arrested.'

Theresa is so shocked that she stumbles backwards into me. I end up supporting her as she tries to regain her balance. She's gasping for air, or perhaps the words.

She manages a breathy: 'I don't understand.'

'We're taking him to the police station at Beaconshead.'

'Why are you arresting him?'

'I'm not in a position to say at the moment.' The officer pauses for a second, gesturing towards the driver in the car containing Atal. 'Now, if you could stand aside…'

TWENTY-FIVE

Theresa and I sit in the same waiting area that I eyed when I was at the police station to look at the clothes that may have belonged to Richard. When I was here earlier for the appeal, I was brought through the back door – but it's still my third visit in a day and a half. Not bad considering I haven't done anything wrong.

'I can't get my head around it,' Theresa says. It's roughly the twentieth time she's said this since we arrived, although I don't blame her. My head's spinning, too. We must be thinking the same thing, although neither of us are brave enough to say it. I'm certainly not – although there's another voice within me that would take whatever this is if it means Richard can be exonerated.

'He *found* Alice's body,' Theresa says.

'I know.'

'You were there.'

'I was… but not at the beginning.'

Theresa spins to take me in with wide, veiny eyes. Our drive here was more of a manic rush to follow the police cars than it was any sort of conversation. Kylie remained at the restaurant to get a lift home with one of the restaurant staff members she knows.

'I *wasn't* there,' I insist. 'Atal knocked on the door and asked me to call the police because he'd forgotten his phone. He was out walking Lucky.'

'Lucky…' Theresa repeats the name and then mutters that she hasn't fed the poor dog this evening. It's only a few seconds until she's back in the room. 'What happened after he knocked on your door?'

'I called the police. I was on the phone to them as we walked back towards Daisy Field and the stream.'

'What then?'

'You already know. We got there together. There was the girl in the red coat. Atal said she wasn't breathing. I was going to check – but then the police turned up.'

'There must be something else…?'

I start to say 'no' as an automatic reaction – but then remember something I'd dismissed at the time.

'Only that Atal's bottom half was wet,' I say. 'He said he'd dragged Alice out of the stream. His trousers and his feet were drenched.'

Theresa nods along, although it's hard to tell whether she already knows. There's nothing overly odd: if he did drag Alice from the water, then he was going to get wet. I suppose the one thing that always stuck with me is that he thought she was dead when she wasn't. He had left her to come to my house and, in that time, she actually *could* have died.

We sit quietly for a few moments before Theresa pushes herself up and crosses to the counter. I don't hear what she says – but I do see the palms-up, apologetic body language of the woman on the other side. It's not long before Theresa sits back down next to me.

'She says she can't tell me much…'

'Do you know if Atal's lawyer is here yet?'

A nod. 'That's about all she'd say. Mandeep's downstairs with him now.' Theresa pauses for a beat and then turns to me. Her next sentence gives me chills. 'This must bring back memories about what happened with your dad…?'

I have to turn away because, now she's mentioned it, the memories feel uncomfortably and painfully close. I spent a lot of hours waiting around for news from solicitors and police officers, none of whom ever seemed to have anything good to say. I thought I was done with police stations and waiting rooms.

'The justice system gets things wrong sometimes,' I say.

'They're wrong about Atal,' Theresa replies. 'He hasn't done *anything*.'

We sit and we wait. Theresa checks in with the woman at the counter twice more, although there are no updates. The only moment of something approaching action is when a uniformed officer brings in a man whose arms are handcuffed behind his back. He has been arrested for being drunk and disorderly and is seemingly doing his best to prove the point. He hurls around a series of swear words, almost falls over his own feet, and then asks the woman behind the counter if she fancies a drink 'when this is all over'. He ends up being shunted off to another room for a chat with the custody sergeant.

We wait some more until, eventually, a large Asian man in a suit appears from the side door. Theresa stands but he beckons her back down as he slots in next to us, putting a case down on the seat. Before Mandeep says anything, he motions towards me but Theresa explains that I'm her friend and that it's fine to talk in front of me.

'Atal's going to be kept in overnight,' Mandeep says.

Theresa shoots up into a standing position before she lowers herself a moment later. '*What?*'

Mandeep rests a hand on her arm, possibly to keep her seated. 'This is perfectly routine.'

'Routine for what? What are they saying he's done?'

'It's all a little unclear and I'm not sure I'm best placed to say…'

'What does that mean?'

Mandeep glances to me for a second and then back to Theresa. 'Atal is my client – and there has to be a certain confidentiality within that.'

The lack of clarity is as clear as can be. I watch as Theresa tries to makes sense of something that must be impossible for her to understand.

'He's my husband.'

Mandeep maintains a tight, controlled smile. He likely learned this on day one of legal training. The measured, wordless apology that isn't an apology.

'You should go home for the night,' he says. 'Check on that lovely dog of yours. I'll be back here in the morning and there will hopefully be news then.'

'But you can't— I mean— You must be able to tell me what he's been arrested for?'

'Perhaps tomorrow.'

Theresa is understandably stunned. It's bad enough that her husband has been arrested – but she doesn't even know why.

'Why can't you tell me?' she asks.

The measured, non-committal smile remains on Mandeep's face. 'I can't tell you anything more than I have, Theresa. I hope you understand. If roles were reversed and I was acting for you, I'd do the exact same thing.'

'Does that mean Atal's told you not to tell me?'

Mandeep straightens his suit and stands. He picks up his briefcase from the seat. 'I really should be going,' he says. 'I'll be back here tomorrow. I'm sure you'll have some answers then.'

We watch him leave. Theresa stares through watery eyes and I can only imagine the mix of confusion and aggravation she's feeling.

'I can drive you back in Atal's car,' I say.

Theresa gazes blankly ahead and then stands, before fishing in her bag for the car keys. She passes them over and we head outside, where we trail along the street towards the vehicle. I get into the driver's side and have to fiddle around with the seat and mirrors to get everything into position. The windows are misted and I struggle to find the correct controls for the heaters. All the while, Theresa sits in the passenger seat and stares directly ahead. It's only as I'm ready to set off that she finally speaks.

'Do *you* think that *they* think Atal did that to Little Alice?'

'No…'

My reply doesn't sound like a 'no', even to me. Why else could they be holding him?

The drive back to Leavensfield is completed in silence, except for when I get close to Theresa's house. She tells me to keep driving through to mine and that we can swap, then, and she'll take herself home. I start to query whether she'll be all right but then stop myself. I wouldn't be in the mood for this question and I doubt she is.

It's a short drive through the now deserted village and up the hill to my house. I reverse onto the drive, making it easier for Theresa to pull back out, and then yank up the handbrake.

'I'll check in with you tomorrow,' I say.

Theresa nods along and then mutters a low 'thank you for coming', before she gets out of the car. We exchange the briefest of hugs as she crosses to the driver's side – and then I watch as she drives off into the night.

I can't reconcile the fact that I'm desperate for it to be true that this is something to do with Atal and not Richard… and yet I don't.

Before I head into the house, I check the phone that came through the door this morning. There's still been no reply since I left the clothes behind the village sign, so I decide to take the initiative.

Me: Are you okay?

I unlock the front door and move into the hall, before locking it behind me. I call out to Kylie, asking if she's home – which gets a 'yes' yelled down from above. By the time all this has happened, there's a reply on the phone.

Yes. Thank you.

It's achingly brief – but then that's Richard when it comes to text messages and technology in general. I would bet I've got dozens of similar replies from him when we've messaged back and forth about far more normal things.

Me: *Can you come home now?*

The reply isn't instant – but it doesn't take long.

Not yet.

Me: *They've arrested Atal*

I stand in the hall, waiting for a reply. *Hoping* for a reply. This could be the reason why Richard is hiding wherever he's hiding. He knows that Atal did something – but he's been waiting for the police to take action.

The grandfather clock ticks around for almost five minutes until I surmise that there's nothing coming back any time soon. It's nearly eleven o'clock – and it's been yet another long day in a series of long days.

I take myself upstairs, to check in on a sleepy Kylie. She's already in bed but asks how Theresa and Atal are doing. I say there won't be much news until morning – and she's seemingly too tired to want more.

When I get into bed, I place the phone on Richard's pillow. It's comforting to have it close and I have a sense that there's more to come. I figure the buzz of the evening will keep me awake – but the length of the day has a greater toll. I remember pulling the covers up high under my chin and then…

I'm drifting and dreaming and yet the world is quaking. I think there's water, or maybe it's grass. Everything is rumbling and jumping and…

I'm in bed and there's something vibrating close to my head. Light bounces around the ceiling and it takes me a moment to realise the phone is pulsing. My eyes strain through the dark, fighting the tiredness. The red digits on the clock beam through the gloom, telling me that it's four minutes past four.

There's a text message waiting for me.

Go to Fuel's Gold for 9am. Wait behind the old fuel tank and don't be seen.

THIRTEEN YEARS OLD

We're at the kitchen table as Auntie Kath puts the plate of toast down in front of me.

'Are you sure you don't want anything on it?' she asks.

I mumble a 'no' and pick up the first half-slice of bread. Of course I want something on it. I'd love jam, or marmalade – except that I keep finding myself saying 'no' to things when I wish I'd said 'yes'. I think my aunt knows this because she always comes back to check, except that I do the same thing again.

'How was school?' she asks. I glare at her, which she seems to take as an answer. 'I need to talk about tomorrow,' she adds.

'I don't want to.'

'I know you don't – but I'm going to say this anyway.'

I bite the toast and then make a point of chewing and chewing, trying to keep my mouth full enough so that I don't have to say anything.

'Court is not a good place for you,' Auntie Kath says. 'Definitely not tomorrow, in any case. I know you want to be there for the verdict but it can't happen.'

'He's my dad.'

'I know he is, love.'

I hate the way she stares at me sometimes, when her eyes are kind and full of pity. At times, it feels like there's nothing worse. I want her to be angry, like I am. I want us to go to court together and let everyone know that this isn't right before it's too late.

'He didn't do anything wrong. Why can't I tell them that?'

'We've been through this. Your dad's lawyers and the lawyers from the other side agreed to accept everything you told the police. They believed every word you said. Because of that, you didn't need to say it all again. They already gave that evidence to the jury. It's called accepted evidence – because they *accepted* it as true.'

I have another bite of toast, chewing and chewing once more as I try to think of a reason that I have to be in court.

'I want to see Dad,' I say.

'I know, love. You will – but not in court. Your dad's lawyer doesn't think it would look good if you're in the public gallery when you're supposed to be at school.'

'But I want to tell them that he didn't *do* anything.'

Auntie Kath smiles that stupid smile she does when she can't think of anything to say.

I put down the slice of toast I'm holding and push away the plate. 'I'm not hungry.'

She doesn't touch the plate. I don't know why I'm saying I'm not hungry. I am – and my aunt knows it. Nobody is fooled and the only person who'll lose out is me by not eating.

I still don't reach for the plate, though.

Auntie Kath is still watching when the phone on the wall rings. She glances up to the clock to see that it's almost half-past four, and then she checks her watch as if making sure.

'Is that—?'

My aunt cuts me off with: 'They said it would be tomorrow…' before hurrying to the phone and plucking the receiver from the cradle.

I watch her, hoping for a big smile to appear on her face that will let me know Dad's on his way back. I'm sure I'll be able to see the result before hearing it.

'Okay.' She's nodding and there's no smile yet. 'I understand. Is that—? … Oh, no, right, I get it…'

Still no smile – though she turns her back slightly towards me.

'Is that everything? ... No more tonight then? ... All right, I'll tell her.'

I wait... but I already know.

Auntie Kath turns and I can see the answer in her face. She steps across the kitchen and crouches, then presses a hand to my shoulder. Which is when I burst into tears.

TWENTY-SIX

THURSDAY

Kylie and I have already run out of things to talk about with one another. Before she left for university, we wouldn't actually see each other that much, largely because she'd either be in her room, or she'd stay on at college to be with her friends. After the reunion between us, it's like those old walls are back. I don't know what to say to her – and that problem seems to be mutual.

We sit at the kitchen table eating breakfast together – toast with jam for me, porridge for her – but she barely looks up from her phone. I don't risk showing her the phone that came through the letter box, although that's largely what's on my mind. She hasn't mentioned Richard – but she has asked if there was any news from Theresa.

I haven't heard anything so far and, if I'm honest, since getting the message overnight about an illicit meeting this morning, I'd almost forgotten what happened with Atal. It's like I can only focus on one monumental event at a time.

'Have you still got coursework to do today?' I ask.

Kylie looks up momentarily from her phone. 'If I can concentrate – and if your internet connection doesn't keep dropping out. What are you up to?'

'I'm probably going to check in with Theresa soon to see what's going on. Do you need anything? Food? That sort of thing?'

A shake of the head. 'I'm good.'

I finish eating and then put on my winter gear again. This ritual is one of the worst parts of the season. Nothing can ever simply happen; it has to be accompanied by ten minutes of hunting down layers – coats, scarves, gloves, hats, extra socks – and everything else.

Kylie passes me on her way up the stairs and asks if I'll message her with any news. I say I will – and then I step out into the cold. I will be checking in with Theresa – but not yet.

I don't want to be seen on the road, so pass through the gate onto Daisy Field and trail the hedge line up the slope. It's the first time I've stepped onto here since Atal and I were here and we saw the red-jacketed shape on the riverbank. I still wish I'd ignored him and gone to check on the girl myself.

There's little sign any of that ever happened now. The area the police were investigating has been cleared and the only indication something odd might have taken place is the tyre tracks that skirt across the hard ground towards the stream. Even those are barely more than a dimple at this time of the season.

There's no bridge across the stream – but there are a series of places where people have dropped large stones to create an easier way across. The water is at a gentle trickle for now but, when the big thaw comes, it will gush down from upstream and cover these stones. Crossing will be a dicey game then – but it's easy enough now as I pass onto the other side of the water and continue along the line of the hedge. I soon emerge back onto the road, a couple of hundred metres down from Fuel's Gold.

The large price board is at the front, with the pumps beyond and then the static building past that. In the age of everything being owned by the usual big companies, this is a throwback to something of years past. Like so much of Leavensfield, I suppose.

I carry on walking and the irony isn't lost on me that this is likely the final part of the route Alice took four days ago when she was here. I pass the price board but ignore the main forecourt as I continue on to the big metal clothes recycling bin on the edge of the property. Beyond this are the woods that stretch up to the top of the hill and most of the way down the other side. It doesn't look like much on a map but there is a few square miles of dense woodland and bracken all compacted into an area where few people explore beyond the edges.

At the back of the main building, along the side from the recycling bin, is the rusting, large cylindrical frame of an old fuel tank. I would assume it goes back decades to when putting petrol in a car wasn't as straightforward as it is now. The only thing I know for sure is that it's large, that the far side is shielded from view – and that this is where Richard wants to meet.

I make sure I remain out of sight from whoever might be in the shop and then I pass around the recycling bank before slotting in behind the tank. There is crumbling tarmac underfoot, with stunted weeds sprouting through the gaps. The only other things of note on the ground are a grey plastic step and what looks like a makeshift fishing rod made out of an old mop handle.

It's ten minutes to nine – and only now that I realise how much I really do miss Richard. It doesn't mean we have a perfect relationship and everything I said to Kylie about making a mistake was probably true... but that's only part of it. He offered me a stability I'd never had before. I don't know if there have been any other students apart from me but, even if there have, it would only be anyone *after* me about which I should be concerned.

I'll have questions for him but that doesn't mean everything we've had together these past few years should be discarded.

I just want to see him again.

And so I wait.

It's five to nine – and then it's nine o'clock. I recheck the message from the early hours of this morning and it definitely says nine. I figure that being a little late is fine – but then it's five-past. Both phones say the same time – and then it's ten-past.

I'm about to text to ask what's happening when there's the sound of a car engine. Out here, in the middle of nowhere, the growl clings to the breeze; growing louder and louder until a car crunches across the gravel next to the recycling bin. I didn't think Richard would be coming in a vehicle – and especially not the type of black 4x4 urban tank that just pulled in.

Harriet drives one, because of course she does.

People justify those vehicles around here because of the remoteness and the occasional bad weather – though the truth is that getting around in a regular car is simple enough. As with anything else, it's a status thing. One person gets a big car, so somebody needs a bigger one. If one person's sitting at a normal height in their vehicle, someone else needs to be higher.

I'm hidden from view, tucked in behind the fuel tank as the driver's door opens… except it isn't Richard who steps down. It isn't even a man.

It's Harriet.

It's not *like* her car, it *is* her car. That's almost the only reason I recognise her. She has a baseball cap pulled down over her face and is wearing loose, grey, jogging bottoms with a matching, zipped-up top. It's only the car and the way she moves that lets me know it's her. There's no way she would have dropped off her kids at school looking like this.

At first I wonder why she delivered the phone – and has been texting me, except she makes no effort to come anywhere near the fuel tank. Instead, she opens the rear door of her vehicle, reaches in and pulls out a pair of stuffed black bin bags. She scurries towards the recycling bank, pulls down the hatch at the front, and then stuffs in the first of the two bags. When that drops, she does the same thing with the second. After that, she quickly glances over her shoulder – without seeing me – and then dashes back to her car before doing a U-turn and heading back towards the village.

Everything must have happened in less than a minute.

I check the phone but there's no new message. It's only when rereading it that I realise there was never a meeting promised. I'd assumed that – but all it offered was a time and a place for me to be.

As if Richard wanted me to see this…

I move out from behind the fuel tank and cross to the recycling bank. The hatch on the side has been built with a stopper attached, so that the deposited clothes cannot be pulled back out and stolen.

Which is when I realise why there's a step and improvised rod that's been left behind the fuel tank. When there's a clothes recycling bin in a place like Leavensfield, valuable goods are likely to get donated because people can't be bothered with the likes of eBay, or even taking them to charity shops. Someone will have cottoned on to this at some point – and I'd bet whoever it is has been stealing from here for years.

I take the step and the rod, feeling exposed in the daylight. If anyone drives past, I'll definitely be spotted – but I don't want to wait for it to be dark again.

Standing on the step gives me the angle to lean into the hatch, while the rod has been built with a hinge in the middle that lets it arch around the security divider.

None of that means it's easy. I feel like I'm on one of those arcade machines when the claw comes down to grab the prize, only to snaffle air.

It's a good five minutes before I finally grab one of the black bags Harriet deposited. I decide to leave the second bag, for now at least – and so take the rod, step and first bag back behind the fuel tank.

The bag is full of something soft and, when I open it, there are children's clothes on the top. The first item is a yellow sweatshirt with a daffodil on the front. It's small and shapeless, probably for a young girl. I return it to the bag and start to reach for something else before I change my mind. The sweatshirt might well be for a girl – but it's not the type of thing Harriet would allow her daughter to be seen wearing. It's too garish and the material too cheap.

I check it over again, spotting where the hem along the bottom has started to fray. There's also a small hole under the right armpit. It feels completely unrelated to something Harriet might have – which is when I see the name tag that's been sewn into the collar.

ALICE PRITCHARD

THIRTEEN YEARS OLD

The visiting room of the prison is like the cafeteria at school – but it's a lot cleaner and quieter. Instead of kids making their chairs screech and the echoing cacophony of people sitting, standing and talking loudly, there's silence.

'Is it always this quiet?' I ask.

Dad shakes his head. 'This isn't the usual visiting hours, Mads. They set this up especially for you. This room would usually be full with people. It's so loud, you can barely hear each other talking.'

He reaches out and I let him take my hand.

'Is this where Auntie Kath visits you?' I ask.

'Yup.'

'Is it noisy then?'

'It sure is.'

Dad's thinner than when I last saw him, even in his face. There's much more grey in his stubble and on his head, too. I think about saying this to him, although I'm not sure if it's the type of thing he'd want to hear. He probably already knows.

'I wrote down the cricket scores for you,' I say as I stand.

The pair of guards over near the door both watch me as I dig into my pocket and remove the folded-up sheet of paper. When I came in, they made me show them the page and someone took it away to read.

I flatten the page on the table and then slide it across to Dad.

'They asked me if it was code,' I say.

'Who did?'

'The man who let me into the prison. He looked it all over and asked if it was a code but I told him it was just cricket scores.'

Dad smiles but it doesn't feel as if he's particularly happy. He reads through the page and then turns it over to check the back.

'This is very good of you,' he says.

'I copied it out of the paper. Then Auntie Kath said I could have just brought you the paper – but it was too late by then.'

He smiles again and then folds the page back up again. 'I think I prefer your writing.'

I wait, wanting him to say something more, although all he does is stare aimlessly towards the wall behind me. I turn to see whether there's something there – but it's only a long stretch of grey brickwork. When I look back, Dad's watching the table instead.

'Are you all right?' I ask.

'Course I am, Mads. How are things with you?'

I only notice his hands are shaking because the table begins to rattle. He quickly puts both hands onto his lap and the sound stops. He won't look at me and instead keeps staring at the table. There's a scrape along his neck that stretches downwards from his ear. It's red and is like the time I skidded across the playground and took the skin off my knee.

'Auntie Kath says we can go wherever I want this weekend,' I say. 'It's supposed to be dry.'

'That sounds good…'

I wait for him to ask where I might go – but he doesn't. His upper arms are rocking now, too.

'Auntie Kath says that, even though the judge said six years, that you'll be out earlier if you're good. She wouldn't say how long – so I didn't know if that meant five years? Or four?'

Dad is nodding but he doesn't reply.

'Does that mean five years?' I ask. 'Or four…?'

'I'm trying not to think about it, Mads.'

He mumbles something else that I can't hear, before lurching into a cough that he uses his shoulder to stifle.

'I know you didn't do it, Dad.'

He gulps. 'It doesn't matter, Mads. The jury think I did.'

TWENTY-SEVEN

I continue looking through the bag, only to find items of clothing that are far more likely to belong to Harriet's children. Gemma doesn't have a son – but there are boys' clothes in the bag. There are also girls' items that are far too small for twelve-year-old Alice and more likely to fit a seven- or eight-year-old, like Beatrice. Among everything, I find two items with Alice's name stitched into the back, plus another two that are likely her size.

It's a simple text that I send to Richard.

Me: *How did you know?*

It's as if he was waiting for this, because the reply is almost instant.

I needed you to see.

Me: *That doesn't answer the question! I don't understand what's going on.*

The reply takes longer this time and I can picture Richard struggling with each letter.

You will.

I wait for a while but nothing more comes through, so I try calling the number but there's no reply. With little clue of what to do, I stuff all the clothes into the bag and then dump it back into the recycling bank. It didn't feel worth emptying the second bag because I've already seen what I was supposed to. No good can come from keeping Alice's clothes, especially with DI Dini sniffing around. The last thing I want is for him to find them hidden around my house.

It's hard to have any idea what this might mean. Harriet and Gemma do seem to be best friends now, so Gemma might have asked Harriet to get rid of some clothes for her? That's as possible as Harriet having access to Gemma's house and taking some of Alice's clothes. Or having those clothes for another, far more sinister, reason.

I can't make sense of it – least of all how Richard knew Harriet would be here. Despite what I saw, there's still disappointment that I didn't get to see Richard. I'd worked myself up to the point that I was looking forward to it and, instead, I got something else.

I head back down the hill, not bothering to stay out of sight this time. I'm only passed by one car in any case. I almost stop to pick up my car from the house – but it's a little warmer today and it feels like I have renewed purpose. I'm practically at a march as I continue on to the village – and then to Theresa's house.

It's a little before ten o'clock when she opens the door – and it's like looking into a mirror as she bats away the yawn. The dark rings under her eyes and the way everything about her seems to sag is an accurate reflection of how I've been feeling since Sunday.

'Any news?' I ask.

'Not yet. Mandeep's at the station. He told me to wait here.'

She lets me inside and then we head through the house towards the conservatory at the back. This is the room to which we always drift when we're at Theresa's house. On a sunny day like today, the rays blaze through the glass, making it feel like summer regardless of the outside temperature. To reflect the sheer amount of time spent out here, there is a faded brown sofa that Theresa got on clearance, along with a matching armchair. This is more of a living room than their actual one.

Theresa sets herself in one corner of the sofa, while I take the other. Lucky is busy dozing in a patch of sun. He lifts his nose briefly enough to acknowledge me but then promptly goes back to sleeping.

'I keep thinking the worst,' Theresa says.

'I genuinely know how you feel.'

'How have you been dealing with it?'

'I'm not sure I have… not really. You're the one who told me I had to keep doing things.'

Theresa sighs and curls her legs under herself. 'I don't think it's gone round the village yet…'

It perhaps shouldn't be a major concern – but I understand why it is. Perception is as important as reality in a place like Leavensfield.

'I read that they can only hold him for twenty-four hours – so he should be released by this evening at the latest…'

Theresa doesn't respond to this – although that might be because, shortly after I've finished speaking, there's a solid clunk from the front of the house. We turn in unison – and then I follow her in standing as the word 'Tee?' echoes through.

Atal appears moments later – and he looks even more exhausted than his wife. His eyelids are barely open as he staggers into the conservatory.

'You're home,' Theresa says. It's somewhat stating the obvious, although understandable.

Lucky stands up from his spot in the sun and trots across to Atal, where he starts sniffing his ankles. Atal reaches down and ruffles the dog's neck. He mutters a 'good boy' and then stands straighter once more.

'Mandeep dropped me off.'

'What's going on?' Theresa asks.

Atal turns to look at me. 'Do you mind if we do this in private?'

I start towards the hall – but have barely taken a step when Theresa calls me back.

'Anything you have to say to me, you can say in front of her.'

'I don't—' My protest is immediately cut short by the volcanic stare in Theresa's eyes. She's gone from shattered and confused to Mount Etna erupting in no time.

Atal's gaze shifts nervously between me and his wife. It probably doesn't help that we're all still standing.

'I lied to the police,' Atal says. He shuffles uncomfortably, wanting to be anywhere that isn't here.

'When?' Theresa asks.

'About Alice.'

The heat is no more. It's like the windows are open and a winter wind is blasting through the conservatory.

'I wasn't just walking Lucky when I found her,' he adds. 'I mean, I *was* walking him – but I'd not been at the restaurant before that, like I said.' He looks down to the dog and Lucky raises a paw, looking for the attention he must have been missing over the past few hours. Atal crouches and ruffles his ears, then Lucky lies back on the ground at his owner's feet.

Theresa is like a statue. 'Where were you?' she asks.

'Don't get mad, but—'

'Don't tell me not to get mad. Where were you?'

'I went to the restaurant as usual – but I left early.'

'Why?'

Atal takes a breath and slinks into the armchair. Lucky follows him and nuzzles his nose into Atal's legs before lying across his feet. Atal rubs a hand over his eyes and then squeezes the bridge of his nose.

'It's going under,' he says.

'What is?'

'The restaurant. It's been struggling for months, probably a year or more. Everything's getting more expensive but we've not been getting as many people in. Last winter was slow but I thought we'd make up for it in the summer. Except we didn't. If anything, this summer was slower than the last. We've not been getting the customers. I should've said something to you before.'

I look between Atal and Theresa, feeling an interloper in something that doesn't concern me. This is the first I've heard of any financial problems, although I suppose there's no reason for me to have known. The only obvious indicators are that, on the odd occasion that Richard and I have been to Atal's, regardless of the day or time, it's been more or less empty.

Theresa starts a reply with 'What does that—?' but Atal cuts her off.

'I was visiting a financial advisor,' he says. 'I know I told you I'd been at work when I picked up Lucky for his walk – but I hadn't. I told the police the same thing but didn't think they'd check. That's why they arrested me.'

Theresa has been standing the entire time but she slumps onto the sofa as if she's been deflated. Her mouth hangs open and I can't tell if she's angry, relieved, confused, or a bit of everything.

'They arrested you because…?'

'I said I was at the restaurant before walking the dog. I suppose they thought I might have been doing something else… especially as it was me who found Alice.'

'Why were you visiting a financial advisor on a Sunday night?'

'We couldn't figure out another time. I went to his house. The police checked it all – and that's when they let me go.'

I suppose that explains Mandeep's reluctance to elaborate last night. He'd have known this but, with the alibi unchecked, he could hardly assure Theresa everything was going to work out fine.

'I swear what happened to Alice is nothing to do with me,' Atal says.

There's a short pause and then Theresa responds with: 'I never thought it was.'

Atal stares at his wife and then bows his head slightly.

I'm not sure how I feel. The good part of me is happy for Theresa and Atal about the fact there's an innocent explanation for his arrest. The devil tells me that it means Richard is back on the hook.

'I should've told you about the money thing,' he adds.

'What happens now?'

'I'm sorting out a loan.'

'I mean with the police!'

'Oh… I don't know. They released me, so I assume that's everything. I'm not on bail. They didn't say they wanted me back.'

'What about the lying to the police?'

He squirms like a child with nits. 'I don't think anything's going to happen about that.'

Theresa takes a large breath and tugs at an errant strand of hair. 'I was so worried.'

'I'm sorry.'

'I slept on the sofa because the bed was too empty. Lucky kept me company.'

Atal scritches the dog's ears as a silent thank you – and I've never felt more of a third wheel than I do now. I mumble something about being glad that everything's all right. I immediately regret saying anything, seeing as though any good news has been tempered by the fact Atal's restaurant might be on its way out of business. Anything's better than prison, I suppose. I've seen the effect of what time behind bars can do to a person.

Atal and Theresa barely look up as I make my way to the front door and, by the time I get outside, I've almost overlooked that it's December. The heat in Theresa's conservatory made that easy to forget. I check the burner phone – but there are no new messages. I don't think I like this one-way relationship of me being fed information at Richard's whim – but it's another thing that very much feels like him. I'm not a subservient wife, although it's a fair statement that many of the big decisions in our marriage are made by Richard. He's the one who decided on our holiday to Cornwall last year and he picked the South of France the year before. There are smaller things, too – like the brands of the food we buy, or the music that plays around the house. I've never really questioned a lot of it – and it's not as if I mind too much – but I suppose it fits with the fact that none of my questions are being answered.

I have to pass through the village to get back to my house. It's a walk I've made hundreds, perhaps thousands, of times – but it's hard not to feel conscious of the stares of the locals. This is probably as busy as Leavensfield gets at this time of year. There are two people with bags coming out of Bob's village shop, plus a good half-dozen others mingling on the corner close to the café. At first I'm not sure why – but then I spy Dini sitting at the table in the window. He's in his suit, with a jacket hooked over the back of a spare chair. It's the perfect spot for people watching, especially in the summer when tourists stop here because they've read about the place in a guidebook. When in the right spot, it's possible to see the looks of 'is this it?' on the faces of people as they get out of the car and take in the two streets they've travelled such a distance to see.

It's uncanny that, as I close in on the café, Dini looks up from the papers in front of him and takes me in. It feels as if he isn't only watching in the moment but as if he's *watching* in a greater sense. I wonder if Richard has gone silent because something's actually happened to him, as opposed to him wanting to control information.

Dini nods towards me in the way someone might when they pass an acquaintance on the street. I find myself nodding back, but it's more a reflex than anything else. I quickly turn away and continue on to the corner, close to the tall stone cross.

It's there that I see Zoe floating along the path on the other side. Her legs must be moving but there's a grace about the way she shifts that I'd find impossible to replicate. She's in an ankle-length dress, with wellies on her feet and an anorak around her shoulders. It wouldn't usually work away from something like a boggy festival site but here, in the middle of winter, it's as if she's invented a new style. No wonder she doesn't appear to care less what anyone thinks of her.

I feel less conscious about acknowledging Zoe's small wave – but, this time, she beckons me across to her.

'Is that detective still in the café?' she asks.

'Yes.'

She nods towards a battered Mini that sits a little up the road on the way towards my house. 'I was thinking about coming to your house,' she says, 'but fate must be working for us because here you are.'

'Why are you looking for me?'

She glances over my shoulder and then leans in close, so that only I can hear. 'I think I've seen your husband.'

TWENTY-EIGHT

I angle away from Zoe, taking her in and looking for some sort of sign that this is a misunderstanding. She doesn't blink.

'Where?' I ask.

'I'll take you there.'

Zoe turns and heads to the Mini. It's old-fashioned, with a blocky, square back-end instead of the rounded edges of the newer models. She opens it by putting the key into the lock and then, after getting into the driver's side, she reaches across to pull up the knob on the passenger's door. When I get in, I'm immediately caught off guard by how low the seat is to the floor. It almost feels as if I'm sitting on the tarmac when she starts the car. It's also got those old wind-around handles that have to be rotated to get the windows up or down.

My dad never drove a Mini but being in a vehicle like this will always make me think of those afternoons we spent driving around the countryside together. In the summer it would be so hot that we'd have to have the windows down and would barely be able to hear the radio or one another. There was no in-car air-conditioning back then.

Then there was that one journey in particular.

'Do you know where I live?' Zoe asks, interrupting those thoughts of Dad.

'In the cottage up near Atal's.'

'Right. There's an old building at the very end of the property. I think they used it to store firewood years ago, back when it was a working farm that was heated by coal and wood. I've only been down there a couple of times because it's run-down and I've not properly checked whose land it's actually on. I think it might still belong to the family who sold the cottage.'

'I didn't know there was a building there.'

'You can't spot it from the road. I can only see it when I'm in the kitchen at the back of the cottage. It's hidden by the trees otherwise.'

'Is that where you saw him...?'

It might make sense considering the texts make it sound like Richard is nearby. If he's been hiding out in a shack, he'd want the extra clothes that I left – especially the jacket. It's been well below freezing every night since he disappeared.

Not only that, getting around Leavensfield on foot without being seen is simple enough. That's partly because there are so few people but also because it's easy to follow hedgerows and the stone walls to get across the fields, instead of using the roads.

I want an enthusiastic, certain 'yes', but, instead, Zoe gives a steady 'Perhaps.'

'What makes you think it's him?'

'I'm guessing. The person I saw down there looked like an older man. I'd not seen him before this week and I know your husband is missing, so...'

'Do you know Richard?'

'Only from around the village.'

The car's engine groans as Zoe drops down a gear to approach the hill. It's amazing the memories that can reappear from such a seemingly small thing. Dad's car used to make the same grinding whimper on long, steep hills. On winter days like today, he'd have to tease the engine with the pedals, while easing out the choke in an attempt to get it to start. I'd try to help by spraying de-icer across the windows, even though I had to stretch to reach the top parts of the windscreen. This was thirty years ago and yet the moan of an engine has me picturing it as if it was this morning.

We crest the hill and the Mini's whines drop to a more palatable level. It's only another mile or so until we reach Zoe's cottage.

'Why did you come to me?' I ask.

'You're his wife.'

'I mean why tell me instead of the police?'

Zoe takes a hand from the steering wheel and twirls it in the air, as if searching for the right word. 'Innocent until proven guilty, right? Half this lot would've strung him up from the tallest tree if they had their way. He might've been in the wrong place at the wrong time. Whoever hurt Alice might have, well… you know…'

She's hit upon the one thing that I've been trying to stop myself from focusing upon. Someone harmed Alice – and, if she was with Richard, who's to say he wasn't hurt at the same time?

Zoe takes the turn from the road onto her gravelly drive. Although her place is a cottage in the sense that it's a single storey, it is as wide as two of the houses from down in the village.

As soon as I get out of the car, I'm hit by the jangling symphony that echoes from the side of the house. I stop to take in the collection of ornaments and wind chimes that are massed in a mini patch close to the corner of the property.

'How do you sleep with all that?' I ask.

Zoe has rounded the car. 'It's to ward off the spirits,' she says. A smirk creeps across her face and I'm not sure if that means she's joking.

I follow her around the side of the house as she unlatches a gate and continues until we're at the back. There's a sprawling allotment that's hidden from the road and Zoe points towards a patch close to the house.

'I've got onions and peas in there,' she says. 'I'm going to be putting in some kale, spinach and carrots when the weather starts to turn. If you ever want anything fresh, just come and knock. There's way too much here for just me and Frankie.'

'I never realised any of this was here.'

'It was used as farmland for years before the owner died and all the kids fell out. I had to clear some rocks from the surface but the soil is good. I always wanted my own allotment. I think I might get some chickens when the winter's over. Frankie would like that. I've been trying to teach him about the seasons and how things grow – but he's a kid and I think everyone hates vegetables at that age.'

Zoe pauses for a moment and we stare out across her patch of land before she remembers why we're here.

'This way,' she says, as she heads off along the side of the allotment.

I follow and she keeps walking towards a copse of trees that is perhaps fifty or sixty metres from the end of the vegetable patch. It's colder here and the soil is stony hard with a frost that hasn't cleared.

'Is this still your land?' I ask.

'I'm not sure.' She points back up towards the allotment. 'I think it ends somewhere between there and here but there's no fence. The cottage was sold with a certain amount of acres included. I think the farmer's children just wanted rid of it in the end.'

Zoe steps past the treeline, where there seems to be a semi-natural trail. The thickness of the evergreens cloaks the light and there's an instant dusk as we continue to where the shack appears almost from nowhere. It's less than thirty seconds from the entrance to the copse but hidden by the dark, even when standing a short distance away.

It's not the sort of fully formed mini house I pictured when Zoe first mentioned the place. It's made from rusted corrugated metal and is probably only just about wide enough for a person to lie down inside. That's about all that could be managed anyway, as the roof is too low for anyone to stand inside. I wouldn't be surprised if a good gust of wind would send the entire thing to the ground.

Zoe stops a few steps away from the structure and points to the ground. Despite the hard soil, there is a pattern of criss-crossed footsteps. I don't need to crouch to see that the size of the feet are bigger than mine. Zoe takes me around to the side of the shack, where there is a small, neat pile of browning apple cores that have been left at the base of a tree.

We check the hut itself – but there's nobody inside, nor any sign that there has been someone. It's a small, dank space with wood chippings around the edges that would provide protection from the wind and rain – but little else. I'm not sure if I can picture Richard hiding here. He's a bit like me in the sense that we like a good bed at night.

I suppose needs must – and all that. It's possible that he's been hiding out here, although I'm not sure how he would have known about the place.

'When did you last see someone?' I ask.

'This morning. It was just a shape in between the trees.'

The wind whistles around the clearing on which the shack sits. It swoops up and around the branches until it feels as if it's coming from all directions.

'I can call you if I see someone again,' Zoe adds. 'It could be kids turning it into a den. I think I'd have liked a space like this when I was young.'

Her final line makes me wonder why she brought me out here but I let it go as we take a few more moments to eye the space. Zoe then clasps her jacket tighter around her front.

'C'mon,' she says, 'let's get inside.'

I follow her away from the trees and can't work out if I'm disappointed that Richard isn't here. The moment we step out from the copse, daylight floods down, leaving me squinting up towards the house.

Zoe takes me through the unlocked back door into a small porch area, where she kicks off her wellies. There's a rack, although the area around it is covered with a mound of adult and child shoes.

I follow her lead and take off my own boots, before trailing Zoe into the kitchen.

She's right about the view. From the kitchen window, I can see the allotment and the trees at the back – and then, beyond that, there's green everywhere I look.

There's also that sense of walking into a new person's house, when there's a smell that the owner has long since become accustomed to. Here, the house smells of adventure and outdoors. Of mud and trees and damp. I can imagine Frankie and his friends on the other side of the allotment, with the fields and the trees as their playground. It reeks of opportunity, perhaps of life itself.

I'm so envious.

'Do you want tea?' Zoe asks. 'Something to eat?' She sweeps a hand towards the kitchen table and the cupboards beyond. 'You can make yourself at home, unless you need to get back…?'

I sense that she's searching for someone to talk to. A friend, perhaps. Maybe this whole thing was concocted to get me out here – although there's a fair bit of self-aggrandising in that I don't know why I'd be so special.

'Tea would be great,' I reply.

Zoe fills a saucepan with water and carries it across to the stove. Everything here is old-fashioned, with nothing like a kettle, microwave or toaster in sight.

'Have a look around,' she says, waving me towards the hall beyond the kitchen. 'Whenever I go into someone's house for the first time, I know I want to explore. Feel free.'

It's an invitation that seems too good to be true. I think everyone has that instinct when entering a person's house for the first time. We want to nose about the cupboards and check the rooms. We wonder why the coats are kept in one place when they'd surely be better off in another. We query the colour choices for the wallpaper, or don't understand how someone can live with no clock in the living room. Something which is perfectly normal for one person is an aberration for another.

'Are you sure?' I ask.

'Go for it.'

Zoe turns on the stove and then crosses to the cupboard, from where she retrieves two mugs.

It feels odd but irresistible as I creep along the hall. I expect it to lead towards the front door – like my house – but it doesn't. One corridor leads into another – and then there are three doors from which to choose. The first is a cupboard with a vacuum cleaner and ironing board on the inside. The second contains a toilet and sink. The third door hides a musty room that contains a piano, plus walls of books.

'Do you take sugar?'

Zoe's question echoes through the house and I call back 'No' before we go through the same ritual about milk. I follow the warren of interconnecting passages back the other way until I come to three more doors. I'm about to try the first when I see the framed certificate on the wall. I almost move past it without thinking – but then the significance dawns.

Zoe completed a degree in English from the same place where Richard teaches. She finished four years before I went there, and about the same time that Frankie would have been born.

And, suddenly, I can't forget what Keith told me about my husband.

Dickie always had an eye for his students…

FIFTEEN YEARS OLD

I'm braced for the telling-off as I let myself into Auntie Kath's house. It will be the same as it always is: Where have you been? School is only half an hour away, so how come it's taken so long to walk home? Who have you been with? It's not that Julius, is it? He's a bad influence.

I've heard it all before.

I close the front door and edge along the hall, waiting for my name to be shouted from the kitchen. When it isn't, the thought does occur that I've finally broken my aunt. She'll give up on asking me these same questions day after day and I… well, I don't know what that makes me.

My aunt is sitting at the kitchen table when I get in, cradling a cup of tea between her fingers. She glances up to the clock but says nothing about the time. There's something in her face that I can't read… like she's happy about something, except… not.

'What's wrong?' I ask.

'I think you should sit.'

'Why?'

She doesn't react to this. Something tingles along the back of my neck and there's an imposing sense that whatever's about to happen is going to impact my life forever.

'I don't want to sit.'

Auntie Kath continues to watch me and, without words, it is as if she forces me into the seat through will alone. When I'm down, she opens her mouth again.

'I'm not sure of the best way to explain this,' she says. 'I'm still trying to get my head around it myself.' She must see something in me because she instantly reaches ahead and grips my hand. 'Oh, love, it's nothing like that. Your dad is fine.'

'What is it?'

'A woman was killed a few nights ago. I'm not sure of the details but it sounds like some sort of domestic that got out of hand.'

'What does that mean?'

'Maybe a husband and wife, or a boyfriend and girlfriend. After the woman died, the police arrested the woman's boyfriend. I don't know how they figured it out – maybe his blood, or something, but they're now saying this is the man who killed that hitchhiker.'

I don't think it sinks in at first. 'The hitchhiker' can only mean one thing, except that I've spent so long trying to remember the specifics of what happened that afternoon that I'm no longer sure of what's true and what isn't. Sometimes, I wonder whether Dad ever got out of the car; other times, I can see the hitchhiker's face so clearly that I can picture the spots around his mouth. Then I remember that I never saw him at all.

Something soars in my chest. 'They're saying that Dad's innocent…?'

Auntie Kath holds up a hand. 'It's early days,' she says. 'Things can move slowly in the legal system. I only heard this from your dad's solicitor today. Nothing is going to happen immediately.' She pauses to sip her tea and then adds: 'It's going to be in the papers tomorrow, so I wanted you to know before that happens.'

I can barely get my head around what she's saying. 'So he'll be free…?'

'I'm not sure. I don't want you to get your hopes up all the way. I'll know more tomorrow. Your dad's solicitor is going to come over and he said he'll answer any questions you have.'

I don't need to hear any more. This is what I've been waiting for all this time. Dad's coming home.

TWENTY-NINE

There's a scuffing from the hall and then Zoe appears with a mug looped between her fingers. She looks from me to the certificate and back again.

'He wasn't my lecturer,' she says softly. 'The course was split in two and I was on the other half of the class.'

'I took that class, too.'

Zoe blinks at me and passes across the mug. I loop a finger through the handle and then try to hold it in the same warming way that she was. The heat means I can only manage that for a few seconds. She must have asbestos fingers.

'Is that where you met?' she asks.

I fight away the shiver. It feels embarrassing to admit that I ended up marrying my lecturer – even if I was a mature student. It sounds seedy, even though it wasn't. I nod because I can't bring myself to say it.

Zoe doesn't reply immediately – which is something for which I can only be grateful.

'I was only half telling the truth earlier,' she says. 'I do know your husband from around the village – but I knew *of* him before that. I was taught by a guy named Geoff who loved himself more than Harriet Branch loves attention. Some of my friends were in Richard's class, though.'

We wait for a second, at a stand-off, and then she opens the door next to the frame, which leads into a long but narrow living room. There's a TV at one end and then two sofas that face each other with a table in the centre. Zoe picks up a framed photograph of Frankie that was sitting on top of the rack of vinyl records at the back. Judging by his appearance, it would have been taken in the past year or so.

'I was in my final year,' she says, as if she knows what I'm thinking. 'It happened at Christmas when I'd gone home for the break. An old boyfriend that I used to have at school. One thing led to another, and…' She shrugs as she returns the photo to the cabinet and then turns to take me in. 'We talked about getting together – but "because I'm pregnant" is hardly a bedrock for a stable relationship. I was almost six months in when I took the final exams.' She pauses for a moment and then adds: 'He lives in Australia now. Married, kids, the lot. Frankie Skypes him once a week.'

I'm not sure if the wild conclusions to which I jumped says more about me or Richard. Probably me.

'There was a song,' I say.

'What do you mean?'

'When we were in the car park outside the hall on Monday. Frankie was humming an old song… one of Richard's favourites.'

Zoe's features crease in confusion. 'I don't understand.'

'It's called "Why Do Fools Fall In Love?"'

Zoe eyes me for a second and then tugs her phone out from a back pocket. She fiddles with the device before holding it up. A second later and the song's opening *oooh-wahs* erupt tinnily from the device.

'Spotify,' she says. 'My dad used to be a doo-wop fan. He played this and other songs like it over and over when I was a girl. I guess some of it stuck with me – and then Frankie.' She stops and then adds: 'Did you think…?' Zoe leaves the question unfinished.

I can't answer her because it's another piece of crushing embarrassment. I'm so quick to see the worst in people. It's as if I learned nothing from what happened to my dad.

She doesn't make me answer, which is one thing. Instead, she says we should go back to the kitchen. I follow her through the burrow to the back of the house, where the sun beams bright through the window. She sits at the table and I follow her lead – and, though we say nothing at first, there's something comforting about it. We barely know each other and yet feeling contented when sitting together and saying nothing is surely a sign of friendship.

It's Zoe who speaks first. 'I read your blog,' she says.

'Really?'

'You shouldn't sound so surprised. I've tried a few of your recipes. Frankie loves the vegan, gluten-free chocolate pudding. He says it's much better than the ones I used to buy.'

The smile creeps through me before I even know it's there. I get emails about my work but it's rare that anyone tells me face to face that they've used my recipes. I'm not sure what to say.

'I'm working on a follow-up,' I reply. 'A treacle pudding.'

'If you ever need a keen taster, I know a little boy that will be happy to eat anything you cook…'

I laugh – and it's strange and wonderful. Something I'd forgotten. The laugh quickly turns into a yawn and I find myself apologising while trying to force it away. I'd so love to sleep this all away. To wake up and find that everything's back to how it was.

'Can I ask you something?' I say.

'Sure.'

I hold a hand up, indicating the house – and then I don't need to say the words.

'Scratch card,' Zoe says. 'It wasn't a massive amount but it was enough. I had a mortgage on a proper house not far from Mum and Dad. That had gone up enough in value that I made a profit by accident. It's not like I never have to work again – but I can get by for a few years while Frankie's growing up. I got an accountant who put me onto a financial advisor. I've got investments and savings accounts all over the place.' Zoe stops and laughs, before adding: 'It's like I'm a proper grown-up!'

I join in. I think every adult has a moment in which they realise that they're suddenly grown up. It might be getting a mortgage, or a loan. It could be marrying, or having children, or moving into a flat. There's a point at which a person has to admit the glory days of youth are over.

'Why here?' I ask. 'Why Leavensfield?'

'I always wanted to live in the countryside. I wanted the isolation and figured Frankie would do better with a smaller class size.' She pauses a beat and then adds: 'I didn't realise moving here would be such a social minefield.'

She laughs again and I so wish we could have had a chat like this months ago. There's little quite like finding a person who sees the world in the same way.

'I've tried to steer clear,' Zoe says.

'It's difficult. There's always the next thing: the summer socials, the garden parties, the Britain in Bloom committee, the St George's Day bash, the harvest festival, the fundraisers, the winter ball… it never ends.'

I'm out of breath having simply listed them all – and I know I've missed a few things.

'I heard tomorrow's ball is still on,' Zoe says.

'Harriet's turned it into a fundraiser for Gemma.'

Zoe turns to look through the window – and it's hard to blame her. She must have the best view of anyone who lives in the village. The fields are endless; the sky perfect.

'I guess Harriet's raised a lot of money over the years…' Zoe tails off but it feels like there's more. When it comes, the words run into one another. 'I shouldn't have said that stuff about her loving attention.' She winces, as if she's said something that's physically hurtful and then turns away from the window to make sure I'm listening. 'Perhaps things aren't great for her…?'

'How'd you mean?'

'I just—' She stops herself and then adds: 'How well do you know Gavin?'

To me, Gavin has always been Harriet's puppet. I can imagine him standing for Parliament with his carefully parted hair and smart suits. Meanwhile, Harriet would be running things behind the scenes.

'Hardly at all. Only that Gavin is Harriet's husband,' I say. 'I don't think we've ever said more than a few words to each other.'

Zoe nods, squints, weighs up the options – and then goes for it. 'He tried it on with me,' she replies softly. 'A few months ago at the harvest festival. Frankie and the other kids were off playing and Harriet was busy running the auction. Gavin came across and squeezed my arse. He asked if I liked it while I was trying to push him away. He laughed about it. Said I knew where he was if I changed my mind. Then he went and stood on stage next to Harriet as if nothing had happened.'

I'm stunned. Lost for words in the truest sense.

Zoe turns to look out the window again while I struggle to find something to say. I don't know Gavin well enough to make any sort of judgement call – but I always thought Harriet had the perfect life she portrayed.

'Did you tell anyone?' I say eventually.

Zoe shrugs but it's answer enough. If no one else saw it, then what would be the point? Like when Gemma slapped me – and I chose to do nothing. Telling anyone or everyone would only create more drama and, in a place like Leavensfield, being in the centre of that is the last place a person wants to be.

'Makes you wonder, doesn't it?' Zoe says.

'About what?'

'About what's going on behind closed doors. I guess we all have our secrets.'

THIRTY

Zoe and I keep half an eye on the treeline while talking about other things. After another hour of seeing no one out there, we swap numbers and she says she'll call if she sees anyone. It's hard to wonder if, maybe, this was all because she wanted someone to talk to. If it was, then I don't blame her.

All the while I picture the way Harriet pulled her hand away from her husband when we were massing around the stone cross during the march for Alice. I'd assumed they'd had a minor spat – and perhaps they had – or, maybe, there's something else. Something related to Harriet dumping Alice's clothes in the recycling bank.

Zoe offers me a lift home but I tell her I'll walk. If Richard's disappearance has achieved one thing, then it's increased my cardio levels.

As I follow the verge down the slope towards the village, I keep an eye on the hedgerows off to the side, hoping to spot the shape of someone trying to stick to the shadows. I want my husband back – and I want easy answers about what's been going on, even though I realise I'm unlikely to get those two things together.

I'm through the village centre and on the way back up the hill towards my house when I spot Harriet and Gemma on the path a little ahead of me. They're walking side by side, with Gemma still wearing Harriet's boots. Neither of them look behind, and I watch as they disappear along Gemma's path and into her house.

I continue walking… and then change my mind and turn around. Instead of heading up the hill towards home, I take the turn that's after the school and then keep walking until the gaps between the houses get larger.

Harriet's house is at the end of a lengthy road that stretches from Leavensfield's main street out towards the lower level of the fields. It's a dead end, with nowhere further to go unless someone was to tarmac over a field or two. There's a stile at the end, which is from where somebody might emerge if they were cutting across Daisy Field.

Before the stile, Harriet and Gavin's property soars tall. Everyone in the village knows this place is theirs. There are three storeys, with curved walls along the two ends with a pinch in the centre – making it something like a figure-eight. The expectation might be that something this big might be surrounded by tall hedges and security fences – but its positioning at the tip of a dead-end is enough.

There are no cars on the drive, and Xavier and Beatrice will both be at school. Harriet is at Gemma's and it's probably safe to assume that Gavin is at work.

I unhook the front gate and head along the path to the wide front door, where I ring the bell. I wait for around thirty seconds, before trying a second time. Curtains have been pulled around the front windows, so there's nothing to be seen through them. I try knocking and then press the bell a third time. After another minute or so, I leave it and move around to the side of the house. There's another gate here – but it's simple enough to lever myself over the top – and then keep going until I'm in the back garden.

As with Zoe's place, I never realised how far back Harriet's property stretches. There's a lawn off to one side that would be perfect for bowling or croquet – and then a separate building on the other. The lower doors at the front of this outhouse make it look like they are either stables, or soon will be. For now, there is no sign of any horses – and I likely would have heard if Harriet had one. Everyone would have known.

There's a wall towards the back of the property that is half built, with a large pile of bricks sitting to the side. There's also a big mound of grey gravel sitting on the edge of the lawn, next to an upturned wheelbarrow. It all feels unfinished… very unlike Harriet.

I'm not sure what I'm looking for… probably nothing.

I check the back door and then try peeping through the windows, all of which are blocked by curtains or blinds. With nothing to see *in* the house, I approach the stables. There are certainly no horses here, although there is a single bale of hay that's been pushed towards the back of the first compartment. The second and third cubicles are both bolted with thick padlocks, with the double doors slotted into place so that it's impossible to see inside.

With little there, I start to explore the rest of the garden. It's quite the building site of half-finished projects, with a pile of fence panels on one side that sit next to a bucket that's filled with crusted, dry cement.

It's as I'm thinking of moving back to the front of the house that I spot the barbecue cauldron that's almost hidden in an alcove close to the fence panels. The drum is full of silvery-dark charcoal, with a smattering of scorch marks on the cement below. It's an odd time of year to be having a barbecue, although I suppose this could be a hangover from the summer.

I almost move on… *almost*. That's when I spot a shred of something white that's buried among the charcoal lumps. I lift out the grille at the top and then reach into the drum itself to retrieve the scrap of material. It looks like a square that's been torn from something like a T-shirt, or vest. There is dark dust on my fingers which is impossible not to transfer onto the patch – except that there's already another stain on the cotton. Something browny-red… something that looks an awful lot like dried blood.

And that's when there's the sound of a car pulling onto the drive.

THIRTY-ONE

I tuck myself in at the side of the stables, where the wall juts out and creates a nook behind which to hide. Unless coming through the house, there's only one route into the back – and that's through or over the gate at the side. The other wing of the house is separated by bushy conifers that are swaying in the breeze.

I'm looking for lights turning on upstairs, which might give me a chance to dash around the side of the house. Instead, it's two or three minutes until Gavin appears from the gated side of the house. He's in a suit and looks out of place among the rubble and discarded building materials. This doesn't seem to bother him as he strides across the courtyard and heads for the stables.

He's two-thirds of the way across when he stops, half-turns, and stares at the barbecue drum.

I've left the grille lid on the floor.

I can almost see the thoughts whirring in his head as Gavin stares from the drum to the house and back to the drum. He sweeps a hand through his hair, mulling it over, before making his decision. Instead of going for the stables, he bounds across to the barbecue and drags the drum over to the back of the house. From there, he unloops the hose that's attached to the wall – and then sprays down the charcoal. Blackened, filthy water streams into the drain below, with squirts of liquid pouring onto the bottoms of Gavin's suit trousers. When he's done he steps away and kicks out his legs, wincing at the damp.

It's a very odd thing for someone wearing a suit to have done.

After that, he drags the barbecue back to where it was, drops the lid onto the top, and then returns to the tap to wash his hands.

He stops to look around the garden, although there's so much clutter that I suspect I could be stood in the open and possibly still be missed. Either way, he sweeps across my position without noticing me – and then he heads towards the stables once more.

I creep out from the hiding place, listening until I hear the solid clunk of a padlock being opened. When I peep around the corner, Gavin has disappeared into the stable – so I don't hesitate in racing to the gate. The first time I look behind, I'm already off the property, along the lane, over the stile, and halfway across Daisy Field on the way home.

The more I look at the stained scrap of clothing, the more I can't be sure if the red mark actually is blood. I've spilled ketchup and spaghetti sauce on tops before – and it's looked more or less the same. Without some sort of scientific test to which I don't have access, it's impossible to tell.

Kylie is busy working in her bedroom, leaving me alone downstairs in the house. I hide the material within the cushion cover on the sofa, figuring nobody is likely to find it there. I'm not sure if it holds any importance – although I can't figure out why anyone would use a barbecue to burn clothing, especially in winter.

There have been no messages on either of my phones – and Richard has been silent ever since he sent me to see Harriet at the recycling bin. I think about messaging him to say what I found at the back of Harriet's house – except I'm not sure *what* I found. Whether it's something or nothing. If I have anything to say, it should surely be to ask where he is – and when he'll be back.

I don't know what to do.

People can sit around and complain about how boring life is but I'd love a bit of normality compared to what my life has become.

I check my emails but even that is a testament to everything that's changed. I've heard nothing from any of the magazines and websites who, between them, send me a commission or two per week. No press officers or publicists have been in contact since Monday, even though I hear from someone most days. Everybody has something to push, or that they want selling, but they seemingly now do not want me to be a part of that.

I'm a pariah.

Even if I wanted to distract myself with work, I couldn't.

I close the laptop lid and am on my way to the stairs to see if Kylie wants me to cook something for tea – but then the doorbell sounds.

There's always that moment of panic now; of wondering if it might be Richard or, worse, DI Dini with bad news. If anything, the person on the doorstep is more surprising than both those options.

It's Harriet.

She's in some sort of designer yoga wear, although the crow's feet under her eyes give her a preoccupied, troubled look.

'Can I come in?' she asks.

We're already along the hall and in the kitchen when I realise that it didn't occur to me that I could say no.

Harriet parks herself at the kitchen table, dropping her bag on the spare seat at her side, as if this is her house and I'm the visitor.

'I'm worried about Gemma,' she says, not bothering with anything like small talk.

I am still on my feet, off guard at the speed with which this has happened.

'Why?' I reply.

'I don't want to tell the police this because I know how it sounds – but she's spending less and less time at the hospital. It's like she's given up on Little Alice.'

I find myself pacing to the kitchen counter and back again. Somehow, Harriet has taken over my house in the way she takes over anything. It's extraordinary and, in some ways, admirable.

'I'm not sure why you're telling me…'

Harriet waits until I've stopped moving. I'm leaning on the counter, looking across the kitchen towards her.

'It's because Gemma keeps talking about you. She keeps threatening to come round here. Silly stuff. I'm worried that she might do something stupid…'

I don't know if I'm any good at spotting a lie but Harriet doesn't flinch when she says this. She's certainly capable of hyperbole and rabble-rousing.

'Why are you telling me instead of the police?'

'Because Gemma has a lot going on with Alice in hospital. She isn't sleeping or eating. I've been trying to keep an eye on her as she doesn't have many friends in the village.'

It's hard to imagine that's the only reason. Harriet always seems to have ulterior motives – not to mention the fact she's one of the reasons Gemma doesn't have many friends.

'What sort of threats is she making?' I ask.

Harriet dismisses this with a small shake of the head, making it clear that she's here on her terms and for her reasons. 'She probably doesn't mean it,' she says. 'But I wanted to warn you just in case.'

'I don't know what you're warning me about.'

'I just—' Harriet sighs. 'I'm trying to help.'

'It didn't seem like that at the school the other day.'

She exhales again and then rubs her eyes. 'I didn't know you were going to be there. I was trying to support Gemma but things spiralled and got a bit out of hand. I don't think people meant the things that were shouted. I tried to calm everyone down.'

I slot in on the other side of the table and lock in on Harriet. The fury of that moment is suddenly upon me again. 'Somebody called me a paedo. They said they didn't want me near their kids.'

Harriet continues scratching her eyebrows and then launches into a yawn that she fails to stop. 'I know…'

For some reason, as quickly as it arrived, the anger has subsided. Perhaps for the first time since I met her, Harriet seems like a real person. I think it was the yawn that did it. Something beyond her control that was real.

Perhaps things aren't great for her…?

Zoe's words have stuck with me. Maybe this yawning, face-scratching Harriet is the real person? Everything else is a front. Like those people on social media whose selfies and photos make it look as if their lives are endless success stories when the truth is that they're sitting at home watching *Bargain Hunt* with a bucket of ice cream and a tube of Pringles.

'Have you heard from Richard?' Harriet sounds hesitant.

'No.'

'Have the police said anything about him…?'

I stare at her and she catches my eye before turning away.

'Sorry. It's none of my business.' She takes a breath and then sits up straighter. 'There's another reason I'm here. We're having a prep meeting this evening about the winter ball. It's kind of a rehearsal. There are lots of little things to be done and I'd love it if you could come.'

'I'm not sure if that's a good idea.'

'It's a small community, Maddy.'

It might be the way she says my name. The 'Maddy' in place of the usual passive-aggressive way she'll say 'Madeleine'. If not that, then it's because I know she's right. I don't know what's happening with Richard and how or when this will ever be resolved. But, if

I'm going to live here, then I am going to have to make an effort to be a part of society.

There's the sound of footsteps from the stairs and then Kylie drifts into the kitchen. She stops dead on the spot when she sees Harriet and does a slow turn between the two of us. It's like a click of the fingers as Harriet instantly returns to her regular smiley, happy confident self.

'Kylie! How great to see you again. I didn't know you were back. How's university? I'm sure you're doing wonderfully.'

Kylie glances back to me. She's smart enough to know that all isn't right. There's tension in the air.

'It's going well,' she says to Harriet, before quickly turning to me and avoiding a follow-up question. 'I was just here to grab a yoghurt.'

She does precisely that, taking a small tub from the fridge and holding it up to illustrate the point. I doubt that's why she originally came down but she takes a spoon and then disappears back up the stairs once more.

Harriet waits until there's the sound of a door closing upstairs and then she stands and picks up her bag. 'I want this to be the biggest fundraiser we've ever had. I want to do right for Gemma.' A pause and then: 'For Alice, as well. For when she's better.' She takes a step towards the kitchen door and then turns: 'I should've let you do the desserts like you wanted. It is your thing, after all. It might not be possible but, maybe, if we get you and Gemma together tonight – when there are other people there – we might be able to smooth everything over.'

I watch her, wondering if there's a kicker to come. This doesn't seem like something that can be smoothed over with a chat and a cup of tea.

'We'll see,' I reply.

'Perhaps bring Kylie? I think it's going to be a bit of a village event. A time for healing.'

This sounds like the other Harriet.

'What do you think?' she adds.

I almost mention the bag of clothes that she dumped in the recycling bank. The ones with Alice's name sewed into the back. Of the two of us, I think Harriet's secrets might run deeper than mine. Despite that, I still feel backed into a corner and I wonder if this is what Harriet wanted. I can't figure her out. Whether she's manipulative, thoughtful, or both.

'I'll be there,' I say.

THIRTY-TWO

Harriet was right about one thing: more or less the entire village has come out to attend the winter ball practice run. The children have massed together towards the back of the village hall and are playing some sort of British Bulldog game by racing widthways across the space while someone in the middle tries to tag the runners. The adults have massed towards the front, where Harriet is on the stage once more.

'Thanks for coming out,' she says. 'I know people outside of the village have been moving on but I want tomorrow to be about Gemma. I think it's an opportunity for us to come together as a community. We support our own in Leavensfield and tomorrow is our chance to prove it.'

I say nothing – but I've not felt a lot of that 'support' in recent days.

She moves on to delegating the various jobs that need to be done. Much of it revolves around putting up decorations of some kind. It's quickly apparent that there's a lot more people than there are jobs to be done, although I suppose the point of the evening is more about community spirit than it is actual work. It's hard to fault Harriet for that. A few sideways looks come my way but I wonder if it's because I'm expecting them and paying too much attention.

When she finishes speaking, everyone separates into their groups and then heads off towards the various corners of the hall. Many of the men are either up ladders, or holding them while trying to string bunting and tinsel across the top corners of the room. There's a lot of 'up a bit', 'down a bit' going on. Kylie and I end up unfurling cloths for the rows of tables that are pressed against the sides of the room. One group is mopping the floor, while another is sweeping it. A quartet of locals is hanging lights at the back of the hall, while some of the men have joined in with the game of British Bulldog.

Kylie and I finish quickly enough and then end up standing around, unsure what to do next. We aren't the only ones. Many of the jobs were small enough that the tasks were completed within minutes. I turn to take in the room. Harriet, Gavin, Sarah, James and Gemma are all on stage, decorating a tree that sits towards the back. Gemma's the clear odd one out. She has her arms across her front and is nibbling her fingernails as she stands to the side, watching as the pair of couples work in unison. Harriet mentioned something about getting us together for some sort of smoothing over of issues – but it hasn't happened yet. I don't blame Gemma for her anger anyway. If roles were reversed – and I thought she or someone close to her had done something to Kylie – then it would need more than Harriet to contain my rage.

Theresa and Atal are towards the back of the room, working with three or four other couples on sticking blobs of cotton wool along the window sills.

When I turn to say something to her, I realise that Kylie has drifted away. I scan the room and she's off talking to Zoe close to the stage. They're laughing about something and I can imagine how someone like Zoe will be the closest Kylie might have to a proper friend in the village. There are almost no older teens around here but Kylie has matured in the months she's been away and they're two of the younger women in the room.

Nobody is paying me any attention now – which is fine by me. I'll take ambivalence over hostility. Those dangerous moments outside the school feel like a distant memory or a dream of something I've remembered incorrectly.

The world continues turning around me as I watch Gemma trail Harriet around the hall. Harriet has a clipboard and is checking on each of the jobs she assigned. Every now and then, she will turn to Gemma and ask her something. I can't hear what's being said – but it's simple enough to see from the shrugged body language that Gemma is deferring to whatever Harriet decides. It's only four days since her daughter was found face-down in a stream – and yet she's here, acting as if it's all fine. I don't want to judge her – especially as I have little idea about how long she's been at the hospital, or the effect that's had upon her, but something seems off. That's not least because of the fact that she's still wearing Harriet's fluffy snow boots.

When I turn back to the stage, I realise that I'm not the only one watching Gemma. As James continues to work on the tree, his wife is behind him, her eyes fixed on where Gemma is standing close to Harriet. I can't read her expression, other than – perhaps – that something doesn't feel right to her either. I'm still not sure why Sarah came to my house, nor why Harriet did so today. Question piles upon question.

When I turn from Sarah back to Gemma, I realise that she's no longer standing where she was. Harriet and her clipboard have moved on to Theresa and the window sills but Gemma has drifted towards the side of the stage. She glances both ways and then disappears through the door that leads towards the kitchen area. Sarah is back at the Christmas tree, having apparently missed this. When I look to the people around me, they're all locked in conversations with one another, either having not noticed, or not cared.

It's probably nothing – there are toilets through that door as well – and yet the way Gemma checked over her shoulder niggles at me. I stride across the hall and through the same door as Gemma. There's a cloakroom area off to the side, with reams of coats spilling out through the open door. Opposite that are the joint doors that lead into the men's and women's toilets. I poke my head into the women's, though all the stall doors hang open, with no sign of anybody inside.

I move back into the corridor and then head along the passage. There's a community noticeboard, advertising various events and things people are trying to sell. Past that is the kitchen. I'm almost reaching for the door when a hint of movement close to the fire exit catches my eye. It's Gemma I see first – but that's only a moment before I realise she's talking to Gavin. Harriet's husband towers over her but there is barely a distance between them as they mutter at a volume that's much too quiet for me to overhear.

I'm not hidden but neither of them pay me any attention as they continue to whisper back and forth. Gavin's standing tall, arching forward intimidatingly. It might be inadvertent but Gemma swiftly takes half a step back and replies with a loud 'no'.

At this, I must shift my weight because there's a creak from the floorboards underneath. Both Gavin and Gemma turn to look at me in unison and there's a moment of inertia before Gavin clears his throat.

'Can I help?' he asks, acting as if this is all normal.

I focus on Gemma. 'Is everything all right?'

She scowls as she takes me in, pauses for a second more and then turns her back on Gavin before striding past me back towards the hall.

'It would be if your husband hadn't thrown my daughter in a ditch.'

SIXTEEN YEARS OLD

I've never stayed in a hotel before. I've seen *Home Alone 2*, where Kevin has that grand suite to himself in New York – but that's nothing like this. There's a desk built into the wall on one side, with a double bed on the other. The sheets are folded tightly underneath the mattress, which is probably what Auntie Kath wants when she tells me to make my bed. Other than that, there's a small bathroom with just enough space for a bath and sink – and that's it.

There's an odd smell that I can't quite figure out. It's mainly lemon but, underneath that, just faintly, it's like someone has been sick.

I hope I don't have to sleep here tonight.

There's a creak from the corridor and I shuffle myself onto the corner of the bed, trying to make it seem as if I've been waiting here casually the entire time. No big deal. The creak becomes footsteps and I brace myself, waiting for the sound of the door opening – except whoever it is keeps walking past this room and away towards the lifts.

I wait, just as my aunt told me to do. She said she wouldn't be long – but I've learnt that adults say a lot of things in order to not commit to a time. 'Soon' is the biggest lie of them all. It can mean anything from a few minutes to a few months. If I have my way, I'd ban the word.

The television doesn't work properly… or not like a proper TV in any case. There's a screen telling me which hotel I'm in – even though I'm literally in it at this moment. Like someone with a sign saying 'You're in London' while you walk around London. I know where I am.

I press a few buttons, hunting for the guide, but then give up. I don't care what's on anyway. That's not why I'm here.

It takes me nine long strides to get from one side of the room to the other. The pattern of the wallpaper has seventeen spirals across the width of the room and thirty-nine along the length. There are five plug sockets. The curtain on the left side of the rail is missing a hook.

Then the phone rings. I'm not sure what it is at first, although that's largely because I'm not expecting it. When I pick it up and say 'hello', there's nobody there.

It's as I'm holding the phone receiver that there's a beep from the door. There are voices and then, suddenly, my aunt appears in the short corridor leading into the room. I put down the phone and she smiles across the room towards me.

'Sorry it took so long,' she says as she turns.

He barely feels real. Like one of my dreams where I'm not sure what happened and what didn't. Where he's in my thoughts and then I wake up and can't figure out whether he was there or not.

It's Dad.

He's so thin now. He always talked about losing weight and I suppose he's achieved that. He's wearing a sweatshirt that hangs off him, with the sleeves covering his hands. His face is so thin, to the point that it's only his dark eyes that let me know with certainty that it's him.

I go to him, wrapping myself around his middle as he pats me on the back gently.

'Hey, Mads,' he says.

I want to reply but there's a lump in my throat and the words are stuck. I don't know what to say anyway.

Auntie Kath stands by the door and says she'll be back soon, that we can take our time, although I'm not sure that Dad's listening.

I close the door and then lock it in place, not wanting him to leave again. After that, I find him sitting on the corner of the bed, in the precise spot that I was minutes before. He's staring at the floor, with his hands resting on his knees.

'Are you okay, Dad?' I ask.

'I am.' His voice is croaky – and I'm not sure that he sounds it.

'How was the journey?'

'Bumpy.'

I want him to look at me, to hug me again, but instead he stands and crosses to the window. He pushes aside the net curtain and stares down towards where I know the car park lies.

'We can do anything you want out there now,' I say. 'The park, the beach. We can go to the cricket, if you want?'

I want a smiling, happy 'yes' but he mumbles something I don't catch and doesn't move from the window.

'Do you want something to eat?' I ask. 'There's a carvery downstairs, or a McDonald's down the road. I think there's a Tesco past that if you want a sandwich or a cake…?'

Dad turns away from the window, although he looks through me as if I'm not there.

'I think I just want some sleep, Mads.'

He moves across to the bed and kicks off his shoes, before sitting on the opposite corner.

'Do you want to do something later? Go out for food then? Or something else?'

He closes his eyes and then lies back on the bed, staring up to the ceiling.

'We'll see, Mads.'

THIRTY-THREE

FRIDAY

When I wake up, the burner phone is the first thing I check. It sits on Richard's pillow but I've not had a single message since the one telling me to go to the back of the petrol station. I send a simple 'hello?' and then wait for a minute or two, hoping for a reply, though there's nothing.

I feel anger now. How hard can it be to send a brief update, telling me what's going on? Or letting me know that he's safe?

I take a shower, spending longer than I usually would in trying to scrub away the injustice of everything from the past week. By the time I'm out, there's a message waiting for me.

Ru going to the ball later?

It's been more than a day since the last message and receiving this now is almost more frustrating than receiving nothing. Always questions and never answers.

Me: *Why?*

You should.

Me: *WHY??*

I wait for a minute and, when there's no reply, I try calling the number. It rings five or six times and then goes silent, so I instantly try a second time.

No answer.

Me: ANSWER THE PHONE

I wait. Maybe a minute, maybe two. Then another text comes through.

Go to the ball later. There will be answers. I promise.

I clench the phone so hard that the plastic digs into my palm. What I really want to do is hurl it into the wall. To watch it crumble into pieces. The only reason I don't is because of those final words. Answers is all I want and, although something feels wrong, I can't place what.

I type out a few replies but delete them all, knowing there won't be another response after this. Richard was right about being behind the petrol station to see Harriet disposing of those clothes – and I trust that he'll be right about this, too.

There's something buzzing through me now; the determination that everything will be over in a few hours, even though I don't know quite what that will mean.

When I get downstairs, there's a gentle humming coming from the kitchen. I can't place the sound and, when I nudge open the door, I'm not prepared for what's on the other side. Kylie is sitting at the table with a sewing machine that I've not seen since we moved in. It used to belong to my mother and is one of those things that I've dragged around with me for years, even though I've never used it. Something I doubt I'll ever get rid of but something I cannot be without.

'Where'd you find that?' I ask.

'Under the stairs. I vaguely remember putting it there when we moved in.'

She checks something on her phone and then glances towards a light blue dress that's on the table next to the machine.

'Do you know anything about sewing?' she asks. 'I need to do some work on this.'

'I can tell you what a needle and thread is – but, after that, you're on your own.' I slot in on the other side of the table. 'What are you up to?'

'Working on a dress for the ball later.'

'You're going?'

'I wasn't – but then I was talking to Zoe last night and we're going to go together and freak a few people out.'

She grins and I can picture the two of them coming up with a plan of how to subvert something the village holds dear. As a villager and, more importantly, a mother, I wholeheartedly approve.

'How are you going to freak people out?' I ask.

'We're going as a punk Elsa and Anna. Y'know, from *Frozen*.'

She speaks as if I'm a ninety-year-old who's not heard of anything that happened since Man stepped on the Moon. Something for which I wasn't alive.

'I've heard of *Frozen*,' I say. 'And why are you going as a *punk* Elsa and Anna?'

'Mainly to see people's faces. We're going the whole hog. You'll see. Do you remember Jane from my halls?'

'Only in the sense that you've talked about her.'

Kylie's not listening. 'She does fashion, so she's shown me a couple of things – plus I Skyped her earlier to ask for some tips on what to do with this.' She holds up the dress. 'First I need to figure out how the machine works.'

'I don't think I can help you much with that. Your grandma tried to teach me once but I didn't really know what she was talking about – plus I wasn't that interested.'

Kylie holds up her phone. 'I found the manual online.'

'In that case, I eagerly await the results.'

She turns back to her phone and squints between the screen and the sewing machine. I almost tell her to keep her wits. The evening is supposed to be a fundraiser – and the village has been through a lot since Sunday – but perhaps this is precisely what people need? I don't think I'm the best person to be preaching about judgement in any case.

I make myself a tea and then leave Kylie to it as I head back upstairs. I've spent almost none of the week thinking about this winter ball. A big part of me is surprised that it's happening at all – especially as Alice is still in hospital. Another part isn't shocked in the slightest. I can imagine any number of villagers talking about 'Blitz spirit' as justification for keeping calm and carrying on.

I suppose, even with it happening, the idea of me being there still feels odd. If none of this had happened, Richard and I would've probably ducked our heads in for a short while. I am on the planning committee, after all – but that wouldn't have stopped us making our excuses after the early formalities were done with. A few hours in and everything devolves into the men heading outside to smoke cigars, while the women are left babysitting and cleaning up. Some things will always be the same.

With everything from these past days, I had no plans to go – but I think Harriet altered that when she visited last night. Especially with Kylie now going, it's probably right that I'm there. As Harriet said, Leavensfield *is* a small community.

Then there's the fact that Richard wants me there.

I pick out something simple to wear and hang it from the curtain rail. I'm not quite sure how it makes for 'winter magic' – but Harriet's themes are only usually for herself anyway. I've never been much of a princess and am not ready to start now.

With plans for the evening apparently in place, I feel a calm that I've not experienced in days. I get a bit of writing done, even though it might never see the light of day professionally. After that, I help Kylie as best I can – despite the fact she's already better than me at using the sewing machine.

I've not stepped a foot outside and, before I know it, the daylight has gone. I think there were even a handful of moments in which I forgot that my husband is missing – and that a hospitalised young girl was last seen getting into his car.

One of those moments is when I see Kylie in her ridiculous dress. It's taken her most of the day to stitch, cut and sew. Instead of the long, light blue gown of a princess, hers is low-cut at the top and short at the bottom. She's interwoven black into the blue and has gone about sixty per cent goth for the occasion. She doesn't look like herself – but I suppose that's the point.

I drive us down to the village hall and park at the front, before we both get out of the car. Someone's hung a large banner across the front of the hall that reads 'Winter Magic'. It could be tacky – but it isn't.

There's a buzz in the centre of the village; something almost indefinable, unless a person has lived here for long enough to spot it. I see it in the way people are getting out of their cars and then stopping to point at whoever's closest and compliment them on whatever they're wearing. Some have gone all-out with the theme and are wearing wintry white or light blue dresses, while others are like me and have gone for something straight and simple.

It's impossible to undersell how big an event it is for the village – and churlish not to mention how important Harriet is for that. She *makes* events happen, she organises people – and she raises money. She does those things time after time. Sure, it has a bit of the trains-running-on-time-1930s-Germany vibe about it all – but she deserves credit.

We've not even made the front door when there's a shriek from off to the side. Zoe is crossing the car park and has spotted Kylie. Zoe's in something black and similarly gothic, albeit intercut with a purple shawl and ginger streaks in her hair. They point to one another and then link hands as they do a mini twirl.

'What do you think?' Kylie asks.

'Freaky.'

She grins and then goes to drag Zoe towards the hall – except that Zoe isn't ready to go.

'Can you take Frankie in for me?' she asks Kylie.

Her son is at her side, dressed in a pair of black trousers with a white shirt and dark tie – like all the other boys. He wriggles, uncomfortable, but he won't be the only one. I'd worry about any young lads who actually enjoy wearing this sort of thing. They're the sort that will surely grow into the type of suit-wearing smart-mouths who bankrupt nations.

Kylie looks quizzically between Zoe and me. 'I didn't realise you knew each other…?'

It's Zoe who answers. 'We know each other a bit…'

Kylie hovers for a moment more but doesn't question it any further as she takes Frankie's hand and leads him inside.

I watch her go and quickly blink away the thought of my daughter with children of her own. It's there and gone.

'Is this awkward?' Zoe asks.

'What?'

'If I'm friends with your daughter?'

'No…' I shake my head but I suppose I don't know what I feel. There was a moment in Zoe's kitchen when it felt like we were kindred spirits. She sits in that bracket that's halfway between my age and my daughter's. She could be friends with either of us, both, or neither. It's like being back at school and courting the friendship of the most popular girl. I should be too old for all this.

'I'm embarrassed,' Zoe says.

'What about?'

'It wasn't Richard that I saw at the shack. I caught a couple of teenagers up there earlier. They're not even from the village, but they've been recreating some sort of Bear Grylls survival thing they saw on YouTube. They've been half freezing to death every night. That and smoking weed.'

'Oh…'

She gives a sad, consoling smile. 'I'm sorry. I didn't mean to waste your morning yesterday. I enjoyed the chat, though…'

'Me too.'

'Maybe we can do something similar again soon? When all this is sorted…?'

'I think I'd like that.'

We step to the side to allow a family to pass. There are two young sons in identical little suits. Both skip alongside their parents, who are bickering about who should look after the car keys for the evening. Small, stupid things.

'Have you heard anything about…?' Zoe tails off.

'No.'

I think of the mobile that came through the door and is now in my bag. It promises answers this evening, although I can't possibly comprehend what they might be.

Zoe nods towards the doors. 'Shall we head in?'

I follow her onto the red carpet and we pass a trio of vertical 'For Alice' banners hanging from the ceiling. The hall itself is incredible. As well as the work done last night, a group of people must have been here all day. The ceiling is covered with silver, white and pale blue streamers that reflect the spinning lights beaming up from below. Along with the glittering tree on the stage, there's a pair of inflatable snowmen at the back of the hall, plus a dusting of white along the edges.

Slade or Wizzard or someone like that is playing through the speakers – though the volume is gentle. Every man that I can spot is in varying levels of suit – either a basic two-piece with a tie, a three-piece with the waistcoat, or a full-on dicky bow get-up.

The women range from ballgowns to expensive-looking princess dresses, to something more simplistic, like mine.

Zoe heads off towards the children's area next to the snowman. Frankie is there with a couple of other boys – but there's no sign of Kylie. The hall is crowded, but she should be easy to spot given her outfit... except that she isn't.

I do a lap of the hall but she's nowhere in sight. I end up asking one of the women manning the appetiser table if she's seen a young woman in a short blue and black dress, only to get a blank look. I keep asking until someone points me towards the front of the hall, saying they saw someone like that heading towards the stage. The ball hasn't officially started yet and the stage itself is clear of people. I'm yet to see Harriet herself.

I'm through the door on the way to the toilets when I hear the shouting. I know what's happening a moment before I see it. Gemma is in the same spot as she was last night, next to the fire exit.

Except, this time, instead of talking to Gavin, she's pinning Kylie to the wall by her throat.

THIRTY-FOUR

'Where's your dad?! Where is he?!'

Gemma's forearm is across Kylie's windpipe as she presses her into the wall. My daughter's eyes flare wide as she spots me and tries to gasp something. I can only see her from the back but Gemma is wearing a smart, sparkly silver dress that I suspect belongs to Harriet. There doesn't seem to be any weapon in her free hand – but that doesn't mean there isn't something unseen.

'Gemma…' I move closer, saying her name and watch as the tension dips in her shoulders. There's a burning furnace of fury within me that someone has *dared* put their hands on my daughter – but the slightly louder voice tells me that calm is what's needed here.

Slightly louder.

'A lot of people really want to help you today,' I add.

Gemma turns to glance over her shoulder. She's still got an arm across Kylie's front – but it's dropped towards my daughter's breastbone and there's little pressure now.

'It's a stupid winter festival.'

I take a moment, pushing away the anger. Keeping my voice level. Ignoring my trembling hand. 'People care about you.'

'Do you think I *care* about the money? This stupid fundraiser? I want my daughter.'

'I know you do. I'd like mine, too.'

Kylie is trying to catch my eye but I'm focusing on Gemma as I edge nearer. They're only a metre or so ahead of me now. Gemma's arm has dropped completely, although she remains between Kylie and me. Her chest bobs up and down rapidly as she pants for breath. Her eyes are wide and unfocused, and I suspect she might have taken something.

'Why did he do it?' Her voice is lower now, slightly more focused.

I keep moving forward until I'm in a position where I can sandwich myself in between Gemma and Kylie.

'I wish I had answers for you,' I say.

Kylie slides around behind me and sidesteps along the hall until she's out of the way. I mouth the word 'Harriet' before she nods and shuffles off towards the main hall, leaving Gemma and me alone in the alcove by the exit.

She's trembling.

'Why did he do it?' she repeats, the words slurring into one another.

'I don't think Richard did do it...'

The words feel dangerous, except that something has changed in Gemma. Whatever anger she had moments before has faded as she steps backwards and slides down the wall until she's sitting on the floor.

'She's not getting better...'

Gemma's words are a whisper and I can't help but flash back to Alice and her red coat lying next to the stream.

'They keep saying positive things at the hospital – but nothing's changing. She's in a coma. They say she was hit on the side of the head.' She clamps her fingers into a fist and grinds her teeth together. 'Someone hit my little girl on the head.'

I'm on the ground next to Gemma, unsure what to say – but knowing more than ever before that this wasn't Richard. Whatever he is, he's not a man that would do this sort of thing. I can't be that wrong about a person.

'I hate being there,' Gemma says. 'I know it's wrong. I should be at the hospital – but I can't stand seeing her like that.'

I'm dumbstruck. I can't pretend I know how she's feeling and I doubt she'd want to hear it from me anyway.

Gemma shifts abruptly and grabs my hand, clasping my fingers into hers. 'He had nothing left to lose. That was the problem. You're free when that happens, aren't you? You can do whatever because you've lost hope anyway.'

I try to absorb what she's said but there's a lot to unpack. Gemma squeezes my fingers so tightly that they throb. Her eyes are so wide that it's like they might pop right out of her head. I can smell booze on her breath.

'I pushed him too far. I know that. I left him with nothing to lose – but Alice didn't deserve what happened. I know it's my fault. Can you tell him that I know I was wrong?'

I don't know what she's talking about.

'Tell… *Richard*?'

Gemma's words blend into one another now, as if her mouth can't say them quickly enough. One long, slurred sentence. 'I know you must be in contact with him. I don't blame you. I *know* what it's like.'

It's the way she squeezes the word 'know' from the depths of her soul that lets me finally see it. Perhaps I already suspected at some level? It's the same mystical infatuation that I once had with Richard. Perhaps the one I still do. It's why, when Keith said that Richard 'always had an eye for his students', I knew it was the truth.

People don't understand unless they've been there, too. The closest thing I can compare it to is being a child, when someone shows a magic trick for the first time. There's that sense of fascination and mystery. Meeting Richard was like that.

'You and… Richard…?'

Gemma shakes her head. She speaks quietly and croakily. 'Not recently. He said he was with you and asked me to respect it. Said he'd lost one wife he loved and couldn't lose another.' She sniffles away a bubble of snot and then gulps. 'Sorry about your door.'

I suppose that answers one question. I wait, and then: 'Were you one of his students?'

'A long time ago.'

'How long?'

I already know. Gemma shakes her head and doesn't answer.

'How old is Alice?'

Gemma dips her head and rests it on her knuckles. 'Twelve,' she says. 'Alice is twelve.'

LAST SUNDAY

RICHARD

Gemma twists in the passenger seat to take in her daughter in the back of the car.

'Put in your headphones,' she says.

Gemma has spoken with the kind of tone that makes Richard wish he could put in his own headphones. The noise-cancelling ones that Maddy bought for him the Christmas before – almost a year ago now. They only fit into one of the three turntables at the house but he has to admit that the precision of every groove from the vinyl sounds spectacular with them. He's been able to listen to his records in a way that wasn't possible before.

Another argument is about to happen.

Richard checks the mirror and watches as Alice does as she's told. She unfurls the earphone cable from the pocket of her jeans and then plugs it into her phone. After that, Gemma turns back to the front. This was all supposed to have been sorted out at The Willow Tree. He'd chosen that pub for a few reasons, one of which was because it was nowhere near Leavensfield; but the other was that he thought the serene surroundings might make Gemma more reasonable. Alice was off playing near the stream while he and Gemma had their conversation.

It did not go well.

It's dark now. The days are so short at this time of year and, with the openness of the area around Leavensfield, they feel even shorter.

'I need more,' Gemma says.

It's a variation on what she's been saying for twelve years – and a repeat of what she was talking about earlier.

'I told you at the pub – I'm struggling. I can only just afford the mortgage on your house along with everything else. Maddy will—'

'I told you not to talk about her when we're together.'

Richard slows for a bend and tries not to let it needle too much. This is his fault, after all. Years and years of mistakes catching up.

'We're not *together*,' he says. 'Not like that. This is *not* a relationship. I made a mistake twelve years ago and—'

Gemma twists theatrically to look towards the back seat. 'Don't you *dare* talk about our daughter like that.'

'You know that's not what I meant. This is one person blackmailing another.'

Gemma turns back to the front and crosses her arms over the seat belt. It's a moment of respite but Richard knows it won't last long. They've been dancing around in these circles for years. Every time he concedes one thing, she wants something else. It's gone so far past simple child maintenance. He thought it might end by paying the mortgage on a house in the village. She'd been pestering him for ages about moving closer. He wasn't even necessarily against it… except that he didn't realise 'closer' meant Leavensfield itself. Gemma did all the legwork in hunting down a place that was available.

Except that, whatever he did, it was never, *ever*, enough.

'I don't want to work at the petrol station any more,' she says. 'It's horrible and it's so cold at the moment.'

Richard checks the rear-view mirror. The road is empty but he looks at Alice, too – making sure she's still got the earphones in. Perhaps she can hear them talking anyway.

'I can't afford to keep you,' he says. 'We've talked about this. I explained at the pub. The mortgage is so much by itself. I can't pay for everything else as well.'

'Alice is *your* daughter. *Your* responsibility.'

'I know – and I'm paying for a house where you both can live. But Maddy—'

'Stop saying her name.'

'She's my *wife*!'

'You had another wife when you got me pregnant and it didn't stop you then.'

Richard doesn't have an instant answer to that. There was an opportunity to tell Maddy about Alice back when they first met – but he missed it. He'd have had to explain about how he cheated on his wife, which isn't a great way to start a new relationship. Then, before he knew it, it was too late. He was left disappearing to meet 'work colleagues' when he was being 'Uncle Richard' to his daughter.

'I've changed,' Richard says.

Gemma turns towards the back seat again. 'You'd rather we went away.'

'No.'

'You've got a big house and I need another hundred quid a week. If you can't afford that, then sell some things.'

'I *have* sold some things.'

'A hundred a week, or I'll tell everyone. The whole village will know. *Madeleine* will know.'

It's too late now – but Richard has realised this is why Gemma hunted down that house in Leavensfield. She said he'd be able to watch his daughter grow up – which was true – but it was more about the way she could use the community against him if need be. There have been so many more demands since she moved to the village, even though he's now paying more than he ever has.

There's not a lot more to say after this. He's going to have to sell some more things to get the money Gemma wants. Maddy doesn't seem to have noticed the little odds and ends that have disappeared so far but he can make up something about trimming his record collection and then see how much he gets. Longer term, he'll have to come up with something better.

Richard pulls in a short distance away from Fuel's Gold and leaves the engine running. 'What time does your shift start?' he asks.

Gemma eyes the dashboard clock. 'About ten minutes.' She twists towards the back seat and waves her hand while saying Alice's name. Richard twists against his seat belt to watch as his daughter undoes hers and opens the back door.

'How's Alice going to get home?'

'She'll walk. It's not far across the fields.'

'It's so cold.'

'Maybe if her Uncle Richard wasn't afraid about being seen with her…'

Gemma clicks her fingers and then gets out of the car, closely followed by Alice.

Richard watches from the driver's seat as they walk the short distance along the lane before passing the recycling bank and stepping into the bright lights of the forecourt.

There's being careful about where and when he might be seen with Gemma and Alice – and then there's outright recklessness.

Gemma and Alice have disappeared into the minimart building but it's only a few moments until Alice emerges. Richard puts the car into reverse and edges backwards until he's out of sight from anyone inside the shop. He's at the rear of the forecourt and there are no vehicles at the petrol pumps.

Alice is in her big red coat and she stops to look across to the far side of the road. The dewy fields lie beyond, with the hazy lights of Leavensfield glowing from the bottom of the valley. On evenings like this, when the sun sets early and frost clings to the verges, the wintry scene from the top of the hill is like a painting.

Alice tightens her jacket's zip – but it won't be much of a match for walking home over the fields in this weather. She's only twelve.

Richard pulls up the handbrake and leaves the car idling as he gets out and then beckons the girl across. She glances quickly at the shop, takes one step towards the road – and then seems to change her mind as she crosses to where Richard is standing. She stands a couple of steps away from him, her arms crossed.

'I can give you a lift home,' he says.

'But Mum—'

'Don't worry about your mum.' Richard glances towards the shop, where, because of the angle, there's no chance of Alice's mother spotting him. 'If she says anything, I'll deal with it. She doesn't have to know.'

Alice bobs from one foot to the other. The cold, dark walk home across Daisy Field can't seem too appealing.

'She's told me not to get into a car with strangers.'

Richard forces a smile, but the icy, needly wind scratches at his face and he ends up offering something closer to a grimace. 'Come on… I'm not a *proper* stranger, am I?'

Alice eyes him and he can see the conflict within her. She should say no – except nobody wants to walk home on a night like this. Besides, what mother lets a twelve-year-old walk home in the dark? Even in a place like Leavensfield?

'It's only down the hill,' Richard adds, nodding towards the village in the distance. 'Not far.'

A car passes on the way down to the village. Alice watches it go and then nods shortly, before slipping into the vehicle.

Richard moves quickly as he returns to the driver's seat. *Just a short ride*, he tells himself. *Just a short ride.*

He wonders if there will ever be a day when he tells her who he really is. If not that, then she's a smart girl and perhaps she'll figure it out herself? He or Gemma – or both – should have done it a long time ago, but one lie turned into another, which turned into another. It's the story of everything from the past twelve years.

Richard reverses onto the road but they've only travelled a short distance when Alice presses herself to the glass and points up towards the hill.

'What do you think that is?'

There is rarely anybody out on the roads at this time on a Sunday evening, so Richard eases off the accelerator and allows the car to roll to a near stop as he ducks down to try to get an angle on whatever Alice has seen. It's hard to tell from the road – but there's some sort of speckled light from up on the hill, towards the woods.

'I have no idea,' Richard replies.

'Can we go and look? It might be aliens!'

It's not aliens but there's something about the glee in Alice's voice that Richard finds hard to resist. They don't get enough moments like this, when it's only the pair of them. There's a track that heads away from the road, up towards the trees. It means driving into a dead end, although it shouldn't be too much of a problem to turn around at the top. The lights on the hill are probably just teenagers with a phone, or something like that. Hard to know, really – especially in the middle of winter. Either way, it will be an extra five or ten minutes where it's just him and Alice.

The track is unmarked and hard to spot in the dark. It follows the line of a hedge and Richard has to slow to a crawl in order to see it. He takes the turn and the car immediately starts bumping up and down across the rocky ground. Alice giggles at this and jolts around exaggeratedly as they continue up.

Richard's going to have to tell his wife about her – and probably soon. The extra money for Gemma is unsustainable and, really, he just wants to be able to see more of his daughter without all the hoops and games. Maddy will understand. He's never cheated on her. Never. He made a mistake twelve years ago, before they even knew one another.

Alice ducks down, pressing against her seat belt to try to look up towards the top of the hill. The light is clearer now and definitely more than a phone.

'What do you reckon it is?' she asks.

'I have no idea,' Richard replies. 'But I guess we'll find out in a minute or so.'

THIRTY-FIVE

'I didn't need the extra hundred quid,' Gemma says. 'I just didn't want to work at that stupid place any more. I shouldn't have asked him for more. The house was enough.' A pause and then a quieter: '*More* than enough.'

I suppose that answers the question of how Gemma can afford to live in Leavensfield. She can't. Richard's been paying for her house, almost certainly from his savings account.

So many questions.

'I didn't know you went to university,' I say.

'I didn't, not really. My parents forced me into going, but it wasn't for me. Then I got pregnant anyway.'

'Richard…' I say his name, even though I already know.

Gemma doesn't respond, not directly in any case.

'I said it was from a boy I met on a night out. Never got his name and all that. Mum said I was a slag but she wouldn't have liked the truth either.'

'Do the police know about Alice and Richard?'

Gemma sits silently for a moment. Her chest is still heaving and she shuffles uncomfortably. It's no surprise: the wall and floor are equally unforgiving.

She doesn't answer the question but, in a way, that's more than answering it. I don't know the whole story but I can figure out much of it. Gemma was hardly going to tell them that she'd been blackmailing my husband for anything up to a dozen years.

'When I saw you yesterday, I thought that maybe you and Gavin…'

Gemma glances sideways to me. There's something dismissively incredulous about her expression. '*Gavin?* He was asking about Alice and the police. I was trying to get him to leave me alone.'

There's the sound of a door opening from the other end and then Harriet appears. Gemma instantly wraps her arms around herself and stares at the wall ahead.

'Are you all right?' Harriet asks as she stands over us. 'We can get you home, or take you to the hospital? Whichever you prefer. You don't have to be here.'

Gemma replies with a long, loud exhalation – and she doesn't look up.

'C'mon,' Harriet says, reaching down. 'Let's get you home.'

I stand and help with Gemma's other shoulder as Harriet and I lift her up. Instead of passing through the front of the hall, Harriet uses her hip to open the fire exit and we edge through that. Gemma is walking by herself now and Harriet mutters, 'I'll take it from here,' leaving me alone and watching as they half walk, half stagger across towards the benches near the road.

Alice is Richard's daughter.

No wonder she was getting into his car. I'm not sure whether to be relieved, annoyed, or both. Whether to be annoyed at him for keeping it secret, or me for missing everything.

With the fire door closed, I have to head back around the hall and then through the front entrance. After that, I make my way through the crowd towards the stage once more. The music has started properly now and a handful of couples are on the dance floor. More are standing around the edges, trying the canapés.

Kylie is waiting near the door next to the cloakroom and toilets. She spins and does a double take as I appear, wondering why I've appeared from the other side.

'Harriet and I helped Gemma out through the fire exit,' I say. 'I think Harriet's going to take her home.' I peer closer towards Kylie's neck, although there don't seem to be any marks. 'Are you okay?'

'I think so. It probably looked worse than it was. What about you?'

I blink at her, relieved she's fine. Wanting to grab her and hold her. I'd not thought of myself. 'I'm fine,' I say. 'We just talked for a bit.'

'It can't be easy for her,' Kylie says.

'Right…'

I should tell Kylie that it's not by blood – but that she has a sister of sorts. I would – except it's not the time. I've not processed it myself yet. I've not decided if I should go to the police first, or check in with Gemma once she's calmed down. Everything is so messy that there doesn't feel like a correct choice.

Kylie glances towards the door and the hall beyond: 'I'm going to find Zoe, if you don't mind.'

'I don't mind.'

She slips into a half smile, half laugh. 'Thanks for saving me.'

'I'm a real superhero.'

Kylie grins, briefly rests her head on my shoulder, and then heads towards the party. The music blares momentarily as the door opens and then dims again.

I suppose Richard was correct in his messages that something would happen here tonight – but he couldn't have known about this. He must have meant something else. I could text him now to say that I know about Alice – although I can't see that it would do any good. It feels like a face-to-face conversation.

At something of a loss as to what comes now, I head back into the party myself. The dance floor is almost full now. It's largely couples, but I spot Kylie and Zoe together on the far side – and there are children as well. I drift around the room, grabbing a canapé from the table, mainly so that I have something to hold. It's some sort of pastry puff, with hummus in the middle.

It's Sarah who catches my eye, largely because the moment she sees me, she quickly turns away towards the children. The younger ones have been grouped together at the very back of the hall and are playing board games across a series of tables. Her two, as well as Harriet's children, are there – as are a good fifteen or sixteen others. In a digital age, it feels like a very Leavensfield thing to be happening.

Sarah's in a bluey-white dress and is clutching a wand with a star on the end. She holds it aloft, almost as if she's going to curse me with it as I approach. I ask her how things are going and get a brief 'good, thanks' as a response. She then crouches to needlessly interfere in a game of Monopoly that's being played by four of the children.

I hover where I am, waiting until her thighs can take it no more and she has to stand.

'How's the chest infection?' I ask.

'Better, thank you.'

'It's just that, when I mentioned it to James the other day, he didn't seem to know a lot about it…'

I follow Sarah's stare across the hall towards the front doors, where her husband is currently in conversation with Harriet.

It takes her a few seconds to reply. 'He always underplays it,' she says. 'You know what blokes are like. They have a sniffle and call it man flu. We have a full-on chest infection and they act like it's nothing.' She tries to laugh it away but her body language is all over the place and she can't stop staring at James and Harriet.

'He didn't know you left the house.'

'When?'

'When you were at mine on Tuesday. I asked him about it and he didn't know you'd come over.'

Another pause, briefer this time. 'It's not like we tell each other everything.'

'Why *did* you come to mine that day?'

Sarah shrinks away from the tables by a step or two. It's not much and probably unconscious. She looks past me towards the main hall and then returns to watching her husband and Harriet, who are still in conversation.

'I was checking in on you after what happened at the school. Plus I had tickets for you.'

'But we've never been friends. You could've put the tickets through the letter box.'

'I was trying to be nice.' She launches into a cough and I wait as she bats a hand in front of her mouth.

'You've not been around much this week,' I say. 'You missed the planning meeting on Sunday. You've missed all sorts.'

She pats her chest. 'I've been getting over it.'

It could be the truth except that her quivering voice and wandering eyes tell another story. I try to remember what we talked about when she came to the house. It all felt so odd at the time – so innocuous – except that she was actually waiting outside in the cold. She might have been there for quite some time before I got home. Why wait?

'Why were you so worried about Richard?' I ask.

'I wasn't… I mean, I was. Everyone was, I mean *is*. We're all a part of the village, aren't we?'

This would be acceptable – except that she hasn't been back in the past three days to see how I'm doing, or to ask any more about Richard. It feels like there's more to this, except I'm not sure where it all ties together.

Sarah's had enough anyway. Two of the children are playing dominoes and, without being called, she swoops down upon them and starts to explain some rules that I'm relatively sure they already knew.

Speaking to Gemma has left me emboldened. It's been a strange week and yet I've accepted much of it because I've felt so shell-shocked by it all.

On the other side of the hall, Harriet and James are leaving through the large doors. I hurry across and follow them out to where James is now helping Gemma into the passenger side of his 4x4. Her foot slips on the step up and she slumps against the frame of the car. James holds her up as she cackles to herself. I amble across the car park, watching instead of participating. Harriet is off to the side and, after James has bundled Gemma into his car, he approaches her.

'Sorry about this,' Harriet says. 'I can't find Gavin, else I'd get him to do this.'

James mutters something about it being no problem – although the way he dabs at a patch of saliva on his suit doesn't make it seem as if it's all fine. He gets into the driver's side – and then pulls away from the car park, heading towards the village cross and, presumably, Gemma's house on the other side. It's not far.

Harriet stands and watches before she turns and looks me up and down.

'Do you think I should call the police?' she asks. 'Do you think she's dangerous?'

'I don't know.'

'What happened with you in the pub toilets?'

'Not much.'

Harriet waits, as if expecting more of an answer. She isn't going to get it. 'I should've gone with her,' she says. 'Just in case.'

'Why did you give her your boots?'

Harriet sucks in her cheeks. We're alone on the tarmac of the car park as the muffled sound of the party music plays behind us.

'Because she asked.'

'That's generous of you.'

Harriet looks to me, probably wondering if I'm being sarcastic. In truth, I don't know myself. I'm not done yet anyway,

'Why did you dump Alice's clothes in the recycling bin up at the garage?'

I haven't turned to look at her but I can see Harriet's head crane back in the corner of my eye. A small ice age passes in the silence that follows. I can sense Harriet's mouth bobbing open.

'How do you know about that?'

'Does it matter?'

I face her now – and she shrinks under my gaze. She's underestimated me but I think I might have overestimated her. She's just a woman, after all. Same as me.

'I had some of Xavier and Bee's stuff that didn't fit any more. I'd taken them to Gemma's and asked if she wanted anything. I thought I was helping but I guess I misread the situation. She went crazy. Started throwing Alice's old clothes at me and saying she wanted them out of the house. She was manic, saying that Alice was going to die and that it was all her fault. I ended up stuffing everything into bags. I was going to keep them but Gavin suggested the charity bin.' She pauses and then adds: 'Were you at the garage, or something?'

This isn't what I expected. It sounds so… normal. So real. I believe every word she's said.

Except that I got a text telling me to be behind Fuel's Gold.

'Who knew?' I ask.

'Who knew what?'

'Who knew you were going to take those clothes to the recycling bin?'

Harriet blinks at me, not understanding why I want to know. 'Just me,' she says. 'Well… and Gavin, I suppose.'

LAST SUNDAY

RICHARD

Richard grips the steering wheel tightly as the car continues to bump along the trail. The car keeps lurching across the stones towards the ditch and he doesn't feel completely in control.

'It's like a roller coaster,' Alice says.

Richard doesn't reply – but only because he's worried he'll bite through his tongue as the car bounces down into one of the many holes. He eases off the accelerator and allows the car to roll to a stop before killing the headlights.

'We can walk the last bit,' he says.

Alice unclips her seat belt and then opens the door as Richard does the same on his side. The trail continues for another couple of hundred metres until it reaches the dead end. Beyond that is a field and then the woods. On the other side of the hedge, the stream bubbles and ripples down the hill towards the village beyond.

Richard is beginning to think the detour wasn't such a good idea, except that there's something about the way Alice skips around the front of the car that leaves him yearning to tell her who he really is. Maddy will surely understand when it all comes out. He had broached the idea of a daughter with India – except that she'd taken it badly and he never got a chance to mention it again. It's different with Maddy because she already has a daughter. She knows what it's like.

By the time this is through his mind, Alice is already a couple of steps further up the slope. An orangey blob is glowing from the tip of the dead end above. The surrounding hedges would make it impossible to see from almost all angles but, for whatever reason, it so happened that Alice was in precisely the right spot, with precisely the right amount of curiosity to ask about it.

The stream babbles on the other side of the hedge as Richard hurries to catch her. They haven't travelled far before it becomes apparent that the glow is coming from an interior light of a car.

'Not aliens,' Alice says, disappointed.

'No…'

They're close enough that Richard has a good idea of what's actually going on – except that Alice is too fast for him. By the time he's reached for her to say that they should go back the way they came, she's already dashed ahead.

The car windows are misted but it's not quite enough of a curtain to block what's happening inside.

Alice stops and turns to look up at Richard. She's only a few paces from the car. 'Are they fighting?'

Richard puts a hand on Alice's shoulder and tries to guide her backwards along the track towards the car. They're not fighting…

Except that it's too late.

The back door opens and Gavin Branch steps out of the car. His shirt is untucked and he's refastening his trousers.

'It's not what it looks like,' he says, talking to Richard.

Alice has stopped and is trying to look past Gavin towards the back of the car – although Richard can see easily enough what's going on, and he suspects it's *precisely* what it looks like.

Sarah Overend's face appears at the back window. She squints to see what's going on but, as she leans in, she shows that the only thing she's wearing on top is a black bra.

Alice giggles in the way children do when they see something naughty. She's a young twelve, which Richard suspects is what happens when someone's forced to move around and has been unable to settle. He thinks children ideally need two parents but then he's old-fashioned like that – and this isn't ideal. It's not her fault that she hasn't had that.

'Hello, Mrs Overend,' she says with a laugh.

Gavin spins to look between the car on one side, plus Richard and Alice on the other. He's stuck in the middle.

'We're going to go,' Richard says, still trying to get Alice to move backwards. 'Alice, come on.'

She doesn't move. She's fascinated by what's in front of her. It's only now that Richard realises how cold it is. Alice is in her red coat, but he is wearing only his regular clothes – and Gavin is wearing less than that. Gavin's frantic, short breaths disappear into the sky as the light from inside the car finally disappears. If only they'd left that light off. If only, if only.

Gavin strides forward, brushing aside Alice as he closes in on Richard and grabs for the other man's shirt. 'You better keep your mouth shut,' he says.

Richard pushes him away, although there's little force to it.

'It's your word against mine,' Gavin adds.

'I'm not going to tell anyone. Just… maybe find somewhere more private next time. Or turn off the lights.'

'Don't tell me how to live my life.'

Richard keeps trying to move away, not wanting any part of the situation. It would likely all be fine if it wasn't for one thing.

Alice laughs.

It's more of a snort: a natural, childish reaction as opposed to anything malicious. Except that Gavin isn't thinking straight. Everything happens in a second as he spins and thrashes a right arm towards her.

There's a splat as he catches her across the temple – and then, as Richard gasps a 'no', she's falling. Her head cannons into a rock and bounces up before she slumps into a lifeless ball. There's silence for a second – and then gravity takes hold as she slides down into the ditch and continues rolling towards the stream beyond.

THIRTY-SIX

If it's only Gavin and Harriet who know that she was taking those clothes to the recycling bank, then it's only Gavin or Harriet who could have told me to be there to watch...

'Where's Gavin?' I ask.

Harriet's eyes narrow. She must know something's up but she doesn't know what. When she doesn't answer, I take the burner phone from my bag and check the last few messages received. Something felt off about the most recent few but I couldn't see what. Now I'm looking for it, the answer is right in front of me. It should have been obvious. I *wanted* it to be Richard who was texting me but it's only now that I realise what I missed.

Ru going to the ball later?

Richard would never have typed 'ru' in place of 'are you'. He's an English lecturer. He's always railing against text-speak and the way the younger students compose essays.

'Where's Gavin?' I repeat.

'Why?'

'Where is he?' I'm shouting now, surprising myself.

'I don't know!'

It's like there's a puzzle in front of me – and suddenly the pieces go together. When Sarah came to my house the other day, the important thing she asked wasn't about Richard, it was about the police. She wanted to know if I knew anything about the investigation.

Then there's Zoe, who said that Gavin tried it on with her.

And Sarah again – who missed Sunday's meeting, which was at the exact time when she knew with one hundred per cent clarity where Harriet was going to be.

Gavin.

It can only be Gavin who put the phone through my letter box and has been messaging me ever since.

But why would he want a bag of Richard's clothes and his coat? That's what I left behind the village sign after all.

And then I see the other thing. In the same way that Sarah and Gavin knew that Harriet was going to be in the back room of the Fox and Hounds hosting a planning meeting for the ball, Gavin knows precisely where I am now. He's the one that encouraged me to be here.

Go to the ball later. There will be answers. I promise.

'I have to go,' I tell Harriet. 'Tell Kylie I've gone home. I'll pick her up later.'

Harriet spins, off guard from what's just happened. 'Why are you going?' she asks.

I ignore her, fumbling in my bag for the car keys and then hurrying across to where I'm parked. I'm already in the driver's seat, trying to close the door, when Harriet stands in the way and blocks me from shutting it.

'What's going on?' she asks.

'I need to go.'

'But why? What's going on with Gavin?'

'Nothing. I just need to go. I'll be back later. Make sure you tell Kylie I've gone.'

Harriet hovers for a moment, before I reach and physically push her away from the car. She allows herself to be moved – but stands and watches as I reverse out of the space and then accelerate towards the hill that leads up to my house.

The phone that came through my door sits on the passenger seat next to my bag and it chimes that old-fashioned *ding-ding-ding*. The road is empty and I slow as I pluck the device from the seat and click to see the new arrival.

I'm at the back of the Fox & Hounds now. Come quickly.

There's a brief moment in which I forget that this isn't Richard – but it only lasts a second. This is Gavin – and he wants me to be waiting at the back of the pub – which means that's the last place I should be.

I continue driving and then turn onto the driveway. The gravel crunches to announce my arrival and then I get out of the car and stand, looking towards the house. All the lights are off, except for the rainbow fairy bulbs on the Christmas tree that wink through the curtains of the living room. I left those on, partly through habit. Richard always says that big social events in Leavensfield would be a godsend for burglars if anyone paid enough attention.

Something feels wrong, although I can't say what. It's only when I get to the front door and insert the key that I turn and spot it. My car is always parked in the same spot – and there are tyre-shaped dimples in the gravel from where Richard always leaves his. It's only gentle, barely noticeable, but now there's a third set in between the two. Someone else has parked here recently.

I let myself into the house and am swallowed by the darkness. The only light in the hall comes from the second phone as I tap 'Where ru?' as a reply to the message about going to the Fox and Hounds. Might as well play along.

There's nothing untoward upstairs, other than that Richard's office is still uncomfortably bare. I wonder if there were any papers in there relating to Gemma and Alice. He's either bought a house, or is renting it – but, if it's in his name, then there isn't necessarily a link. Does Dini know? Has he known all this time, but he's kept it from me?

Back downstairs, I edge into the living room, where the Christmas tree lights continue to blink. There's no one here, so I head for the kitchen. The blinds are up and, because of the position of the moon, it's almost like a bluey daylight has descended. There's nobody here, either.

The house is empty.

I start to turn to head back to the car, unsure of my next move, when I feel drawn to the shed at the end of the garden. It was empty when I looked a few days before and sat in Richard's rocking chair.

There's dew on the lawn; a gentle dusting of fine white across the grass – except that's not all there is. There are footprints, too.

I go to grab the shed key from next to the back door – except that it isn't there. I search the surrounding surfaces and look on the floor but there's no sign of it. It was definitely in place earlier. I open the back door anyway and step onto the lawn. The footprints that lead to the shed are only visible because they're recent: a series of long outlines on top of the grass. As the dew continues to build, they'll be gone in minutes.

I'm halfway across when my phone starts to ring. My *proper* phone. It's Harriet's name on the front but I ignore her as I silence the device. It instantly starts to vibrate from her repeat call.

There's no need for a key to enter the shed – because the padlock sits on the low wall at the side, next to the key. I reach for the door and the hinge creaks noisily into the silent night as I pull it open.

I spot the rocking chair first, untouched in the back corner, next to the pile of blankets. It's all so normal… until I turn and look the other way – and stare into hell.

LAST SUNDAY

RICHARD

The blood appears instantly. It's on the rock where Alice hit her head and, as she slides limply towards the stream, there's a speckling of red across the stones.

Richard watches, frozen to the spot. It doesn't feel real and yet it's in front of him. He steps towards her but a hand snags his arm and drags him backwards. Gavin's eyes are wide and there's saliva bubbling in the corner of his mouth.

'We need an ambulance,' Richard gasps, as he tries to wriggle his arm free from the other man's grip. When Gavin continues holding on, Richard reaches forward and pushes him. He succeeds in making the other man let go – but also in leaving himself off-balance. As Gavin staggers in one direction, Richard tumbles in the other. His knee has twisted in the attempt to get away and the small stones graze his palms as he tries to right himself.

Alice is on the other side of the path – or she was. Richard can't see her now because she's disappeared below the line of the verge. He starts patting his pockets, hunting for his phone. She needs an ambulance and it's going to take long enough to get one out here as it is. Unless it's better to carry her back along the track and get to a hospital himself…

He pushes himself up, trying to ignore the pain in his knee. The last time he twisted it was coming down the stairs when he realised he'd left something in his office. The type of innocuous adjustment he'd have made tens of thousands of times through his life. Then he found himself in a crumpled heap, wondering how it had all come to this. The doctor said there wasn't much he could do. He recommended a physio and gave a speech that basically came down to 'age, huh?'

Richard tries to stand but it's hard to put weight on the knee. The best he can do is half-limp, half-hobble across the lane towards where he saw Alice disappear into the ditch.

Gavin's standing there, staring down towards a gap in the hedge, where the stream is flowing on the other side.

'Al—'

Richard doesn't get the name out because Gavin turns and punches him in the face. Richard reels backwards, knee collapsing in on itself. A pair of teeth rattle around his mouth and the metallic taste of blood swills across his tongue. Not a punch... something else... something harder. Gavin must have been clutching a rock, or something like that. Stars swirl across his vision but Richard sees Gavin drop an object to the ground. Or maybe he hears it? It's hard to tell as the thoughts all disappear into one another.

Then there's black. Someone's dragging him across the ground, then he's being lifted and dropped into somewhere dark. There are muffled voices – a woman who's trying to speak through a series of cries that seem to be getting louder and louder. There's a man's voice, too. Maybe Gavin's? He says something about 'it has to be this way' and 'just get yourself home'.

Richard only realises he's in a car boot when he tries to sit up and cracks his head on the low ceiling. He must be in the back of Gavin's car, although the man's voice from the other side then says 'I'll move his car'. Richard closes his eyes and tries to focus on the words but then he's being bumped up and down. The vibrations scorch through his body and everything aches. It even feels as if his mind is thumping. Thoughts appear and disappear but none of them seem to fit together. He closes his eyes again.

There's a clunk and then light. Not much light but enough to make those green stars swim in his eyes. Or maybe that's because something hit him in the head?

Someone's in front of him. A man. Someone he knows.

'Time to get out.'

It's Gavin who's speaking. Of course it is. It was Gavin who hit him. It was Gavin who shoved his little girl into that rock.

'Where's Alice?'

Gavin clinks something on the edge of the car boot and Richard squints through the gloom to see the long barrel of a rifle pointing towards him.

'It was my father's,' Gavin says. 'This thing can put down a deer, and it can definitely do the same to you. So let's get out of the car nice and slowly.'

Richard's knee aches as he tries to spin himself around. He wants to get to Alice but there's no obvious way out. His back hurts and so does his head. In fact, it would be quicker to list the body parts that don't throb. He thrusts his legs out the back of the car and then rocks forward to propel the rest of his body out. As soon as he hits the ground, Richard's body crumples underneath him.

'Oh, get up,' Gavin sneers. 'I didn't hit you *that* hard.'

Richard tries but everything is spinning. Gavin is suddenly closer than he realised – and is thrusting some sort of white cloth towards him.

'Press that to your head,' Gavin says.

'Where?'

Gavin frees one hand from the gun and taps his own temple, indicating the spot.

Richard copies and then realises that he's bleeding. Something gloopy is clinging to his ear and the side of his face. When he presses the cloth to his face, jolts singe through him from ear to ear.

'Walk.'

'I can't, I—'

'*Walk!*'

Richard stumbles in the direction indicated by Gavin. It turns out to be through a gate at the side of a house and then across what looks like a building site. There's a separate, smaller house in the distance, although it's hard to tell in the murk. No, not a smaller house. Stables.

When they reach the stables, Gavin opens one of the doors and ushers Richard inside with the rifle. There are hay bales against the back wall and stray threads of straw across the hard ground.

Richard rests against the wall as Gavin crouches and puts the gun on the floor. His brain tells him that this is the chance. He can spring across and grab for the weapon, while making as much noise as he can.

Except his body won't obey. By the time the thought has occurred, it's already too late. Gavin has lifted a hatch that Richard hadn't seen, and then picked up the gun once more.

'Down there,' he says.

'What is it?'

'An old food storage area for the horses. Now get in.'

Richard eyes the rifle and knows there are few options.

'What about Alice?'

'I'm dealing with it.'

'What does that mean?'

Gavin lifts the gun, not exactly pointing it but making it clear that he can. 'Get in.'

There's a ladder that's attached to the edge of the opening – and Richard does as he's told, despite the ripples of pain through his knee and back. Anything to keep Alice safe.

The area underneath the stables isn't quite tall enough for him to stand. There's more straw across the floor, although little else he can see in the darkened corners. He imagines rats or mice – although it feels enclosed. Corner to corner, there might just be enough room to lie down.

Gavin closes the hatch, leaving Richard in darkness. His eyes sting and it takes a few seconds for him to realise that there is the faintest of light coming from the edges of the hatch to create a perfect square above his head. Gavin is pacing across the top. There are more muffled voices, perhaps a phone conversation, and then the hatch opens once more. The quick switch from darkness to the gloom of night leaves Richard blinded.

'I don't know what to do with you,' Gavin says with a huff.

'Let me go…?'

'You're a funny man.' Gavin steps away and then instantly back as he waves the gun into the air. 'You're going to stay down there and you're going to be silent because, if you're not, I'm going to put a hole in Maddy.'

It's already cold – but Richard feels a bristling spike of ice pass through him. 'You wouldn't risk everything you have.'

'Are you joking? Do you know what a mess I've got to clear up? Your car, that stupid girl, those rocks, Sarah. Maddy would just be one more thing for the list. So you're going to stay down there and you're going to shut up.'

'You can't keep me here forever.'

Gavin bites his lip and then: 'Have it your way.'

He slams the hatch and then there's the sound of something being dragged. There are footsteps above and then, eventually, silence. The only light remains the square around the hatch but, when Richard gently presses the underside, it doesn't budge. It's so much effort anyway. Richard's body is ready to shut down – and the only reason he's stopping himself from curling into the corner is because of Alice. And Maddy.

Richard pats his pockets, looking for his phone. He tries all of them, inside and out, but it's gone. His wallet and keys have been taken as well, although he doesn't know when that might have happened.

It's hard to know how long passes, although it doesn't feel like much. There's a scrabbling from above and then the hatch pops open. Gavin is there, out of breath and wearing a heavy coat.

'Come here,' he says.

Richard is pressed into the corner furthest from the hatch and struggles to move.

'Don't make me come down there,' Gavin says.

Richard reluctantly shuffles across the floor until he's directly underneath the hatch. Gavin is sitting above and reaches down with a large soft disc that he presses into Richard's hand.

'Swallow that.'

'What is it?'

Gavin drops a bottle of water through the space and it lands with a plop on the ground. Richard ignores it for the moment until he turns around and spies the gun on Gavin's lap.

'It's not you I'll shoot,' he says. 'It's Maddy. Now swallow it.'

The disc is squishy in Richard's hand, yet firm as well. Like a jelly bean but significantly larger. There doesn't seem to be another option, so Richard puts it in his mouth. Swallowing it is going to be harder than suggested and it's definitely going to need some chewing.

The taste is hard to describe. Not bad, more… nothing. Like dust.

Richard chews and sips at the water until it has all gone. Despite the water, his mouth feels dry.

'What was it?' he asks.

'Horse tranquilliser. It used to be the only thing that could calm Puddle back when Beatrice was going through her horsey phase.' He shrugs and there's a moment in which he seems like a normal father. 'It won't hurt you,' Gavin adds. 'I checked. It will just help you sleep.'

'I could freeze to death.'

Gavin shakes his head and then stretches forward, before dumping a pile of blankets through the hatch.

'I'll be back,' he says. 'Just remember that if you consider doing anything stupid, it's not you I'll hurt, it's your wife.'

SIXTEEN YEARS OLD

Dad is sitting in the kitchen with the newspaper spread across table in front of him. He hasn't turned a page in a good few minutes and, even though he's looking at the pages, I don't think he's reading.

'Can we do something?' I ask.

He doesn't seem to hear, so I slot into the seat on the other side of the table and repeat myself.

Dad still doesn't respond, not at first anyway. He continues staring down and blinks his way up as if he's a few seconds behind me.

'We could go to the park?' I say. 'Or the beach? Or the cricket. I checked and it's the last county home game of the summer…'

Dad mumbles something that I don't catch. He's barely left Auntie Kath's sofa in the week since we were in that hotel room together. I thought he might have just been tired, but very little about him has changed since then. He spends a lot of time staring at the walls and he hardly ever talks. There are a lot of times in which it feels like he's running a little behind the rest of the world. Where Auntie Kath or I will ask him something and then, ten seconds later, there's a reply. My aunt says he needs time, that he's been through something traumatic.

'Is there anything I can do to help?'

He shakes his head. 'You wouldn't understand, Mads.'

'You can try telling me…'

Another shake. 'You're too young.'

'I'm sixteen.'

'I know.'

I reach for his hand, except he pulls away. He's not looked up from the paper at all.

'Are you sure you don't want to go somewhere?' I ask.

'Maybe tomorrow.'

EARLIER

RICHARD

Days have passed. It's hard to tell how many while underneath the stables because there is no light. Everything is marked by when the hatch opens and Gavin appears with food, water, or more of the tranquilliser chews. It always seems to be dark when the hatch opens – although it is that time of year where the sun rarely hangs around for long. It's definitely been three days, possibly four. It could even be five.

In between the blankets and the straw, Richard has made something close to a nest. It doesn't make the floor that much comfier but it's better than nothing. The worst thing is the smell. Gavin will swap the buckets once or twice a day – but that's not much of a help.

Where is this all going to end? Surely nowhere good. The only reason Richard goes with it is for Maddy. Gavin has stopped making threats any longer – not that the inherent menace has gone anywhere. Richard wonders how she's doing without him. She's not the type who'd go to pieces – but he'd like to think she's missing him.

There's a bigger worry, too. He knows how it must all look.

The hatch opens as it always does and the light burns. Richard's become used to the darkness now – and the various shades of black within it. Gavin's silhouette is standing in the space above the hatch. He lowers down a large bin bag that, when Richard examines it, seems to be full of his clothes.

'Where did you get these?' he asks.

'Doesn't matter.'

Richard holds up the coat that he's had for something like twenty years. He bought it from an old outdoors shop at the seaside that had closed down the next time he visited. 'This was at my house.'

Gavin doesn't reply, instead reaching into a separate bag for three Snickers bars that he drops down.

'Have you hurt her?' Richard asks. 'You better not have. I—'

'I've not touched her. I've not even spoken to her this week.'

'So how did you get the clothes?'

'Don't worry about it. I thought you'd appreciate something warmer.'

That's true enough. Richard assumes that Gavin used his key to break into the house at some point. It's hardly comforting – but Gavin's claims of leaving Maddy alone does seem true. Richard has to believe something, after all. This is all he has.

He reaches for the Snickers bar and struggles to tear across the top. It takes four or five tries until the wrapper comes free. The chocolate bar is devoured in barely a few bites.

Gavin sits on the edge of the drop and watches as Richard sweeps the other two bars away to the corner.

'You care for her, don't you?' Gavin says.

'Who? Maddy? Of course.'

'It's just all those rumours about your other wife… I suppose I believed them.'

Richard shuffles away towards the corner. The past few days has been one humiliation after another – but this is one thing about which he won't talk.

'Why was the girl in your car?'

Richard ignores the question. It's not the first time Gavin's asked and it's not the first time he's been ignored. He might be able to force Richard to take the tranquilliser tablets by threatening Maddy – but he can't make him talk about things he doesn't want to.

'What have you done with her?'

Gavin doesn't answer this.

'Is she alive?'

No answer.

'Do they think I hurt her?'

Still no reply, not at first. And then: 'Are you a paedo?'

'What sort of question is that?'

'Are you?'

'Of course not.'

'So why was she in your car?'

Richard doesn't answer – but neither does Gavin reply to any of the questions. The two men are stuck staring at one another.

'Maddy won't believe I did anything to that girl.'

There's a hesitation that's almost nothing – except it's enough to let Richard know that he might be right.

'What makes you so sure?' Gavin replies.

'Her father was convicted of something he never did.'

Gavin rocks backwards, taking it in. In an odd way, Richard feels as if he's come to know the other man somewhat in the past few days. He knows all about Stockholm Syndrome and of course it's true that he'd rather be free. None of that changes the fact that he also knows this is something that's got massively out of hand. A stupid affair that has spiralled way beyond anything that could have been predicted.

He also knows there's no simple way out of this. He could promise not to tell anyone – but how realistic is that? He's been gone for three, four, or five days. People are going to want to know where he was. And then there's the far more important question of what's happened to Alice. To his daughter. He wants to know those answers, too – but every time he asks, Gavin is silent. Sometimes, he simply leaves. As awful as it is, these few minutes are the only times Richard gets to talk to another human. It keeps him sane, in between the woozy moments of sleep brought on by the tranquillisers.

'What happened to Maddy's dad?' Gavin asks.

'It's not my place to say.'

Gavin nods slowly and then passes down the next squishy disc.

Richard is so used to them now that he doesn't mind the taste. He even anticipates it.

'When will you be back?' he asks.

'Do you miss me?'

It's humourless and neither of them laugh.

Richard does the thing he always does – and puts the disc in his mouth. He doesn't need the water any longer. The discs are like gum and he chews it until it's gone, when he opens his mouth to show Gavin.

It won't be long before the giddiness hits and then he'll drift off to sleep. 'You can't keep me here forever,' he says.

'I know.'

'If you're going to kill me, just do it.'

Gavin's features are stony and unreadable. He doesn't move for perhaps a minute – and then he stands and lowers the hatch back into place.

THIRTY-SEVEN

Richard is dangling from a noose made of thick, blue rope. He's wearing the clothes I dropped off behind the village sign that I now know he couldn't have collected himself. It's only a couple of steps towards him and I reach around his middle, trying to support his weight.

Not again. Please, not again.

'Richard?'

His eyes are closed and I can't tell whether he's breathing. If he is, then it's too shallow to notice. It's dark and I can't see properly. He's heavy and yet, in the days since I last saw him, he seems thinner. I get myself underneath him to the point that I'm almost giving him a piggyback as I attempt to support his weight with my back and shoulders. When we're in that position, I reach up and try to get my fingers into the knot.

I realise almost straight away that this will do no good. The rope is too thick and the tension too taut.

It's not only that: Richard weighs too much for me and I'm being pushed down to the floor. I lower myself all the way and there's a stomach-grinding moment in which I feel the rope take my husband's full heft once more. I dash the few steps across to the other side of the shed and then drag the rocking chair across the floor until I can manoeuvre it underneath him. The chair squeaks as it bobs back and forth – but it does the job as I manage to manipulate Richard's body so that the back of the seat is taking his weight.

It takes me a few seconds to find the light switch. I don't come down to the shed often enough to have any muscle memory of where it is but eventually find it hidden behind the door. Pressing it doesn't get the expected result – largely because it's not only the yellow bulb within the shed that turns on. There are strings of white bulbs that criss-cross the garden; a hangover from two Christmases ago when Richard spotted a load of lights on offer at B&Q. We ended up wiring all the lights to the same source. It's all so bright that the back of the house is lit up as if it's daytime.

Back with Richard and I still can't tell whether he's breathing. There are reddy-purple scratches around his neck but the noose is no longer digging in. I need to get him down.

With the lights on, I can see the shears resting in the corner along with the rake and spade. The blades look rusted but it's as good as I'm going to get. I scissor the shears around the blue rope that's been nailed to the roof – and then I squeeze as hard as I can.

Nothing happens.

The shears are wrapped around the rope, except the blades are not doing the one thing they're designed to do. I try to crush the handles together but only succeed in twisting the rope, which makes Richard's limp body start to spin. My chest is heaving from the effort and my palms feel raw from the wooden handles.

I stop, take a breath, and then try again.

This time the blades catch. It's like the first moments where scissors go through cardboard. There's a gentle, creeping amount of give – and then the shears slice through the rope as if it's soft butter.

Richard flops across the chair but the curved legs mean that he rocks instead of falls. I lower him to the floor, onto his back, and then press my fingers to his neck to try to find a pulse.

Nothing.

I rest my ear next to his chest, then his mouth, listening for a sign that he might be breathing – but there's still nothing.

I don't know what I'm doing, not really, but I start pumping his chest, remembering the poster from the police waiting room as I silently play the *Stayin' Alive* chorus in my head. When I'm through that, I pause and press my ear to his mouth, before moving onto the chorus of *Another One Bites The Dust*.

I'm almost the whole way through it, my forearms burning, when Richard's upper body convulses. He almost jumps upwards with a cough before his eyelids start to flutter. When he falls back to the ground, I watch as his chest gently rises.

He's a mess, with deep red marks around his neck and a scabbed indent on the side of his head near his ear. His eyes are closed once more and there's a wheezing, groaning noise creaking from his lungs.

He's alive.

I fall back until I'm sitting next to him. There's sweat pouring from my face that has pooled along the top of my dress. That's when I spot the piece of folded paper sitting on top of the blankets. My name is written on the front and, inside, there's a simple 'Sorry about the girl'.

I don't think it's Richard's handwriting… although it is in block capital letters, so it's not beyond all possibility that he wrote it.

I say Richard's name but he doesn't reply. The sound of him wheezing is comforting enough for now, but I need to call an ambulance and the police. I had my phone not long ago, so it is somewhere in the shed – although I can't immediately see it. Somehow, the shed has become a battleground of rope, shears, an upturned chair – and my husband's body.

I shuffle back towards him, still scanning for my phone – which is when a shadow lurches across the floor. From nowhere, Gavin is in the doorway, blinking from the lights that criss-cross the garden. He must have come around the side of the house… and he's holding a rifle across his front.

He looks from me to Richard and back again, his features wrinkled with confusion. 'I thought you were at the back of the pub…?'

THIRTY-EIGHT

'Have you had him this whole time?'

Gavin is dazed from the lights behind and the gloom of the shed. He stares down towards me and the white behind him almost makes it look like he's glowing. In the distance behind, the side gate hangs open.

'Wrong place, wrong time,' Gavin says. 'I've got too much to lose.'

He sounds matter-of-fact as he glances down towards Richard's unmoving body. If there's any emotion there, then it's a resigned sadness.

'I don't understand,' I say.

Gavin gets no opportunity to respond because my phone starts ringing. It's on the floor to my side – hidden almost right in front of me. I don't need to move to see Harriet's name flashing across the front.

'It's your wife,' I say.

He looks at the phone and then back to me. 'She never could keep her nose out of everyone's business.' Gavin sighs and then lifts the gun. 'If it's any consolation, this isn't what I wanted.'

'What isn't?'

'Husband couldn't live with the guilt of what he did to a little girl, so he killed himself and his wife. It's a tragedy, I know.'

My phone buzzes and a text from Harriet appears on the screen. I reach for it but Gavin whispers a solid 'don't'. It doesn't matter because the message was short enough that I could read it anyway.

When I lean backwards away from the phone, Gavin must see something in my expression.

'What did it say?' he asks.

'I didn't get a chance to read it.'

He frowns, knowing I'm lying – but then he apparently reasons that it has no bearing.

There's a moment of silence until Richard moans and tries to roll onto his side. Gavin looks between us and raises the gun.

Behind him, unseen by anyone but me, there's movement from the gate at the side of the house. It's not surprising, I suppose. Not after what Harriet texted me. Not with the way the lights will be beaming out towards the road.

'Did you mean to do it?' I ask.

'Do what?'

'Did you mean to hurt Alice?'

Gavin lifts the rifle and levels it towards Richard, who is on his back once again: wheezing but not moving. It's easy to think of people as good guys or bad – and Gavin's doing a very good impression of a bad guy. He has all the power here and yet, when he looks to me and sighs, the only thing I see is sadness. It could be for himself but perhaps it is for that little girl. Nobody wanted this.

'No,' he says. 'I never meant to hurt her.'

It's the truth – and it's also the words that finish him.

The shadow creases across him but by the time Gavin turns, Gemma is already upon him, having heard every word. Harriet's text of 'Alice is dead & Gemma's missing' meant there was only one place she was going to come. Gavin tries to spin the gun around towards the flailing, hissing beast that leaps upon him – but it's far too late for all that.

Gemma is possessed.

The rifle clatters to the ground, closely followed by Gavin and Gemma. Intermingled limbs flail as she ends up on top of him and then connects with three or four sharp punches. She's wailing and shrieking. There are no words there, only fury and grief.

I shuffle across towards Richard and cradle his head. I should intervene, I *could* intervene... except that I don't.

Another punch rattles into Gavin and his head bounces onto the floor. He's not fighting any longer.

'Gemma...'

She's straddled across him and it's like she's in a trance. She's focused entirely on Gavin and starts slapping his chest as she screeches a banshee-like scream of 'No'.

'Gemma...'

If she hears me then she doesn't react.

I make a movement towards her but her focus has switched from Gavin to the thing that's on the floor next to her.

The shears.

I'd discarded them after cutting through the rope holding Richard and, before I can say or do anything, she picks them up. I see it happening a moment before it does. Blue spinning lights now swirl at the side of the house and there are more figures in the garden. Someone in a uniform, a man in a suit. They all see what I see – and we're each equally powerless as Gemma grips the handles and then slams the point of the shears down into Gavin's chest.

THIRTY-NINE

CHRISTMAS DAY

If frost counts, then it's a white Christmas in Leavensfield. The wintry blanket descended through the early hours of Christmas Eve – and the thermometers haven't troubled anything above freezing since. With the patches of ice stretching across many of the roads leading both into and out of Leavensfield, there's something of a bunker mentality in the village at the moment.

When my phone beeps, I look through the front window and then give the figure at the end of the drive a small wave before I head through to the kitchen. Richard is sitting at the table, with his walking stick leaning against an empty chair. He's not one of those men who'll insist that any degree of medical help is a slight on his masculinity. When they gave it to him, I think he was secretly upset he wasn't going to get a wheelchair.

He removes his glasses as he looks away from his book and takes me in.

'I'm popping out for a walk now,' I say.

'Is that with—?'

'Yes.'

Richard bows an acknowledgement and then returns his glasses to his head. 'It's cold out,' he replies.

'I know.'

'Not going to warm up until January, they say.'

'I won't be long. I was thinking you and I could maybe go down to the village later when the pub opens?'

He doesn't look up although he freezes momentarily. 'Maybe,' he says.

It's an obvious 'no' – and perhaps it isn't a good idea, except that he's not left the house since we got back from the hospital. That will be a conversation for a day that isn't today.

I head into the hall and put on my coat, scarf and gloves before heading out into the cold. Harriet is waiting at the end of the drive. It's the first time I've seen her since the night of the winter ball, although we have been messaging. I was so wrong about her, although I guess it's too late for any of that. There are no designer goods on show now – only jeans, a heavy coat, wellington boots, and a beanie hat.

'Merry Christmas,' she says – although the forced smile is obvious. Hard to blame her for that, although I don't know how I never saw the front before. It was Zoe who brought it up.

'Merry Christmas to you, too,' I say.

Harriet leans in and we hug awkwardly before we turn to the road. 'Where would you like to walk?' she asks.

I look up the hill and it's impossible not to identify the spot where Alice was attacked, close to the woods, at the end of the track. Everyone now knows where and how it happened now – and the end of the lane is a quilt of flowers.

Not that way.

'Daisy Field?' I say.

Harriet doesn't reply but she turns and heads off along the verge. I follow in single file and it's hard not to remember this is how it all started, with Atal and me walking this same route. It's only a few minutes until we head through the gate and emerge onto the field. We end up side by side as we amble towards the stream on the far side.

'How's Kylie?' Harriet asks.

'She's gone to Zoe's for the morning to help give Frankie some sort of Christmas treat. She's been there a lot this week.'

'I didn't know they were friends.'

'They weren't. I guess sometimes people just get on.'

Harriet doesn't reply, although it feels like she wants to. I wonder how many friends like that she's ever had.

'My two are with Mum,' she says. 'Mum and Dad have been staying over this last week – but they've taken them back to their house for a couple of hours.'

The stream has frozen, which is only a surprise in the sense that I didn't expect it. If it had been like this on that night Richard was driving Alice home, then her body would never have drifted down to here. There are so many what-ifs. Harriet must notice it, too. We've both gone silent because what is there to say? In the space of a week, a twelve-year-old girl was killed – and then her mother ended up on a murder charge for impaling the man responsible.

Harriet's lost her husband and her best friend.

It's the story of two affairs: Gavin's with Sarah – and Richard's with Gemma twelve years ago. So many secrets in such a small place.

'I'm not allowed to visit Gemma,' Harriet says.

'Why?'

'If it goes to trial then I have to be a witness. I asked about seeing her last week but they said it can't happen at the moment. You won't be able to visit her either.' A pause and then: 'Not that I'm saying you should.'

Gemma's parents died a few years ago and she now has no next of kin. She is the end of the line. Harriet and I will have both heard the rumours about temporary insanity pleas and the like. It all feels a long way off but the Leavensfield grapevine has cleared up some things for me. Gemma was in James's car during the winter ball when her phone rang. He only heard one side of the conversation, although everybody knows what was said by now. Someone from the hospital asked if she could go there right away. Gemma immediately replied with: 'Is she dead?' – and the moment of silence was enough for her to have her answer.

She jumped out of his car while it was still moving and then dashed off into the night. I more or less know the rest. She came to my house, followed the lights around to the back… and then she did what she did. Everybody seemingly knows that part, too – even though I haven't told anyone in the village about it.

Harriet and I follow the curve of the frozen stream as we arc down towards the village. If we keep going, we'll end up at the stile to the side of her house.

'Can I ask you something?' Harriet says.

'Okay.'

'How did you know I dropped those clothes off?'

I'm surprised that this hasn't got around yet. I've told the police – and given them the device – but I guess the leak isn't them.

'A phone was put through my letter box,' I say. 'Gavin was texting me, pretending to be Richard.'

'Oh…' We keep moving for a few more steps and then: 'I told him about Gemma wanting me to get rid of them and he suggested I go to the recycling banks after dropping off the kids at school.' She sighs. 'I don't get why he was texting you.'

'I think for a degree of trust. To let me see something I shouldn't.'

'But you already thought it was your husband…?'

I start to answer and then stop myself. It's not clear in my own mind. 'I was sure and I wasn't. I think I wanted it to be him. It was seeing you that had me sure it was Richard. I was probably going to skip the ball until he texted and convinced me to go. Gavin needed me away from the house so that he could get Richard into the shed.'

'He was making it look like suicide…?'

Harriet makes this a question, although she probably already knows. Theresa definitely does – and she didn't hear it from me.

'Right…'

We are almost at the bottom of the field but, instead of crossing the stile, Harriet keeps walking past it, following the line of the hedge, where the ground is crusty and hard. It doesn't feel as if either of us are ready to stop talking. I think we'll do a lot more of this in the months to follow. She'll need a friend who understands what she's going through and I suspect I will, too.

'I'm just so angry…'

Harriet lets it sit but it isn't only words. They're spat through clenched teeth and I can hear the righteous fury bristling through her.

'He can't hurt you any more.'

'Not him.' She hisses the reply and then quickly adds: 'I can't believe she stayed quiet after everything Gavin did.'

That's the other family destroyed. It's not only Sarah's affair, it's concealing the crime that Gavin committed. I've not seen, or spoken to, James since it all came out but I can't imagine he's taken it too well – and then there is their kids.

'People do strange things when they're scared of losing everything,' I say.

'That's no excuse.'

'No.'

'How did you stand by Richard through that week?'

We reach the next corner and Harriet turns and starts back up the hill once more. I follow, unsure if I'm ready for this conversation.

She doesn't get the answer, so Harriet continues: 'Everyone thought he'd done something terrible and then run off – but you always believed in him.'

'I'm not sure that I did. Maybe…'

'You never let other people get the better of you, though.'

'He still had an affair and a secret child…'

Harriet doesn't respond to this. Richard and I haven't quite had it all out yet, largely because I know he's grieving from losing his daughter. I don't necessarily blame him for the affair, because I don't know what his circumstances were with India at the time. I do blame him for hiding away both Gemma and Alice for all that time. It's a conversation we'll have another time. Perhaps our marriage will survive, perhaps it won't. I don't think I'm ready to think about that yet. I need to stop seeing Gemma with those shears whenever I close my eyes before I make any major decisions.

'But you believed in him,' Harriet says. 'You must have done.'

'I suppose.'

'That's what I can't get my head around. You're so strong-willed.'

'Or it's because I've been there before.'

SIXTEEN YEARS OLD

It looks like there are three keyholes as I try to unlock Auntie Kath's house. My key scrapes around the edges of the lock before I finally manage to get it into one of them. When the key turns and the door shifts inwards, I almost fall inside.

It's all very funny and I can't stop myself from giggling, even though I should probably be quiet. I shush myself – but that only makes it funnier. Auntie Kath is on holiday and because Dad never wants to do anything, it means I've had more or less free rein in the past few days. I wish I hadn't had those final few vodkas at Julius's party, though. I was already tipsy and that tipped me over the edge.

There are no lights on in the hall and I presume Dad has long since dozed off on the sofa. He's been sleeping there ever since he got home and shows no sign of wanting to move anywhere else. Kath says we can't stay here forever but I don't know if that means we'll actually have to move out at some point.

I creep through the hall as quietly as I can and then move through to the living room. I'm expecting the television to be on, with Dad asleep in front of it – except the room is dark and neither of those things are true.

Perhaps he's finally listened to us and has taken himself up to bed? All it took was for me to leave him alone for an evening.

I move back into the hall and stumble towards the stairs. I'm already on the second step when I realise there's something blocking the way up. My muddled mind is blank of explanations until I back up and reach for the light switch.

Something tells me I shouldn't press it – except my finger is already there – and then it's too late.

Hanging from the light fitting above, dangling in the centre of the staircase, is my father's limp, lifeless body.

What My Husband Did publishing team

Editorial
Claire Bord
Ellen Gleeson

Line edits and copyeditor
Jade Craddock

Proofreader
Liz Hatherell

Production
Alexandra Holmes
Caolinn Douglas
Ramesh Kumar Pitchai

Design
Lisa Horton

Marketing
Alex Crow
Hannah Deuce

Publicity
Kim Nash
Noelle Holten

Distribution
Chris Lucraft
Marina Valles

Audio
Kelsie Marsden
Arran Dutton & Dave Perry –
    Audio Factory
Alison Campbell

Rights and contracts
Peta Nightingale
Martina Arzu

CPSIA information can be obtained
at www.ICGtesting.com
Printed in the USA
LVHW091317080222
710582LV00010B/47

9 781838 888602